THE
CLEARING

BOOKS BY SHALINI BOLAND

THE OUTSIDE SERIES

Outside

The Clearing

The Perimeter

VAMPIRES OF MARCHWOOD SERIES

Hidden

Taken

Hunted

PSYCHOLOGICAL THRILLERS

The Secret Mother

The Child Next Door

The Millionaire's Wife

The Silent Sister

The Perfect Family

The Best Friend

The Girl from the Sea

The Marriage Betrayal

The Other Daughter

One of Us Is Lying

The Wife

My Little Girl

The Couple Upstairs

The Family Holiday

A Perfect Stranger

The Daughter-in-Law

SHALINI BOLAND

THE
CLEARING

SECOND SKY

Published by Second Sky in 2023

An imprint of Storyfire Ltd.
Carmelite House
50 Victoria Embankment
London EC4Y 0DZ

www.secondskybooks.com

ISBN: 978-1-83790-014-5
eBook ISBN: 978-1-83790-013-8

PROLOGUE

They're coming for me. I won't be able to outrun them. Better if I stop now and let them take me. But something urges me on. The black night presses down and I can hardly see. My lungs burn in my chest and my breath comes in shallow gasps.

I shiver and sweat in my thin cotton dress. It billows out around me as I run, the grass damp and cold under my bare feet. The whispering in my ears grows louder until it becomes a soft humming chant. Then I realise I'm muttering and singing to myself – a fear-induced mumbling that I can't seem to stop. My eyes water in the cold night air, mixing with tears of terror which dry in tight tracks along my cheeks.

I shouldn't do it, but I turn to look and make out their faint outlines behind me. The shape of them fills my mind with a deeper panic that's almost paralysing. But I will myself on and soon I reach the tree line where low branches claw out, desperate to trip me. Somehow, I stay upright, keep going, evade their mossy grip.

My pursuers are gaining on me from all sides. Their quiet, effortless chase deafens me with its silence. They accept the inevitability of my capture, just as I know that I will not escape.

The forest grows more dense and tangled until I stumble onto a narrow track. Time is running out. There is a strangled gurgling of running water to my left. The stream is widening out, the ground becoming boggy with sucking mud. Within seconds, too soon, I find myself in a large grassy clearing. A small herd of wild ponies are startled awake by my sudden arrival. They snort, whinny and trot away into the forest. Retreating.

Take me with you, I silently plead. But they disappear and the clearing lies empty, except for me. A cloud moves to reveal a quarter moon. The stream bubbles its toil and trouble and the branches creak and moan.

They are coming...

They are here.

I have let myself be herded like a helpless lamb. Somehow, I know this is where they wanted me to be captured.

From out of the trees, the dark hooded figures silently glide towards me; not running, but taking their time. I'm rooted to the spot, surrounded. I gaze up at the racing clouds as they smother the briefly hopeful moon again. And everything goes black.

CHAPTER ONE
RILEY

This was not an idyllic trip to the seaside. There was no time to take in the scenery or smell the salt tang in the air. The blue sky and warm October sun meant nothing to any of us. We were here to trade. And trading was a serious business.

Cutter's Quay was a narrow strip of broken concrete by the ocean. Pa said it used to be a place for holidaymakers, with brightly coloured beach huts and ice cream kiosks. But the beach huts were long gone, ripped down and burned for fuel. Now it was jammed with vehicles and makeshift stalls which seemed to stretch on forever. Traders bartered out of wooden rowing boats and trucks tied together with bits of string. There were crafters and farmers, dealers and pirates. You could get anything you wanted if you knew who to ask.

If you had items to trade, this was the place to come, but you better be armed and you better hold your nerve or you'd come away empty-handed. You might not come away at all.

Today I was here with Pa, my Kalashnikov on full display, slung over my body. I loved this place even though it also terrified the living daylights out of me. It made me feel alive. The first time I'd come, I'd stuck to Pa's side like a barnacle on a boat.

But now I felt confident enough to make trades of my own. And Pa trusted me enough to let me get on with it. After my trip with Luc outside the Perimeter last month to try to track down my younger sister's killer, I'd shown Pa that I wasn't the sheltered little girl he thought I was. At sixteen, I'd suddenly grown up and discovered what sort of a world we actually lived in. And I realised I didn't want to hide from it anymore.

Today, my task was to barter for salt and our usual supplier wasn't here so I'd been directed to a man named Milton Hardy, a well-known local character who was doing quite well for himself.

He worked out of the back of a horse-drawn wagon and had set up behind a group of fishermen. The stink of fish was overpowering, and I held my breath as I sidled past.

I knew Milton by sight but had never dealt with him before. He leant against the back of his wagon, sucking down the dog-end of a roll-up.

'Hi, are you Milton?' I called out.

He beckoned me over with a leer and tossed his roll-up onto the ground. I sighed and approached him, wary of walking into such an out-of-the-way spot. My hand shifted automatically to my weapon and I left it there, finger millimetres from the trigger.

Milton wore a suit, frayed at the hems and shiny at the knees. His hair had been combed back into a greasy quiff and half his teeth were missing, which made me wish he would stop smiling.

'Who are you?' His grin widened. 'Haven't seen you round here before. Never forget a pretty face.'

'I'm Riley,' I replied. 'I was told you trade salt.'

'Among other things,' he said. 'Best human-grade rock salt in Britain,' he said. 'Best prices too.' He undid the neck of a large blue polythene sack and scooped up a handful, holding it out for me to see.

I took a step forward and pinched some of the crystals between my thumb and forefinger. I tentatively licked them.

'Okay,' I said. 'How much of this have you got?'

'As much as you need.'

'I'll take it all.'

He laughed. 'Might be a bit rich for you, sweetheart. You don't know what I want for it yet.'

I waited.

'I've got thirty-two bags of premium-grade salt. They're going for five hundred silver bits each, but I can let you have the lot for fifteen thousand.'

I turned and walked away.

'Told you they was too rich for ya,' he called after me. I ignored him and carried on walking. 'Hey! Come back,' he cried. 'We've only just got going. I can do you a good deal. Maybe you can have it for twelve.'

I stopped and turned around. 'I'll give you a thousand.'

'What? For thirty-two bags? That's less than I paid for it.'

'We all know you didn't pay a bean for it, Milton. So I'll give you a thousand, take it or leave it.'

The smile left his face. 'Come back at the end of the day. If I haven't sold it, you can have it for five thousand.'

'I won't be here at the end of the day,' I said. 'My offer's a one-time deal. A thousand now or I find someone else to do business with.'

Milton scowled. 'Fine.'

'Sorry? Is that a yes?'

He nodded.

I did a silent victory dance in my head and headed back towards him, drawing out my knife with my left hand. His smile vanished.

'What you doing?' he asked.

'Checking the merchandise.' I gave him my best smile as I stuck the knife into the bottom of the sack.

Milton immediately went to reach inside his jacket, but with my right hand I jammed the nose of my machine gun into his gut, making him raise his hands skyward.

'Hmm, funny,' I said. 'Why's there no salt running out of the bottom of the bag, Milton?'

I sliced into the sack some more and out dropped a chunk of wood shavings and a stream of dirty gravel.

'Nice,' I said, pocketing the knife. 'Deal's off.'

'Can't blame a man for trying,' he said. 'I got the good stuff in the wagon.'

I stepped back, still aiming the Kalashnikov at his skinny body.

'Wait here,' he said, his hands still raised. He turned and crawled under the tarp in the back of his wagon and dragged out another sack. This bag was clear and I could see the salt through the plastic. He sliced through the top and held it out for me to try.

We finally did the deal and he rode his wagon over to Pa's AV. He looked from the AV to me and back to the AV again. His face dropped.

'You're Johnny Culpepper's daughter?'

I nodded.

'Oh. Look, sorry for all that stuff back there. I never would've tried to—'

'What?' I cut him off. 'You never would've tried to rip me off if you knew I had a father who could squish you?'

'Basically, yeah,' he replied with a sheepish grin.

I watched and counted as he loaded the sacks of salt into the boot.

'Hello, Milton.' Pa appeared round the side of the AV, carrying a couple of crates on his shoulder. 'I see you've met my daughter.'

'Yeah, chip off the old block, JC.'

'Can we go now, Pa?' I said. 'I'm supposed to be meeting Luc at one.'

'Did you get my salt?'

'Yeah. Milton here did me a good deal.'

'Barely enough to feed my kids, Johnny.'

'You haven't got any kids, Milton.'

Pa dumped his crates on the back seat and we climbed into the AV.

'And?' Pa said.

'I got thirty-two sacks for a thousand.'

'Nice work,' Pa replied.

I glowed under his praise.

'All right,' Pa said, starting up the engine, 'let's get out of here.'

As he drove, I stared out the window at the scrubland scrolling past, butterflies building in my stomach. The adrenalin from this morning's deal had faded and now I was facing an even more nerve-wracking situation: I was meeting Luc Donovan for a picnic lunch. With his dark hair and blue eyes, Luc always got me flustered. But it was complicated. He used to be my sister Skye's crush so I'd promised myself I wouldn't act on my feelings. I'd pushed him away, even though I wanted him. And now... now I had no idea how he felt.

CHAPTER TWO

RILEY

Luc and I still hadn't spoken properly since our 'trip'. There'd been no talk of how we felt. We'd teased and chatted, but it all felt superficial. We never seemed to have enough time together. No time to talk about anything meaningful. So today was a big deal. At least it was for me.

What if Luc had completely changed his mind about us? Maybe everything that happened last month had been a heat-of-the-moment thing. The thought made me sick. I wanted to get to Coy Pond before he did. To make the most of the short hour before he had to go back to work. I looked at the speedo; Pa was cruising at 20 mph. I sighed.

Half an hour later, I ran down the steps and onto the path which ran alongside the gushing stream. A couple of moorhens swam over so I reached into my drawstring bag and tore off a crust of bread, breaking it into crumbs and scattering them across the water. More ducks appeared and I left them to their soggy treasure hunt.

Luc hadn't arrived yet, so I hoisted myself up onto the warm stone wall, dumping the bag next to me. As I waited, I tilted my face up to the sun and closed my eyes. Unwelcome memories rushed at me. Snapshots of the summer. A summer that would remain in sharp focus for the rest of my life. The summer when my little sister was murdered; when Luc and I had risked our lives to track down her killer.

'Hey, Riley. Having a little nap?'

His voice made me jump and I snapped open my eyes to see him smiling in front of me, his blue eyes twinkling with humour. My stomach went into freefall and I put my hands on the wall to steady myself.

'Hey, Luc. How's it going?'

He picked up my bag and peered inside. 'Wow, you actually made a picnic. I'm impressed.'

'Yeah, well, I could lie and said it was me, but Ma made it all.' I slid off the wall, brushing the stone dust from the backs of my legs.

'Thought it was too good to be true,' he drawled. 'Unlike your lazy highness, I actually made sandwiches and a flask this morning.'

'Suck up,' I replied, and leant out of the way as he pretended to push me into the stream. 'Hey!'

'What!' Luc replied with a grin that made my pulse quicken.

'You are such a... a...' I couldn't think of anything fitting enough.

'A... a...' he mocked. 'I know, but that's why you love me.'

My heart lifted irrationally at his words, but I'm sure he didn't mean them like *that*. I didn't know what to think about us anymore. It was all so complicated, but all so simple at the same time.

He hoisted my bag over his shoulder alongside his rucksack and tilted his head for me to follow him. 'Shall we walk for a bit?'

'Sure.'

'How was this morning at Cutter's?' he asked.

'Good,' I said. 'We got what we went for. I like it down there. It's fun.'

I stopped walking as we'd reached a part of the track that had cracked and flooded.

Luc used one arm to hold back the bushes at the edge of the path. 'Here,' he said, 'grab my hand.'

His skin felt warm. He gripped me tight as I skirted the puddle and jumped across the last bit. I wished I could keep hold of his hand, but I let it go. My fingers tingled.

'Thanks,' I said. 'How about you? Was work okay?'

'Work? Yeah, nothing too exciting. Couple of thefts over at Southampton and an interview for a new guard.'

We walked in silence for a while, the ducks on the stream keeping up with our progress.

'Riley...'

'Hmm?'

'We're nearly at the wall. Shall we turn round?'

I glanced up to see the towering red-brick wall ahead and, beyond it, the familiar mesh of the fence encircling us, keeping us safe. I briefly wondered if anyone was passing by outside, imagining what it was like in here. This part of the Perimeter was the most heavily fortified. Only a mile from here lay the Upper Gardens, one of the most dangerous parts of Bournemouth.

We turned and headed back in the opposite direction. With limited places to walk inside, we always found ourselves coming up against the fence. I thought back to our time outside the Perimeter where we could walk or drive for miles without boundaries. With nothing to hold us back but our fear of the unknown.

After walking for a few minutes, I pointed to a spot by the stream. We spread the rug out under the low boughs of a weeping willow. This was my favourite tree. The one my sister and I always used to climb as it had such twisty branches, the low ones dipping their woody elbows into the stream. Skye used to swing upside down by her hands and feet from the larger branches, making monkey noises. She always ended up making me laugh till the tears streamed down my face.

I couldn't believe she was gone. Sometimes the realisation hit me with such force it made me dizzy. I wished I could find her killer, I still wanted to avenge her death, but I had nothing to go on. No clues, no murder weapon, no motive. Nothing. Maybe I never would find out who did it.

'This is great,' Luc said as we sank down onto the rug. 'It's so peaceful here.' He stretched out his legs and gave a sigh.

The butterflies in my stomach were going insane. We were here, alone together, but all we could talk about was mundane stuff. Half-formed sentences flew around my brain, but I couldn't utter the words I needed to tell him how I really felt. To ask him if he still felt the same about me. I was too scared of the answer.

'You okay?' he asked, pushing his hair out of his eyes. His fringe had grown longer and it suited him. Made him seem more vulnerable.

'Yeah, fine.' I reached across to grab our bags stuffed with food.

We relaxed and began tucking into our lunch of fruit, cheese sandwiches and homemade cakes. We were lucky to have out-of-season fruit. Pa always made sure he got us the best of everything.

'I can't eat another thing,' I said. 'I shouldn't have had that last cake.'

Luc held a strawberry in front of my mouth.

I shook my head.

He raised an eyebrow.

'No,' I groaned. 'Too full up.'

'Last chance,' he said, dancing the bright red berry in front of my face.

I shook my head again, so he dropped it back into the bag.

Our lunch break was nearly over and, although it had been great spending time together, we still hadn't spoken about anything meaningful. We'd lost that closeness from back when we were on the road. I sighed and shivered. The sun had slipped behind a thick bank of cloud. The blue sky was already dissolving.

'You're cold,' Luc said.

'I'm okay.'

'It's the north wind,' Luc said. 'Coffee will warm you up. Come here.' He patted the empty space next to him and I scooched around, my heart pounding as he rubbed his hand up and down my arm. 'Riley, you're freezing.'

I gave a nervous laugh. 'Got that coffee?'

He took his hand away from my arm and pulled a metal flask out of his rucksack. I could have cursed myself for opening my big mouth.

'Here.' He handed me the metal lid of steaming liquid and I blew across the top of it.

I looked up and caught his eye, but I wasn't brave enough to hold his gaze. If only he would lean down and kiss me. Obliterate all my doubts.

'I can't stay,' he said. 'I have to get back in a minute. Work.'

'Okay,' I replied, tucking a stray piece of hair behind my ear. The time had gone too quickly and now disappointment threatened to overwhelm me. But maybe it was a good thing we couldn't spend longer together. Maybe it would have all been too awkward. I knew I should forget about Luc and me. I didn't have the strength or the energy to have my heart broken on top of everything else.

'Are you all right?' he asked. 'You seem a bit...'

'Yeah, I'm fine.' I shook away the longing and flashed him a smile.

'Riley...' he began.

'Yeah?'

'I need to...'

'What?'

'Can I talk to you about something?'

My heart sped up. Was he about to tell me something good? Or something I didn't want to hear? I searched his face to see if his expression held any clues.

'Who's that?' he asked staring past me.

Turning and squinting into the distance, I saw a figure coming towards us – a man in uniform.

'Looks like Liam.' Luc jumped to his feet. 'Must be something to do with work.'

'What were you going to say?' I asked. 'Before.'

'Nothing. Doesn't matter.'

I desperately wanted to know what he wanted to talk to me about before Liam showed up, but it looked like I was going to have to wait. Liam was one of the Perimeter guards who worked with Luc.

'He's running,' I cried. 'Maybe something's happened.' I began stuffing everything back into our bags.

'What's up?' Luc called out as he hurried over to meet him.

'Hey, Luc.' Liam slowed and they walked towards me.

'What is it?' Luc asked again.

'You're needed back home,' Liam said. 'You too, Riley.'

'Both of us?' I replied, attempting to fold the picnic rug, but the corners kept slipping out of my clumsy fingers.

'Yeah. You've got some visitors. Just don't do anything stupid when you find out who.'

'What? Why? Who is it?' Luc said. 'Why would we do anything stupid?'

'You'll see.'

'You're freaking me out, Liam,' I said. 'Who is it?'

'You won't like it,' Liam replied, shaking his head.

'Tell us, mate. Who is it?' Luc's voice was sharp.

'Be cool, Luc. You'll find out back at the house. Come on.' Liam took the rucksack from me. 'Your folks are waiting. We're gonna have to run.'

CHAPTER THREE

LISS

It was a hot and dusty day, and the two children weren't anywhere near finishing their chores.

'You're such a chicken.' The boy made clucking noises and bent his elbows to imitate the plump birds that scratched around the yard.

'Shut up! I am not. I'm just trying to get this done before Mum comes back. She'll kill us if we haven't finished. Come on, FJ, help me. Please.'

He screwed up his face. 'Urgh, it's so boring. And hot. Do this with me and then I'll help you finish really quick. I promise.'

The girl looked at her older brother, weighing up whether he was to be believed or not. She usually went along with his plans and nine times out of ten they backfired, getting them both into trouble, which is why she always began by disagreeing with him. But she knew, no matter how much she argued, she would always back down in the end. She loved FJ and he *was* good fun. Even if Mum was going to go mad when she came back from the milking and found the yard still in a mess.

'Okay,' she agreed. 'But you'll have to work double hard afterwards to get this lot finished.'

'Yeah, yeah,' he replied. 'Come on, before Mum gets back.'

Liss followed her brother down the path. The air smelt sweet and fresh, even with the field's underlying scent of damp cow. It was nice to do something fun and interesting for a change. Living on a farm was hard work. One job after another, day in, day out. Most days she didn't mind, but when the sun shone and the air shimmered like it did today, it felt like she was missing out on something, like something magical should be happening...

Maybe it was.

They headed over to the small stand of trees in front of their fence. This area had been left to grow wild; the fence bordered by dense undergrowth. FJ grinned at her, crouched by the bushes and heaved up the large wooden board by its handle. Liss experienced a shiver of fear. If Dad caught them, they would be in so much trouble she didn't even want to think about it.

FJ groped around inside the hole and pulled out a torch. He clicked on the beam and shone it right up close into Liss's eyes.

'Hey!' she cried, closing her eyes against the sudden glare.

He laughed and turned away, pointing the beam down at the ground into the tunnel he'd just uncovered. Then he disappeared down the hole.

'Wait for me,' Liss called to the top of FJ's head.

Their parents had told them that under no circumstances were they to go into the tunnel without them. In fact, they weren't even supposed to be over near this part of the farm. The whole property was surrounded by a high electric fence as well as a deep ditch. This secret tunnel was the only easy way in and out of the place. Their parents had cleverly constructed it to take them from one side of the fence to the other. It had taken ages to build, but it was well done – once inside, their dad only had to stoop slightly to avoid hitting his head.

Liss followed her brother, carefully placing her feet one after the other on the narrow steps. As she left daylight behind, she shivered inside the gloomy damp tunnel.

'FJ, wait! It's dark. I can't see down here without the torch.' Her voice sounded odd and muffled. Then Liss gave a shriek as FJ roared at her. He had the torch pointed up at his own face which was screwed into a scary-monster impression.

'Freddie Junior!' She shoved him, but he kept his balance and doubled up, laughing so hard he could barely breathe.

'Your face, Lissy! That was well funny.'

'It's not funny at all.' She almost felt like crying. 'I'm going back to the—'

'No, no, no. I'm sorry, Liss. I'm really sorry.' He put his arm around her and squeezed her into a bear hug. 'I was only mess-ing. Come on, hold my hand.'

She wanted nothing more than to strop off back to the yard but instead, she took her brother's outstretched hand and let him lead her through the short, narrow tunnel. The walls were lined and secure with built-in shelves, the contents of which couldn't clearly be seen in the dim torchlight. But Lissy knew there were cans of food and tools and stuff.

They climbed up the steps on the other side and FJ shoved open another wooden hatch. The children climbed out of the tunnel into a clump of dense undergrowth buried under a thick stand of trees. Parting the foliage, they took a few more steps and found themselves standing on the grass verge. It was nice to be back in the warm sunshine, but the unsettling difference was that this time they were *outside* the fence.

Freddie Junior walked a little way along the verge, next to the crumbly road. Liss bent to touch the pitted tarmac. It felt warm. The chances of seeing a vehicle out here were almost non-existent and, even if they did, it would probably be Army. Nevertheless, she felt quite breathless with fear in case someone should choose to come along now, while they were out here alone.

'FJ, we better go back now,' she called, trying not to be too loud.

But he didn't reply. He seemed to have vanished.

'FJ?' She looked up and down the road again, trying to spot her brother, feeling her scalp prickle with worry. Where was he? She cast anxious glances over her shoulder, checking there was no one else around.

Suddenly she felt a hand come over her mouth from behind and another grip her arm. She thought she might faint with terror.

'Shhhhh,' a voice whispered in her ear. Warm breath on her neck.

She struggled. Tried to squeal.

'Liss, shh. It's only me.' He let her go.

'FJ?' She spun around to see her brother, but he wasn't smiling. 'FJ, you scared me really badly—'

'Shut up, Liss!' he hissed. 'There's something over there, further up the road.'

She clamped her mouth shut and opened her eyes wide.

'I think it's an armoured vehicle.'

'Army?' she mouthed.

'Don't think so. Looks civilian. Heavy duty though.'

'We should go back,' she whispered. 'Tell Mum and Dad...'

'Are you joking? They'd kill us for coming out here.'

'Okay, we won't tell them, but we'd better go back. It's too dangerous to stay.'

'I'm going to have a closer look,' FJ said. 'You stay here. Keep an eye out.'

'What! Are you mad? No way.'

'It doesn't look like there's anyone inside it,' he continued, a tinge of excitement creeping into his voice. 'It could be abandoned. There might be some really useful stuff in there.'

'Why would anyone abandon an AV?'

'Maybe they ran out of fuel or got sick and died. Maybe they're lying dead in there.'

'That's it, I'm going back.' Liss turned towards the tunnel, desperate to be on the other side of the fence once more.

FJ grabbed her arm. 'Please, Liss. Just for a minute. I just want to see, that's all. There's no one in it. It's not dangerous.' He smiled at her, a pleading, sweet smile.

'How do you know there's no one in it? No. I'm going back.'

His smile melted into disappointment. His shoulders sagged and he gave a cross frown of acceptance.

At his expression, she relented, knowing he'd sulk for days. 'Okay then. Just for a minute and then we'll go back. Promise?'

'Course.' He grinned. 'Come on then. You keep watch while I check it out.'

They trod cautiously along the grass verge.

'I can't see any vehicle,' she said.

'That's because it's hidden behind the bushes. Here.'

Liss almost walked into it. The AV had been camouflaged with greenery, but she could now glimpse its black paintwork beneath the leaves.

'Someone's hidden it here,' she said in surprise.

'I know.'

FJ began pulling branches away from the huge vehicle. It was badly beaten up, the paintwork flaking with patches of rust.

'Do you think it's been here long?'

'No.'

'How do you know?' Liss looked up. She realised she could see part of the yard from here. She had thought their house was supposed to be hidden from the road. 'Do you think they were spying on us?' she asked, her heart beginning to thump uncomfortably.

'Could be,' FJ replied.

Something suddenly dawned on Liss.

'You knew!' she cried.

'Knew what?'

'That's why you wanted to come out here today. You saw the AV from the yard.'

FJ smiled and Liss tried to punch him on the arm, but he caught her fist in his hand. 'So?' he said with a shrug.

'So you could've told me.'

'You would've blabbed to Mum.'

'It's dangerous out here, FJ.'

'Oh, stop being such a baby. We'll check it out and then we'll go back.' He peered in through the window. 'See, I told you. There's no one even in here. Whoever was here has gone now.' He tugged on the passenger door handle. 'Locked. Maybe we can force it with something.'

Liss shivered. 'Please can we go? I don't care if you think I'm a baby. I want to go. I'm really scared.'

'Don't be scared,' came an amused voice from behind her. A man's voice.

Liss froze, not daring to turn around. In all her seven years she didn't think she'd ever been as terrified as she was right now.

FJ instantly looked up at the man with a challenge in his eyes. 'Who are you?'

'I was about to ask you the same thing,' the man replied.

Liss had a feeling of spiralling doom. The man's voice was not aggressive, but she didn't like it, nonetheless. It was posh and a bit mean sounding, and she had the feeling he was making fun of them.

'I asked first,' FJ replied without a trace of fear in his voice. 'Who are you?'

The man laughed.

Liss was shocked at FJ's insolence. He wouldn't dare have talked to Mum and Dad like that. But she was glad FJ was brave because she felt like jelly. She backed up towards her brother and turned around to face the man. He was quite short and totally bald. But his clothes were smart and he didn't look too scary.

'Very well, my name is Mr Carter,' the man said. 'Your turn.'

'I'm FJ. I mean Frederick.'

Liss looked at her brother. She would have burst out laughing if she wasn't so scared. He never used his long name; it always sounded way too grand and grown-up.

'Hello, Frederick,' said Mr Carter. Then he turned his gaze to Liss. 'And who might you be?'

'This is my sister, Melissa,' FJ replied. 'What are you doing here? Outside our farm.'

'*Your* farm? Well, that's a stroke of luck,' Mr Carter said. 'We were just coming to talk to you. Well, to warn you actually.'

'Warn us?'

'Yes. There are raiders on their way here. I'm afraid they want to take your farm away from you.'

'No!' Liss cried.

'They can try,' FJ said, 'but they won't be able to get in. Our fence is electrified.'

'Alas, that will not stop them,' Mr Carter said.

'FJ.' Liss tugged on her brother's t shirt. 'We'd better go back. Warn Mum and Dad.'

'So, it's only you and your parents here, is that right?'

'That's none of your business,' FJ said.

'Now, now. No need to get testy. I'm just being friendly.'

'Right. We'll be going back now,' FJ said, 'to tell our parents. Thanks for the warning.' He took Liss's hand and they began to edge past Mr Carter.

Liss turned back to the man as something had occurred to her. 'You said "we".'

'Sorry?' Mr Carter replied.

'You said, "*we* were coming to talk to you". Before.'

'So I did. You're a sharp one.'

'Does that mean someone else is with you?'

'Yes, my brothers are here with me. They'll return momentarily. Aah, talk of the devil.' Mr Carter gazed beyond FJ and Liss. He smiled and nodded. 'Meet Cassius and Mark, my brothers.'

Before Liss had a chance to turn around, she felt a hand come around her waist and another hand tape something across her mouth. She was then lifted into the air before she could even scream.

The same thing was happening to FJ and she locked eyes with him for a fleeting second. In that brief moment, he gave her a look of panic, defiance, apology and... something else... something which seemed very much like excitement or... triumph.

Liss would remember that look in the months which followed, as it was to be years before she laid eyes on her brother again.

CHAPTER FOUR

RILEY

When Luc and I arrived home, we were out of breath. Ma and Pa were waiting for us wearing serious expressions. Liam didn't tell us anything more on the jog back home and left as soon as we reached the house. We'd pressed him for information, but he wouldn't say.

I had that lurching feeling in my stomach, a feeling I'd come to know too well.

'What is it?' I asked my parents. 'Just tell me.'

'It's okay, Riley,' Pa said. 'No one's hurt.'

I immediately relaxed. For one horrific moment, I'd been transported back to the day when they told me my sister had been killed. They'd had similar expressions on their faces that morning.

'You've got some visitors,' Pa said. 'From the outside.'

'Liam told us that already. Who is it?' I asked.

'They're at the guards' house,' Pa continued.

'I don't think they should see them at all,' Ma interrupted. 'We should let Eddie and the guards deal with them. After what they did... who knows what could have happened.'

'Who is it?' Luc and I said at the same time, desperate to know.

'It's that couple – Fred and Jessie,' Pa replied grimly.

'What!' I cried. 'What the hell are they doing here?'

Luc shook his head in disbelief. 'What a nerve. They must be crazy coming here after all the crap they pulled. Sorry for the language, Mrs C.'

I couldn't understand why Fred and Jessie would come here. They betrayed us. Why would they want to see us again? It didn't make any sense.

'Come on,' Pa said. 'Let's sort this out.'

My heart was hammering, but whether from the run back home or the news I'd just received, I couldn't tell. I grabbed a hoodie off the end of the banister and caught sight of myself in the hall mirror. My eyes were wide and scared-looking and my hair was a mess, curly chestnut strands escaping from my pony-tail. I pulled the hoodie over my head and joined Luc and Pa who were already halfway out the door.

Ma squeezed my arm and watched us leave.

Pa threw his arm around my shoulders and Luc walked on the other side of him. It only took ten minutes to reach the guards' house, but it felt like forever. Why were Fred and Jessie here? It made no sense. I realised I didn't want to see them. I'd rather forget they ever existed.

'I'm coming in with you,' Pa said in a tone that no one would argue with.

We entered the two-storey red brick building and Pa nodded to several of the guards.

Roger Brennan came out of his office and greeted us with a touch of his cap.

'Hello, Roger,' Pa said. 'Have they told you anything else? Said why they're here?'

'Nothing,' Roger replied. 'Keep insisting they only want to talk to Luc and Riley.'

'Let's find out what it's all about then,' Pa said.

'Follow me,' Roger said. 'I've got them in one of the cells. After what they did to these two, I'm not taking any chances.'

We followed him along a short corridor and waited while he stopped outside a metal door, unclipped a bunch of keys from his belt loop and fitted one into the lock. The door groaned as it opened, the sound echoing down the corridor. We entered the cold, gloomy room and Roger closed the door behind us with a clang.

Fred and Jessie were sitting on a narrow bed, but they rose to their feet when we walked in. Fred wore his usual tweed jacket with a checked shirt underneath. He'd aged a bit since we last saw him and looked a little thinner, but I was shocked when I saw Jessie. The previous month she'd seemed youthful and fit, but the person sitting across from us was a completely changed woman; all skin and bones with sunken cheeks and hollowed-out eyes. She'd grown old. How could she have changed so much in such a short space of time?

The room felt cramped and claustrophobic with all six of us standing inside. It was chilly and musty. A window sat high up on the wall, but it had no glass, just thick metal bars. A damp breeze blew into the room making a low whining noise.

'Thank you for seeing us.' Jessie looked embarrassed and so she should. She caught my eye and flushed. 'I'm glad you're both all right.'

A million retorts hovered on my lips, but I didn't reply.

'Sit down,' Roger said, motioning them back towards the bed.

They glanced around awkwardly, but did as he asked. Fred now held his cap in his hands. He looked small and a bit pathetic.

Roger called out into the corridor, 'Need some chairs in here!'

A few seconds later, the door opened again and a guard

brought in a stack of four plastic seats. We tugged them free from one another and the four of us sat facing the worried-looking couple.

'Make it quick,' Luc said. 'What do you want?'

'If it's worth anything, we're genuinely sorry,' Jessie said. 'We hated doing what we did.' She turned to Fred, whose eyes were resolutely downcast. Her eyes filled with tears.

'You've tried the tears routine with us once before, so you can save it,' Luc snapped.

Fred reached across to take Jessie's hand.

Just looking at them brought back an avalanche of memories. We thought these two had been our guardian angels. They had showed me and Luc the warmth of their hospitality after we'd been attacked by raiders. At the time we'd been so grateful.

'How could you!' I cried. 'We trusted you. We wanted to help you and you sent us to that awful place to be brainwashed.' I stumbled over the words, now so upset that I could barely speak. If I opened my mouth again, I knew I'd cry, and they would be tears of anger. I glanced across at Pa, who had a grim expression on his face, but he didn't speak and I was grateful he was trusting this conversation to me and Luc.

'You might not believe us, but we're happy you escaped,' Fred said. 'I know we don't deserve a hearing, but will you let us tell you our story? And then you can decide whether or not to send us packing.'

I glanced at Luc who looked unimpressed and tight-lipped, but he gestured with his hands for the man to continue.

Fred nodded and began his story.

CHAPTER FIVE

LISS

Liss tried to scream, but her mouth had been taped shut. What was happening? And where was FJ? She tried to see where the other man had taken her brother, but they had seemed to vanish into the undergrowth. Her heart thumped so violently, she thought it might beat its way right out of her chest.

She was held tight by the man as he walked, her arms pinned to her side. But because she faced away from him, she couldn't even see what he looked like. Maybe that was a good thing. She didn't think she wanted to see his face. What if he was a monster?

Why oh why had they come out here alone? She'd known it was dangerous, but she had stupidly let herself be talked into it. Were they going to die now? Were they going to be shot? Hot tears slipped out of her eyes and she tried to sniff them back. It was so hard to breathe with this thing over her mouth.

That Mr Carter man had disappeared too. Maybe he'd gone with FJ. If only she didn't have her mouth taped she would scream and scream and shout for her mum and dad to come. They would surely hear her from here. And then Dad would come running out with his shotgun to rescue them. Liss tried to free one of her arms, but the wriggling only made her captor squeeze her even tighter. It was hopeless.

The man grunted and set her down on the ground. He twisted her arms painfully behind her back and tied them up with something sharp that dug into her skin. She gave a soundless whimper. Her hair fell over her eyes, but through the mousy strands she saw that she was standing in front of a vehicle. It looked like an army truck.

The man moved around in front of her. He was ordinary looking. Brown hair, not fat, not thin, not a monster. Just a man.

'Sit down,' he said softly.

She stared at him.

'On the ground. Sit down. I ain't gonna hurt ya.'

Liss manoeuvred herself onto the ground. It was tricky with her hands tied behind her back, and her backside landed with a thump on the grass verge.

The man took some kind of plastic strip out of his trouser pocket and used it to tie her ankles together.

Liss wanted to ask him if he was going to kill her.

Once her ankles were secured, he stood and opened up the back of the truck. Then he bent back down and hoisted her up in his arms like a lamb for shearing.

'You're going to a good place,' he said as he set her down in the back of the truck, swung her legs around and slammed the door shut.

Now Liss sat in total darkness. She thought she might've caught a glimpse of some other children in the truck, but it had been so fleeting she couldn't be sure.

She realised she was shaking uncontrollably. Shaking and shivering and crying like a baby. She wondered if FJ was afraid. And if he was, was he keeping it hidden? Or was he crying and shaking too?

Maybe he was here in the truck with her. It was dark, but she could make out some dim shapes. The sour smell of vomit and sweat made her feel suddenly nauseous. She drew her legs into her body. Her arms were aching badly. How long would she be left in here like this?

A door slammed and the engine started up. A deep throaty rumble. Liss braced herself against the wall of the truck, splaying out her bound hands. As the vehicle began to move, she absorbed every jolt and judder from the road, but wasn't able to steady herself. She was going to be bruised black and blue.

Her fingers brushed against something soft. Someone's leg or maybe an arm? Perhaps it was FJ. But with her mouth taped, she couldn't ask.

The journey was long and uncomfortable. She drifted in and out of terror, her mind circling around the same questions. Where were they going? Would she ever see Mum and Dad again? What about FJ? Was he in here with her or had they taken him somewhere else? Liss wished more than anything that she had stuck to her guns and not followed her stupid brother through the stupid tunnel. In fact, if she was wishing for stuff, she wished she'd been a telltale and told her mum exactly what FJ was planning to do. Even if he had refused to speak to her for a month, it would be better than this.

Liss felt like she'd been sweltering inside the truck forever. She couldn't breathe properly with this horrible tape over her mouth and she worried about how much it was going to hurt when they peeled it off – like a plaster, only much, much worse.

Suddenly the truck stopped with a lurch and Liss was flung sideways. Her head landed on something soft. The engine grumbled for a moment and then everything went quiet. Had they reached their destination? Wherever that was. Liss shuffled upright again and cowered away from the door.

On the one hand, she was so tired and her arms ached so badly that she was dying to get out of here. Plus, the smell was terrible. But on the other hand, what if what lay out there was worse than being in here?

And now that the engine had stopped, Liss could tell there were definitely other people in here with her. She heard muffled coughs and sobs and felt the movement of people shifting about, probably trying to get comfy. Apart from that, it was quiet. She heard no sounds at all from outside.

Her stomach gurgled with a mixture of nerves and hunger, but she knew that even if her favourite food had been placed in front of her right now, she wouldn't have been able to choke any of it down.

After what seemed like an age, Liss heard a voice outside. It sounded like the man who had tied her up and bundled her into the truck. Seconds later, the door creaked open, letting in a violent flood of light.

Squinting and blinking, she glanced around the truck into the faces of other children, all bound and gagged with fear in their eyes. She desperately tried to see if FJ was among them but, from what she could tell, these others were all girls. Most of them were raggedy and scrawny. They looked like real outsiders with matted hair and dirty, angry faces. But she did make out one with brushed hair and clean clothes.

Suddenly another person was dumped next to her, a young girl who couldn't have been more than four or five, fresh tears streaking down her chubby red face.

Then the door slammed shut again and darkness descended. The engine started up and she felt the new girl lean into her, her little body shuddering and shaking like hers had done earlier. Liss wished she could comfort the girl, but she couldn't talk and couldn't even put her arm around her.

She shuffled her bottom around and reached out her fingers. She felt the ridged metal truck floor and the edge of some carpet. Then her fingers came upon material – the girl's T-shirt. She scooched around a bit more until finally she found the girl's bound hands. She took them in her own and gave them a small squeeze.

Liss felt the girl's body stiffen next to her, felt her fingers freeze and then retract. Liss felt for them again and rubbed her thumb along the back of the girl's hand, trying to reassure her. But the girl really went crazy, like she'd been given an electric shock, and tried to shift away so Liss gave up and inched backwards.

The truck soon stopped again and this time two more girls were put into the truck. As the door opened, Liss quickly stared around at the other prisoners. The small girl from before looked up at her with wide eyes and Liss tried to smile, but it was impossible with her mouth covered like this.

As they were plunged back into blackness, Liss felt the girl shuffle towards her and she took a grain of comfort from the small body.

The truck stopped several more times and on each occasion another girl was dumped inside. Liss's eyes soon grew heavy, and despite her fear and worry about where they were headed, she eventually fell asleep.

Waking from a dreamless slumber, Liss tried to stretch out her limbs, but they seemed to be stuck.

And then she remembered.

In that brief second after waking, she had thought it had all been a dream, but as the terrible stench of fear and pee and vomit hit her nostrils, she knew it was all too real. She was here in the truck, kidnapped, taken from her family and heading who knew where.

Her body cramped with stiffness and the darkness crowded in on her like a living breathing thing. If she could have opened her mouth, she would have screamed. She took a deep breath in through her nose, realising that the truck was now still and the engine had stopped. Maybe the man was putting more girls in the truck.

What would her parents be thinking by now? Were they cross or worried? Maybe they were looking for her. Perhaps FJ had managed to escape...

The truck door opened. It was dark outside, but the fresh air felt good on her sweaty face. She heard voices. A man and a woman talking. No... two women. They were talking about numbers and about boys and girls, but she couldn't make proper sense of the words. The voices merged like mashed potato and butter all swirled around together. She realised that was a strange thought to have, but she felt very strange. Not so scared anymore, just tired and odd.

A face loomed above her. It was a woman. She was quite young and Liss couldn't work out if she was friendly or not. She didn't smile, but she didn't look mean either.

The woman was saying stuff, but Liss didn't think she was talking to her. No. She wasn't. She was talking to a man next to her. They were arguing.

'Was this tape really necessary?' the woman said.

'I'd like to see you try driving all day with a lorry-load of screaming kids,' he replied.

'Poor dear.' The woman took the corner of Liss's tape in her fingers and gently began to peel it off.

The skin around Liss's lips stung as the tape pulled away, but it didn't hurt as much as she'd thought it would.

'What's your name?' the woman asked.

Liss took in a gulp of air through her mouth. It was such a relief to get rid of that horrid tape.

'Liss. Melissa,' she replied.

'Hello, Melissa. My name's Sarah.'

Liss stared up at the woman.

'Let's get you out of this nasty truck. I'm sure you could do with a wash and some food.'

The woman climbed up into the vehicle and began peeling the tape off all the girls' mouths. But it was strange, because even though everyone was now free to talk and cry and scream, not one of them said a word.

CHAPTER SIX

RILEY

I stared at the middle-aged couple in front of us. Even after all that had happened, I still had trouble believing they'd lied and sent us into a trap. They just didn't look the type. Showed how much I knew.

As he began talking, I wanted to tell Fred to shut up. I wanted to storm out of there and leave him and Jesse to rot in their cell. But, of course, I didn't.

'Now,' he began, 'what we told you young 'uns weren't all a lie like you might of thought. We *have* got two children, same ages as you two and they *are* with Grey. But we didn't tell you everything. We've done some things we're ashamed of. We shouldn't have done 'em and for that... well... we're sorry.'

As he said sorry, he looked into my eyes. I stared back for a split-second before looking away. But now I was becoming a little intrigued.

'Our kids went missing nine years ago,' he continued. 'Vanished without a trace. Then, about a year ago, we found out that Grey might have been the one who took 'em. So Jess and me, we went to Salisbury to see about getting 'em back. We had no plan like, we just wanted to see if it were really true and to beg for 'em back.

'Well, we never met the big man himself, but another man called Mr Sadler, he said our kids wasn't there. We insisted. We said we'd met someone who used to be there and they knew for definite that our Lissy and Freddie Junior was there. We said we wasn't going nowhere till we had our kids back.

'This Sadler man, he kind of smiled in a horrible way and I wanted to kill him, but Jess held me back and she spoke nice to him. She begged and said we'd do anything to get our babies back. Sadler made us sweat outside those gates for days, but just as we was giving up hope he comes back and makes us a proposition.

'He tells us they're growing their city bigger and they need more hands. Not old hands like ours, but young energetic kids. Well, I know that's cos kids is easier to brainwash and I want to punch his smarmy face as he's telling us, but I hold my fists down tight and I keep listening. He said if we can send him a hundred kids, we can have our two back. Now, Jess and I think he's joking or sommat. I mean, a hundred kids? What's he on?

'He said it would be easy. There's loads of orphans out there living rough with no sorta life. Just trying to survive, we'd be doing those kids a favour. We said if it were that easy, why didn't they do it theirselves. He said that they were doing all they could, but it wasn't enough. They're looking to get thousands. They're trying to take over the country.

'Well, Jess and I didn't feel too comfortable about it. We asked if there was another way, or could we move in too and stay in the Close with our kids. But Sadler laughed and he flat out refused. So we asked if we could at least see our kids and couldn't believe it when Sadler agreed. He brought our babies out, separately, to see us the next day.

'They was grown-up, teenagers, but you could tell it were definitely them. They looked well, but they didn't look at us and we weren't allowed to talk to 'em. Can you imagine being so close, but not allowed to put your arms around them and feel your little 'uns after all them years? It was like torture.'

Jessie let out a sob and Fred rubbed her arm.

'We had no choice,' he said. 'We had to think about doing what the man asked. We tried going to the army first and seeing if they'd help us, but they didn't wanna know. I tell you, that lot are as good as useless. We didn't have no one else to turn to, so we kidded ourselves that what we were doing weren't so bad. That the kids we sent would be better off there, looked after and fed proper with kids their own ages; but we knew it was wrong.

'We went home and then we went out trying to find children who was in a bad way, who wouldn't have made it without Grey's help. But we both felt sick at what we was doing. I kept seeing my kids' faces in my mind and it kept me going. I'm ashamed and I feel like I ain't going to heaven for what I done.

'When you two turned up at our place and came up with the idea of rescuing Lissy and FJ, we wanted to go through with it. But we'd nearly reached our target of a hundred kids and it was too much of a risk to let you try out your plan when we knew our two was almost free anyway. So we added you to the list of one hundred and we told Sadler about your plan.'

My heart raced as I discovered how they'd deceived us from the start. I felt like a gullible fool all over again. Luc's fists were bunched. Pa's chair scraped back a fraction, and I thought he was going to get up and start yelling. But no one said a word.

Jessie also stayed quiet. She'd stopped crying and her face now showed no emotion. She looked vacant, like she wasn't even listening. Fred continued.

'We kept telling ourselves that we was doing it for our kids. They was relying on us. We couldn't just leave 'em there. We're their parents. We're supposed to be there for them. Who else, if not us?'

Luc cleared his throat.

'Say for a moment that I believe you – and I'm not saying I do – that's a horrible situation and I can kind of see why you did what you did.'

'Well, I can't,' Pa said. 'There's no excuse for it. None.'

'You got kids?' Fred asked Pa.

'Riley's my daughter.'

'Aah,' Fred said. 'Well, in that case, I'm very sorry 'bout what happened. But wouldn't you have done the same for your Riley? Wouldn't you suffer eternal damnation if you could save your kids?'

Pa didn't reply.

'So, have you got your children back now?' I asked.

'Well, that's just it,' Fred replied. 'We went back there after we got 'em their kids. And we asked for ours back. Another man comes out, and tells us that we done so well, they want another hundred kids from us before they let Liss and Freddie Junior out. We couldn't believe it. We done all that, more or less sold our souls to the devil, for nothing.

'We can't carry on getting more kids for 'em. And, anyway, I reckon they ain't never gonna let our kids go.' Fred paused and darted a glance at us. Then he looked at Jessie. It seemed like he wanted to say something else, but he remained quiet.

I couldn't help but think they were telling the truth. When we'd first met Fred and Jessie on their farm, near Salisbury, I had instantly liked them and now I remembered why: they had come across as genuine and warm, but with a sadness that couldn't easily be faked. That was why, later on, I found it so hard to believe they'd betrayed us. But we couldn't afford to take them at their word. Not after last time. It could have all been another elaborate ploy and James Grey was not a man I wanted to meet again.

Jessie said something, but her voice was so quiet I couldn't hear her. She spoke again, slightly louder this time.

'We've no right to ask, but we need your help.'

'You're our only hope,' Fred added.

Pa finally spoke. 'That's all very well, Mr...'

'Just call me Fred.'

'That's all very well,' Pa continued. 'But, even if what you said is the truth, why the hell would we put ourselves at risk to help you and your family after what you did to Riley and Luc? In fact, give me one good reason why we shouldn't have you both shot. If you were in my position, would *you* trust you?' Pa got to his feet and took a step closer to the couple.

'Those is all fair questions and I'll answer them as best I can,' Fred replied calmly. 'We've reached the point where we really don't care what happens to us. Without our kids, what's the point of anything anymore? That's why we weren't really afraid to come to you to ask for help. We're desperate. *But* we've come across something you might want to hear. Something that puts you and your settlement in danger.'

'I hope you're not threatening us.' Pa stood in front of me, blocking my view of the couple.

'No, no, you've misunderstood,' Fred replied.

'Well, you'd better explain yourself more clearly.'

'How much do you know about what's going on behind them walls in Salisbury?' Fred asked. 'It ain't good. When we was last there, we got talking to some folk. You can't believe how many people are hanging around outside them walls now, for some reason or another. It seems like James Grey is preparing himself for sommat big. It's part of the reason we thought you might help us. We've got information that is particularly pertaining to you, down here on the coast.'

'Okay,' Pa prompted. 'Go on.'

'Well, first I need an assurance from you.'

'You're not in any position to ask for assurances,' Luc said, standing and moving next to Pa.

'Let's all sit back down, shall we,' Roger Brennan said.

Pa nodded and returned to his seat. Luc did the same.

But Fred stood up. 'My information is vital to all your safety and the only assurance I need is that you won't hurt Jessie and that you'll help us get our kids back.'

'Sit down,' Roger barked.

Fred flushed and sat back on the bed. Jessie squeezed his arm as he carried on talking. 'If you agree to that, then I'll tell you what you need to know.'

'Getting your children back from Grey won't be easy,' Pa said. 'And do you even know where they are? That place is huge. It's a city inside a fortress.'

'We think we know roughly where they are. But we still need your help,' Fred said.

'If your information's good, we'll try to help you formulate a plan,' Pa said. 'If your information's worthless, you'll stay locked up until we decide what to do with you.'

Fred and Jessie glanced at each other.

'My information is solid,' Fred said. 'And we need more than a plan. We need to know you'll do everything in your power to rescue our children.'

'Very well. You have my word.' Pa nodded his assent. 'As long as your information is as good as you said it is. Now, tell us what you know.'

CHAPTER SEVEN

LISS

Liss soon found her voice.

'Where's my brother?' she asked.

'Shh,' the woman called Sarah replied. 'Let's get you all out of the truck and we can talk later.'

'But my brother was taken. He's called FJ, Freddie. He's not hurt, is he?'

'Shh. I'm sure he's just fine,' Sarah said.

Then the other girls began to talk too. Asking questions about their families, asking where they were and saying they wanted to go home. Strangely, one girl with short hair started swearing and shouting at the others, telling them to shut up and stop being babies.

'Enough!' Sarah cried, and clapped her hands twice. She hadn't exactly shouted, but she sounded strict and her voice filled the truck.

The girls fell silent.

'Those who wish to leave this truck and eat tonight will stay quiet. Those who wish to remain tied up inside may do as they please.'

The little girl next to Liss gave a hiccupping sob and Liss shushed her, worried that Sarah would leave her in the vehicle.

'Good,' Sarah said as the girls fell silent. She set to work with a small knife, cutting through the girls' wrist and ankle ties. 'When you are unbound, you may stand outside the vehicle forming an orderly line,' she said. 'Please remain quiet unless I request otherwise.'

As Liss's ties were cut, she tried to stretch her arms out in front of her, but they were so stiff it was virtually impossible and they hurt so bad. Her legs weren't as sore, but her bottom had gone numb, full of pins and needles.

She climbed down from the truck and stood next to a tall girl who must have been about FJ's age. It was dark out, but lanterns glowed and Liss could see that she was standing in a yard in front of a huge building of some kind. The yard was bordered by a long high wall and so there was nowhere to run even if she felt brave enough to try.

Liss suddenly caught sight of the man who had kidnapped her. He was leaving with the other man who had been talking to Sarah. She tried to see where they were going, but soon their figures melted into the darkness, the echoing ring of their footsteps receding.

She turned back to the truck. Sarah was still working her way through the ties. The small girl sat on the floor of the truck even though her ties had now been cut. She looked dazed. Liss turned and held her arms out to her and the girl stared for a moment before shuffling into them. Liss lifted her down, her stiff arms aching in protest. Once on the ground, the girl stuck her thumb in her mouth and held Liss's hand.

'I'm Liss,' she hissed. 'What's your name?'

'Annabelle. I want to go home. Where's my mummy?'

'Shh,' Liss whispered. 'We have to be quiet. Don't worry. I'll look after you.'

Annabelle stepped closer to Liss and gripped her hand tighter.

Sarah had now finished her task and had left the truck. She came and stood at the end of the line of girls. Another woman appeared in front of them, older than Sarah. She didn't really look at them, but began to count them instead. When she was done, she glared along the line.

'My name is Leah,' she said. 'Follow me.' She strode towards the building and the girls followed without hesitation. They all walked in single file except for Liss and Annabelle who held hands. Liss worried they would be told off, but Annabelle's hand was clamped so firmly onto hers that she didn't even try to let go.

Even though she was scared and tired, Liss was glad to be in the fresh air again. The smell and the heat and the discomfort of the truck had been awful. She kept glancing about in case she spotted FJ, but it was so dark she could only see a few yards ahead. She really wanted to ask someone about him again, but the thought of being sent back into the truck was enough to keep her quiet for now.

There weren't as many girls as she had first thought. She did a quick head count. There were eight including her and Annabelle. In the truck, she was sure there had been more like twenty. But it had been dark.

Glancing down at Annabelle, she was relieved to see that the girl had stopped crying at last, even though her eyes and cheeks were still swollen and red. She was a pretty thing, her clothes new and smart and her hair all shining brown curls. Liss wondered how she had managed to be caught. Her beautiful clothes meant she must have come from a rich Perimeter.

The older woman, Leah, had now stopped at a wooden door. She took a key from her pocket and slotted it into the lock, turning it once and pushing the door open.

'Follow me inside,' she called. 'There are wash-hand basins

to your right. Scrub your hands using the soap provided. I will be checking to see they are cleaned thoroughly.'

Liss waited in the queue, the sound of running water making her want to pee. As the queue moved along, she found herself inside a dimly lit hall with flickering wall lights. A row of wooden benches ran along the left side of the wall and above them hung a line of coats and hats on pegs.

Soon it was her turn at the sinks. There were three in a row attached to the wall. She let Annabelle go first and helped the girl wash her hands properly. The water was freezing and it was hard to get any lather out of the small, cracked tablet of soap. There didn't appear to be a hand towel, so Liss shook the drips off her hands and wiped them on her jeans. Annabelle wiped her own hands on the front of her dress.

Sarah followed them, washing her hands and giving them a quick smile.

The queue of girls disappeared through a set of double glass doors. Liss hurried to catch up, dragging Annabelle along with her.

They now found themselves in a large hall which smelt of warm stale food. Women in aprons and white caps were wiping down long wooden trestle tables laid out in rows.

'Eight more for supper!' Leah called out to one of the women.

'It's too late for anything more than broth and bread,' the woman called back.

'Broth and bread is fine,' Leah replied.

What Liss wouldn't give to be at home with Mum and Dad and FJ right now. Sitting at the kitchen table, chatting about the farm and which animals had escaped or were ill or were about to have babies. Laughing with Mum about what Hadley the goat had eaten or answering one of Dad's history quizzes. Would she ever see them again? A tear threatened to fall from her left eye, but she managed to wipe it away before anyone saw.

'Line up and hold out your hands,' Leah said.

Liss looked to see what she should be doing, but, like her, the others were also looking around nervously. After a few seconds' hesitation, they formed a raggedy line and held their hands out in front of them. Leah walked along the line inspecting their palms, the backs of their hands and their fingernails.

The tallest girl was sent back to wash her hands again. As she turned, she banged her leg on the table and her face flushed bright red. She scowled and marched across the floor, her bare feet slapping the tiled floor as she walked.

The rest of them sat at a clean trestle table next to a serving hatch in the wall. They waited in silence until the girl returned. She had to hold her hands out for inspection again. Leah still didn't seem very happy at the state of the girl's nails, but she bade her sit down.

'Sarah, we are ready,' Leah said.

Sarah bowed her head and began to speak:

'Father, pardon our sins and accept our thanks for these and all other blessings. We thank you for leading us here to him and for delivering more of your children unto his care. In Christ's name we ask, Amen.'

After Sarah had spoken, one of the women in aprons came over to the table and placed bowls of soup and drinking cups before each girl. Then she returned with thick chunks of crusty bread. The woman poured water for each of them before placing the tin jug on the table.

'Eat, children,' Leah said. She had no food in front of her, just a cup of water.

Liss gulped down her water and then blew on her soup spoon before tasting the hot liquid. She motioned to Annabelle to do the same.

'Quietly,' Leah said. She frowned at two other girls who had begun slurping their soup down. 'We eat quietly and slowly. We give thanks for every mouthful.'

The girls looked back at Leah but did as they were told. Liss made sure she made no sound as she ate; she didn't want to attract any undue attention.

Once the girls had cleared their bowls and eaten their bread, they sat quietly waiting for whatever was to happen next. Liss was acutely aware of her own breathing and tried to make it quieter. But the more she tried to stifle it, the louder it sounded. She was sure everyone was looking at her.

Then she heard a whimper. She glanced down and saw that Annabelle's face had turned red again and huge fat tears were rolling down her cheeks.

'I want my mummy,' the girl sobbed.

'Shh, shhh,' Liss soothed. She was terrified that Leah or Sarah would become cross if she carried on crying.

'I want to go home!' Annabelle cried. Her voice echoed across the dinner hall. 'Mummy! MU-U-UM!' She was screaming now, her face red and tear streaked.

Leah stood and marched around to Annabelle who had now worked herself up into a total frenzy. Liss put her arms around Annabelle, but the younger girl was in such a state that she barely noticed.

'Is this your sister?' Leah asked.

Liss didn't know what to say.

'Well?'

'Yes,' Liss said. 'Yes, she is. She's just tired. I'll get her to be quiet.'

'See that you do. We do not tolerate such brattish ungodly behaviour here. This is Grey's Church, not some barbaric heathen den.'

Sarah rose from her chair. 'Calm yourself, Leah. I shall show them to their room. They're tired, that's all.'

Leah flushed but didn't reply.

Sarah motioned to Liss to follow with Annabelle.

Liss ignored the wide eyes of the other girls. She took hold of Annabelle's hand and had to almost drag her across the floor to keep up with Sarah who seemed to glide across the tiled floor.

'Come on, Annabelle,' Liss pleaded quietly. 'You can stop crying now. We'll have a rest and you'll feel better, I promise.' But even Liss didn't believe those words. In fact, she felt like joining Annabelle in her tantrum. She wanted to scream for her mother and cry and wail, but she was seven years old, nearly eight. She had to be brave. Crying wouldn't get them out of here. It would only make things worse.

Wherever this was and whatever these people wanted from her, she made a vow to herself there and then that she would not accept this fate. She would do whatever it took to get out of here, find her brother and go home to Mum and Dad. And she would take Annabelle with her.

CHAPTER EIGHT

RILEY

I shifted in my chair. The backs of my legs were numb and my hands were freezing so I sat on them. I was glad I'd grabbed my sweatshirt earlier. I wondered what this news was that Fred was about to tell us. I hoped it was nothing too bad, but I was pretty sure it would be.

'Grey has gathered himself an army,' Fred said. 'He's got guns and the like. Trained up all them kids and adults to march to war. They're coming down here. He wants the coast. He wants your oil.' He looked at Pa.

Pa stared back then shook his head with a disappointed smile. 'That's your information?' Pa said. 'Well, I could've told you *that*. Grey's been threatening to build an army for the past ten years and he's never so much as knocked on our door. In fact, I don't think he's set foot in Dorset, or Hampshire for that matter.'

I realised I'd been holding my breath. For a minute I'd thought we might have been in real danger.

'I'll admit, you had me worried for a second,' Pa continued, 'but that information is not *new* information.' Pa gave a dry laugh.

I tried to catch Luc's eye, but he wasn't looking in my direction.

'You can mock,' said Fred, with a note of anger, 'but you don't know what you're talking about, no offence like.'

Pa raised his eyebrows.

'Jess and me have been to Salisbury a lot and we ain't seen nothing like what we been seeing these last few weeks. It's supposed to be a Christian settlement, but it's more like a military training camp. You won't believe what they got in there. The army shoulda sorted that place out years ago, before it had the chance to grow.'

'But we were only there last month,' I said. 'We didn't see anything like you're describing.'

'I know, Riley,' Jessie said. 'But you were only in one small part. Grey's Close is massive. He controls almost half of Wiltshire and his training camps are unbelievable.'

'We think he must have a weapons factory and we know he's training kids to fight.' Fred shook his head sadly. 'I can't believe what this country's come to, what we've sunk to. And I know me and Jess ain't blameless in all this.

'All the talk up there is of your oil out on that island of yours. Hook Island, that's the name, ain't it? James Grey's attack is coming.'

There was a pause while we all digested Fred's news.

'Say this is true – what sort of numbers are we talking about?' Pa asked.

'Thousands,' Fred replied. 'I dunno how well trained they are, but he's certainly got the numbers. I spoke to this one chap outside the Close and he said Grey done a deal with some West Dorset pirates and got access to boats. Someone else said they seen a couple of copters 'n' all.'

'That's all just hearsay, surely,' Luc said uncertainly.

'I seen the training camps with my own eyes. It's quite an

operation. They're already on the march. They've almost reached our farm and that's not far from here – only outside Fordingbridge. They're taking one Compound at a time, leaving their priest guards behind in each one. They're taking control of the south I reckon. So it won't be long till—'

'Wait a minute,' Pa interrupted. 'They're already on the march?'

'Yeah. I seen 'em at night in their spooky long cloaks, moving all quiet like. Hundreds of 'em. It's like they're floating or sommat.'

A chill settled on me as I remembered the guards from Cathedral Close. Those faceless figures in hoods. And Fred seemed to think they were heading this way.

'They don't bother with outsiders though. They ignored Jess 'n' me when we was on the road. I think they're just after the Perimeters and Compounds. God knows how many places they're already controlling.'

'So they're marching at night?' Luc asked.

'Yeah. We never seen 'em during the day. We heard they've already taken Romsey and Sixpenny Handley—'

'Romsey?' Pa cried. 'Romsey's one of *Eddie's* Perimeters. They haven't taken Romsey. He was only up there a couple of—'

'You got a two-way radio?' Fred interrupted.

'Of course,' Pa replied.

'You try calling them up at Romsey then. See if what I'm saying ain't true.'

Pa got to his feet. 'I'm going to talk to Eddie.' He turned to the door and beckoned for us to follow him out.

'What about our deal?' Fred called after us. 'I gave you good information! You gave me your word...'

But Pa was too preoccupied to answer. I followed him and the others out of the door. My mind was racing. Were James

Grey and his religious army really capable of taking over our Perimeter? What if they were? What if we had to leave our beautiful house? What if our way of life came to an end and we were forced to live a different way?

Everything suddenly seemed more fragile and precious. We couldn't lose our way of life. We just couldn't. I'd seen what life was like on the outside. It was harsh and relentless. And there was no way I would conform to Grey's way of living.

'Do you believe him?' I asked Luc.

'Sounded pretty convincing. Dad's going to be livid if they've taken Romsey. We've got some really good people stationed up there.'

'Let's get Romsey on the radio,' Pa said to Roger. 'Find out if it's true.'

'It might take a while. They don't always answer straight away.'

'Fine. You do it, Roger. I'll be at my place with Eddie and Rita. Come and get us if anything's amiss. In fact, check in with all Perimeters and Compounds within a hundred-mile radius. And double the guards at Hook Island. We need to warn them all. Without causing a panic.'

Roger nodded and locked the cell door.

As we headed back outside into the deepening dusk, the ground beneath my feet felt unsteady, like it was moving. I stumbled and Luc caught hold of my arm.

'You okay, Riley?' Pa asked. But I could see his mind was elsewhere.

'Fine. I'm fine.' But I wasn't fine. I don't think any of us were. What were we supposed to do against an army of thousands? I didn't want to lose everything. I didn't want Grey to make us live a half-life worshipping a god of his creation. And I didn't want to die. If he was coming for us, then I needed to be strong. We would need to fight him. It was the only way we would keep our freedom.

Had I always known this day was coming? Had it been waiting for us all this time? We thought we'd been so clever, that we had tamed the world again, or at least our small corner of it. We thought we'd kept the chaos out and left the rest of the world to deal with it. But the chaos was coming to find us. It was seeking us out again. Had this day been inevitable all along?

CHAPTER NINE

LISS

Sarah led them out of the dining hall through a door at the rear and they found themselves heading along a dark musty corridor. Annabelle's cries had eased into whimpers and thankfully she no longer resisted Liss's attempts to hold her hand.

Sarah kept walking. They passed no one else. It was eerie to be in such a large empty building.

'Do any other people live here?' Liss asked.

Sarah did not reply and Liss felt too unsure of herself to ask again. They came to a door and walked through into another large unlit hall. One wall was made up of floor-to-ceiling windows. Liss's gaze was caught by the small, curved moon that hung outside in the black sky. Was this the same moon that shone into her bedroom window at home? Liss didn't think so.

Beyond the hall were yet more corridors lined with doors that led into unknown rooms. Liss yawned. The truck ride seemed an age ago. She realised they were now climbing a wide staircase with a smooth wooden banister. The wood felt warm under her hand and she caught a whiff of furniture polish.

The floorboards on the landing creaked under their feet. A bell chimed outside.

'Hurry now.' Sarah quickened her pace. 'I have no wish to be late. Hurry, girls.'

Annabelle had slowed almost to a stop, so Liss hoisted her up into her arms and half ran after the woman.

Eventually, Sarah stopped outside a door. It was unlocked and she turned the tarnished brass knob, pushed open the door and walked inside.

Liss followed and deposited Annabelle back down on the floor. They now found themselves in a large-ish room with rows of small metal beds.

'I must go,' Sarah said. 'There's a bathroom to your left. I suggest you go straight to sleep. The others will be along shortly and Leah will not be pleased if you aren't in bed.'

'Which one is—'

'Any bed will do,' Sarah interrupted. And with that, she left the room and closed the door behind her.

Over the chime of the bells, Liss heard the click of a key turning. She waited a moment until Sarah's footsteps had died away, and then she tried the handle. She had guessed correctly – they were locked inside.

Despite the locked door, Liss felt a little calmer, less panicked. Maybe because she was finally away from the grownups. Things felt a bit fuzzy though. Her earlier fear had softened and now she simply felt exhausted.

A large window beckoned at the end of the dark room. The girls walked over to it, Annabelle's hand still gripping Liss's. Metal bars striped the outside of the glass. An old fashioned street lamp stood in the courtyard below, throwing up a soft yellow light.

Liss pressed her nose against the glass, inhaling the dusty window smell. Her mind felt blank. She couldn't seem to think anymore. Every time she tried to latch onto a thought, it slipped away like a wriggling fish.

Annabelle was quiet too. Liss gazed down at the girl, who stared out of the window. Dirty tear tracks lined her cheeks.

'Come on,' said Liss. 'Do you want to choose a bed?'

Annabelle nodded and sank down onto the one closest to the window. Liss took the girl's shoes off and lifted her legs up. She pulled the brown scratchy blanket out from under her and laid it across her body. Annabelle's dark curls splayed out over the sheet. There was no pillow. The little girl turned on her side, stuck her thumb in her mouth and closed her eyes.

Liss sat on the edge of the bed and stroked the girl's hair back from her face, gently soothing her to sleep like her mum did for her when she was ill. The bells had stopped chiming and the room now sat in silence apart from Annabelle's regular breathing. The younger girl's mouth had fallen slightly open and her face appeared relaxed. She was asleep.

Standing up again, Liss returned to the barred window. Beyond the courtyard lay a patch of grass and beyond that towered a high brick wall with tall trees behind it. Their leafy silhouettes were unmoving, like a painting.

Liss suddenly remembered what Sarah had said about how Leah would be unhappy if she and Annabelle weren't in bed when she arrived with the other girls. Liss had no pyjamas. Not even a toothbrush and her mouth tasted horrible. But she thought she'd better at least try to go to sleep. She was tired, but awake. Scared, but strangely not panicky anymore.

She eased off her trainers and lay on the next bed along from Annabelle's. Resting her head on the stiff cotton sheet, she wondered if she would ever fall asleep. What were Mum and Dad doing now? They must be mad with worry. And what about FJ?

This place was creepy and weird. Why had those people brought her here? What did they want from her? She was just a girl. Maybe this was all a terrible dream. She should close her eyes and try to sleep and maybe when she woke up she'd be back at home and she could tell FJ about the awful nightmare she'd had. She closed her eyes and willed sleep to come.

Liss dreamed of dark places and dimly lit corridors. She tried to run, but her legs felt heavy as if they had been stuck to the floor with gungy glue. She should be able to run faster than this. She was good at running – almost as fast as FJ. But it was no good. The darkness was closing in on her like a thick cloud. And there were voices hidden inside the blackness – whispers and mumblings.

She crouched down to try to shield herself from the dark, but it was no good. The blackness was now in her hair and on her face, crawling up her nose and into her mouth. The muttering was growing louder and more insistent. She tried to scream, but no sound came out of her mouth. And the voices in the darkness suddenly merged into a single clear voice:

'Silence,' the voice said.

Liss awoke, sweating and shivering. She realised the voice in her dream had spoken in real life. With a spasm of dread she remembered where she was and forced herself to lift her eyelids a fraction. The room was still dark save for the light from the streetlamp outside. The other girls were now here in the room, climbing into the empty beds.

The woman, Leah, stood in front of the bedroom door like a sentry. It was she who had spoken, waking Liss from her nightmare. Leah's face was hidden in the shadows, an eerie image, and so Liss squeezed her eyes shut again. Her skin was hot and her throat was so dry. She needed water, but she daren't get up or ask. Maybe when Leah had left the room, she'd be able to creep to the bathroom and fetch a drink.

It seemed like it took an eternity for all the girls to fall asleep. For all the coughs and sighs and sobs to stop. Finally, the room was still, save for the occasional creaky bedspring. Leah remained at the door like a soldier or a statue. She was standing so still, Liss began to wonder if she was actually real, but eventually she moved, making Liss jump.

To Liss's dismay, Leah walked into the bathroom. After a couple of minutes she emerged wearing a long nightdress, her hair in a loose braid down her back. She carried her clothes neatly folded in a bundle which she placed on the floor at the foot of an empty bed. And then Liss's heart sank even further as the woman climbed into one of the beds and turned on her side, facing away. Leah was going to be sleeping here; she was going to be here all night.

The need for a drink of water was now so great that she was prepared to risk the wrath of anyone to get it. With trembling fingers, Liss pushed back the bed covers and stood up. A couple of the girls eyed her, but Leah stayed still. Liss tiptoed past the beds and pushed open the door to the bathroom.

The stone floor was freezing, but there was a sink with two taps and Liss made her way across to it with relief. She twisted the right hand tap and stuck her face under the thin trickle of water, gulping the liquid down. Once she'd had her fill, she crept back to bed, pulling the blanket back up to her chin. Annabelle was still asleep in the adjacent bed, her face flushed, her hair plastered around her face, light snores drifting from her open mouth.

Liss watched the girl's face, and the sight of it eventually soothed her back to sleep.

Liss was used to waking up with the sun and didn't mind getting out of bed before dawn. But the other girls were finding it much more difficult. She had managed to rouse Annabelle and now the two of them were sitting on the edge of the bed, the small girl's arms wrapped around Liss, a dazed expression on her face.

Leah was already up and dressed and poking at one particular girl who was still in bed, her eyes scrunched up tight, the blanket pulled up to her nose.

'All of you are to shower quickly and quietly,' Leah said. 'There are towels on the table outside the bathroom. Leave your old clothes in the basket by the door. There are fresh clothes on the table.' She turned her attention back to the sleeping girl.

'Get. Up. NOW.'

The girl opened her eyes. The expression on Leah's face told her all she needed to know, and so she slid out of bed and staggered over to the others, rubbing at her eyes.

There seemed to be some confusion. Leah had said there were towels on the table, but the first two girls had taken one each and now there were none left.

'Um, there's only two towels,' a girl about Liss's age said to Leah.

'Then you must share,' Leah replied.

Liss and Annabelle were fifth and sixth in the queue. They went in together and showered quickly under the lukewarm water. There didn't appear to be any soap. The two small towels were both already sopping wet and so they used their old clothes to dry themselves.

The new clothes were homespun – rough cotton shirts and shapeless pinafore dresses. Annabelle's was much too big and the skirt of the pinafore hung down past her ankles. Liss helped her to roll up the sleeves of the too-long shirt and then she put on her own.

'It's scratchy and horrible,' Annabelle said. 'I want to wear *my* dress.'

'Keep it on for now. We can pretend we're dressing up.'

Annabelle thought about it for a couple of seconds. 'Okay. Are we Cinderella?'

'Yes. And Leah's the wicked stepmother,' she muttered.

'I don't like this game.' Annabelle's bottom lip trembled.

'Nor do I, but we just have to play for a little bit longer.'

'And then can we go home?'

'I hope so.' Liss pushed out the thought of home in case it made her cry.

'Each girl is to take one of these,' Leah said, her hand outstretched.

Liss waited her turn and took an elastic band from Leah's sweaty palm.

'Hair must be tied back from your face. No loose strands or I will cut them off with my scissors.'

Liss fixed her own pale locks into a ponytail, before helping Annabelle, whose curls were trickier to tie back.

'Ow!' Annabelle cried.

'Is there a problem?' Leah asked, walking over. 'Are my scissors required?'

'No,' Liss squeaked. 'It's okay.'

'You've a mark on your neck, girl,' Leah said, pressing her forefinger painfully against Liss's throat. 'Did you not use the soap provided?'

'Sorry,' Liss said. 'I must have missed a bit. Oh, wait, do you mean the half moon shape? That's my birthmark.'

Leah pulled and pinched at the skin where Liss's birthmark sat. 'Looks like the devil's mark to me.' She crossed herself before doling out the rest of the elastic bands.

Once all the girls were showered and dressed, they followed Leah out of the room and back down to the now-crowded dining hall. There must have been well over two hundred people sitting at the tables and they were nearly all children. Liss's heart skipped a beat – maybe FJ was here... but she quickly realised the room was full of girls. No boys at all. No FJ.

You would have thought that with all those people, there would have been plenty of noise. Chatter and clanging cutlery and all that type of thing, but Liss was spooked by the almost total silence of the room. Just the occasional throat being cleared and the scrape of cutlery.

The girls followed Leah to a wide service hatch where three women were dishing out breakfast. Lissy followed what Leah and the others girls did. She took a bowl from a stack on the side and held it out as one of the women dumped a couple of ladles of porridge into it. Then she collected a spoon from a deep cutlery tray. She made sure Annabelle did the same before following their roommates to the trestle table from the previous night.

Once they were seated, a voice rang out across the room. Liss raised her eyes to see where it was coming from.

At the far end of the room, several women sat at a table on a raised platform. One of the women stood, her voice clear and strong, carrying across the heads of all the girls. It looked like Sarah, the woman from last night.

'Father, pardon our sins and accept our thanks for these and all other blessings. We thank you for leading us here to him and for delivering more of your children unto his care. We ask you to help them in this unsettling time and help them tread the path of righteousness to glory. In Christ's name we ask, Amen.'

'Amen,' echoed the voices in the room.

Sarah sat down and everyone began to eat. The porridge was surprisingly good, piping hot and sweetened with a little honey. Liss and Annabelle cleared their bowls quickly. Still nobody talked. Was it always like this? Did nobody ever speak here?

Liss cast quick glances at the other girls on her table. None of them looked her way. They all kept their eyes down, focused on their breakfast. There was the tall girl with the dirty fingernails, the sleepy girl who hadn't wanted to get out of bed this morning, three outsiders who still had matted hair and dirty faces despite showering, an older girl with short hair and a permanent scowl, Annabelle, and her.

At the next table, a small pretty girl with pale blonde hair flashed her a quick smile. This startled Liss and she immediately looked around to see if anyone else had noticed. She glanced back at the girl and gave her a nervous smile in return. The girl raised her eyebrows, smiled again and then turned her attention back to her porridge. She looked a bit older than Liss. Maybe she would get to talk to her later. Find out what was going on. And, more importantly, discover if there was a way to get out of here.

CHAPTER TEN

RILEY

'Sounds like Fred and whats-her-name might be a couple of crackpots,' Eddie said. 'We can't do anything drastic on the word of two people. Especially two people with *their* track record.'

Twenty minutes had passed since we'd been in the cells with Fred and Jessie, and we were now gathered in the large formal dining room of our Edwardian family house. Luc's mother, Rita, and Ma were also here, as well as my uncle Tom, who was a Perimeter guard, and Roger Brennan, Head of Perimeter Security.

Everyone was seated around the fruitwood table as Ma served up a hastily thrown together supper of chilli and salad. Luc sat opposite me, but we hardly acknowledged each other; this afternoon's closeness had evaporated.

Eddie had done most of the talking so far. Luc's parents, Eddie and Rita Donovan, were responsible for setting up Perimeters around the country – constructing the huge electrified fences, supplying trained guards and constantly monitoring and maintaining them. Eddie had wanted to go straight over to talk to Fred himself, but Pa persuaded him to wait.

'I've told Roger to tap up all our contacts to see if Fred and Jessie's story checks out,' Pa said. 'We need to sit tight for a while longer.'

'Whatever the situation, Grey has to be stopped,' Eddie replied. 'We've let this go on for too many years. The man's out of control. We need to act. We need to cut the head off the snake.' He leant across the table and stared at Pa. 'Johnny, you know what I'm saying. You've never been one to shy away from doing what needs to be done.'

Pa didn't reply.

'Okay,' Rita chimed in. 'So if we have to eliminate Grey, how do you propose we actually do it? How easy is it to get to the man?'

'Hold on a minute,' Ma said. 'Before we start on the "hows" and "whens", we need to agree whether this is the right thing to do. Is there another way that won't involve a war? Can we reason with the man? Offer him an alternative?'

'Eleanor,' Pa said. 'He's not the sort of man you can reason with. And even if he was, you can't trust him. We've been putting this off for too long, ignoring the danger. It's been building and building while we've been sitting around pretending his plans will come to nothing. But I was wrong to laugh at Fred. He's probably right. We're facing a war and it's one we're not prepared for. Grey's already on the march, for Christ's sake. And if he's taken a Perimeter already... well, that's an act of aggression.'

I didn't know what to think. My head was spinning. I'd lived in the Perimeter my whole life and our safety had never been in such jeopardy before. Were we really in as much danger as Fred made out?

'We'll be okay down here though,' Luc said. 'We've got trained guards.'

'Yes, Luc, but thirty or so guards against thousands of brainwashed crusaders with weapons, is not a fight I think we can win.' Pa's expression became grimmer with every word.

Luc's expression matched Pa's.

'But there must be hundreds of Perimeter guards around the country,' I said. 'They'll come and help us, surely.'

'Riley, we can't bring those guards down here. They're needed where they are. What do you think would happen to those Perimeters without the proper defences in place?' Pa replied.

'Oh. Yeah,' I replied, feeling foolish. I stared past him at the window where the heavy brocade curtains were still tied back even though it was dark out. The dining room reflected back at me from the cold black glass. Behind our reflections, charcoal clouds skimmed past the moon.

Suddenly, Liam barged into the room without knocking.

'Sorry,' he said. 'I've got news.'

We all transferred our attention to him, noting his flushed face and glittering eyes.

'Romsey aren't replying. No one's on the radio over there. Mr Brennan's still trying to get through. But, worse than that, I spoke to Pete over in the Southampton East Perimeter. He managed to send out a mayday before the channel went dead. And the same thing has happened at Blandford. We think it was a coordinated attack. Grey must've taken those Perimeters at the same time.'

Everyone was silent for a moment, all eyes locked on Liam.

'Christ almighty,' Eddie said, his voice low and furious.

'Clever,' Pa said grimly. 'A pincer movement. We need to make sure they don't get any closer. I'm talking about Southampton West and Poole. And we'd better warn the Compounds too. Any news to the north?'

'Ringwood and Fordingbridge Perimeters and Charminster Compound are still intact as of ten minutes ago,' Liam said. 'We warned them all and they're tightening security.'

'Damn it!' Eddie scraped his chair back and stood up. 'What a mess.'

My mind spun. What did this mean? The enemy was sitting to our east and to our west. If Grey captured the Perimeters to the north of us too, we'd be surrounded.

'We have to go north to defend Fordingbridge,' I said.

'She's right,' Pa said.

I was happy for his praise despite the fear in my belly.

'I think we may be too late for Fordingbridge,' Rita said. 'We'd be better off going to Ringwood. It's closer and that will give us more time to prepare.'

'Okay. Agreed,' said Pa.

'We can't leave Talbot Woods undefended,' Eddie said.

'We won't,' Pa replied. 'We'll recruit from Charminster, strengthen our defences here and take a shitload of weapons up to Ringwood. If we can hold them off there, then we can stay safe. He can't be allowed to get to Hook Island. The oil is everything. I'd better warn Poole to triple security around the island.'

'At least there are no more roads from the west,' Luc said. 'They'll have a hard time getting here from that direction. It'll take days.'

'But what about the eastern Perimeter towns?' Uncle Tom asked. 'Southampton West, Brockenhurst, Christchurch, Boscombe...'

'Yeah,' Luc replied. 'They'll be next on Grey's list.'

'I'll have to send them more guards,' Eddie said. 'Christ knows where I'll get them from. If only the army weren't so bloody useless, they could help out.'

'They're only useless because we pinched all the good soldiers to work for us,' Rita said drily.

'Well, we'll have to get some help from somewhere.'

'I'll see to it,' Rita said, standing. She kissed Ma on the cheek. Ma, who had begun to look pale and terrified.

'I thought we were safe here, Johnny,' she said. 'You promised we'd always be safe.'

'You'll be fine, hon,' Rita said, stroking Ma's hair. But I saw the look Rita gave Eddie. 'Okay, Liam and Tom, you're with me. Roger, you coming?' Rita swept out of the room. Liam winked at me before following his boss out of the door with Tom.

Pa shuffled his chair closer to Ma and whispered something in her ear. She looked slightly less worried. They kissed and she left the room.

'So,' Eddie said, pushing himself up from the table with his fists. 'We go to Ringwood. It's like I said, we cut the head off the snake. It's the only way.'

'Let's just hope it doesn't grow a new one,' Pa replied grimly.

CHAPTER ELEVEN

LISS

Once the girls had finished breakfast, they returned their bowls to the serving hatch and followed Leah out of the dining hall. This time she led them through a different door, out into a long courtyard in front of a grey stone building. Out here, the weather was as bland as the people and the place. Neither hot nor cold. Not sunny or raining. Just a dull day with not even a breeze to ruffle their hair.

Sarah stood at the entrance to the building, in front of a set of thick dark wooden doors. The girls were made to stand in lines.

'First row!' Sarah's voice carried through the courtyard, clear and loud.

The first row of children walked into the building, led by a woman.

'Second row!'

The second row of children filed inside. This went on until Sarah called out the fifth row. This was Liss and Annabelle's row, led by Leah. The girls in Liss's line followed Leah into the building.

Once inside, Liss glanced around and saw several doors to

unknown rooms. A wide sweeping staircase curved around away from the entrance. They followed Leah up the stairs and found themselves in a large classroom with wooden desks facing a blackboard. Most of the desks were already occupied with other girls who all faced forward and didn't even glance back to look at Liss and the others as they filed in.

Liss had an overwhelming surge of panic. Her stomach lurched and tears gathered behind her eyes, threatening to spill out. What was she doing here in this weird place? She should be at home sitting at the kitchen table right now with Mum and Dad and FJ. Dad would be telling FJ to stop drumming his feet against the table and FJ would stop for a moment before starting up again. They would be sipping tea and eating scrambled eggs on toast. And then she and Mum would go off to do the milking while FJ helped Dad.

They had promised them a trip to the local Compound today. Mum was going to trade some of their old clothes for new ones. But, instead, she was here in this quiet scary place. She was alone. No one cared about her here. At least she had Annabelle.

A tall woman stood at the front of the classroom. Her hair was as grey as her clothes. Even her face looked grey. Liss presumed she must be some kind of teacher.

'Find an empty desk and sit,' she said in a clipped voice.

Liss guided Annabelle to a chair and then glanced around in a panic trying to find her own place to sit. She was now the last girl on her feet and broke out in a sweat as she tried to locate an empty desk. No one spoke or tried to help her find a place; not even the teacher. Eventually, she spotted a free desk at the back in the corner. She squeezed her way past the other chairs and desks and sat, not daring to look up, the blood roaring round her head.

Staring at the worn grain in the wooden desk lid, Liss tried to make her mind go blank. But the fear and dread would not go away. Why had they brought her to this awful place? There seemed no good reason for it. Why hadn't anyone told her what was going on? She desperately wanted to speak out and ask questions, but the thought made her legs tremble. The teacher would stare at her, tell her to be quiet or worse. What could she do? How was she ever going to be able to get back home?

Stop thinking like that. She couldn't start crying. She couldn't. If she cried, they would shout at her or even worse, ignore her. She remembered what Mum said to do when she felt scared – to think of nice things. Or, failing that, think of food beginning with A and then B and C and so on. Something monotonous to clear all the nasty things away. It worked and she gradually got her feelings back under control. All the scary thoughts that had threatened to overpower her had been pushed to the side – for now.

After Lissy's momentary panic, the day passed in a blur of sleepiness and boredom. Lessons were all to do with God and religious stuff. Different women taught them, but their voices all merged into one monotonous drone and Liss could hardly keep her eyes open.

They stopped for lunch – soup and bread. And then for supper – soup and bread again followed by a casserole of meat, potatoes and vegetables.

As they plodded back to the bedroom with Leah, Liss felt as though she was being smothered by a thick woollen blanket, her mind all foggy and strange.

None of the girls had spoken to each other all day. It was like they were too tired to bother. They hadn't exactly been forbidden to speak to one another, but everywhere was so quiet that speaking felt wrong. Liss's thoughts kept wobbling around, not staying in one place for more than a couple of seconds so that even when she'd wanted to say something, the words just slipped away.

Once or twice, she had caught sight of the blonde-haired

girl from breakfast, but there had been no opportunity to catch her eye. It was odd though, because each time she saw her, her mind temporarily cleared and she felt a teensy bit more normal.

Annabelle seemed a little better today. She wasn't upset anymore and Liss was always aware of her on the edge of her vision, placidly following instructions. She no longer seemed to need Liss's reassurance. But Liss somehow knew that this wasn't a good thing. She didn't know why, but it had been better when Annabelle was crying and screaming. Better that, than this nothingness.

Now, as they were following Leah along the corridor back to their room, they stopped to let another column of girls pass by. Liss stared at them, all silent and similar in their grey pinafores, all with their eyes cast downward, all clean, pale-faced and expressionless, except for one – the blonde-haired girl.

As they passed each other, the girl whispered something to her, jolting her out of her stupor. It sounded like: 'Don't drink the soup.'

Could she have heard right? But what did that mean? Was she trying to be funny?

Don't drink the soup?

Liss turned back and saw that the girl too was staring back in her direction, mouthing the word 'soup' and drawing her finger across her neck while shaking her head.

Liss felt a slice of fear. Maybe the soup was poisonous. And she had wolfed down two bowls of it today. She didn't feel sick or ill though; just a bit... odd. Maybe these people wanted to kill them. But that didn't make any sense. Why would they bother kidnapping them if they were going to kill them? And then what would be the point of all those boring lessons?

They had reached their bedroom again, the sound of church bells following her in. All that thinking had tired her out. Liss's brain felt muddled again. The bells filled up her mind with their chiming echoing sound, chasing away all other thoughts.

A nightdress lay on her bed. She changed out of her clothes and took her turn in the bathroom to wash. Then she climbed beneath the blanket and tried to remember what she had been thinking about, but all she could think of were the ringing clanging bells and the pattern they made in her head. A metallic looping sound that pealed from high to low and back again, in a never-ending cascade.

The following day, Liss found herself staring at the blonde girl again. It was lunchtime already and she was seated at the familiar trestle table in the dining hall. But she couldn't remember waking up or getting dressed or having breakfast, or even what she had been doing before lunch. It was only now, looking at the girl, that she had some sense of time and of who she was.

Liss's spoon hovered below her lips and she blew on the soup to cool it. The girl was shaking her head and pointing to her own bowl. Liss then saw the girl tip her soup into her neighbour's bowl. She did it so quickly, Liss thought she might have imagined it. She gasped and the girl smirked. Leah snapped her head up, and Liss cast her eyes down and blew on her soup again.

A moment later, Liss risked glancing back at the girl. Liss saw her rub her nose and discreetly point to her. Did the girl want her to dispose of her own soup in the same way she had? But the soup was delicious and she had been really looking forward to putting the spoon of hot liquid in her mouth. The girl put some bread in her mouth and chewed.

Liss felt her heart beating. How could she tip away her soup without Leah or one of the others noticing? Surely she would get caught. Annabelle sat on one side of her. There was no way she would tip it into her little friend's bowl. To her right sat one of the outsiders, her face scrubbed clean now, her hair brushed to a smooth caramel gleam. The outsider girl had almost finished her soup.

Everyone at the table was focused on their food. No one was looking in her direction. Quickly, she lifted her bowl and up ended it into her neighbour's. Some of it splashed onto the table, but miraculously no one seemed to notice. Liss's heart thrummed and she felt almost elated. She stuffed a piece of bread in her mouth to quell an urge to giggle.

The blonde girl's eyes widened and Liss could tell she was really pleased. The outsider was now slurping down her second bowlful without even realising what had happened. Liss felt hunger stab at her belly, but she made do with the bread.

She would have to find an opportunity to speak to her dangerous new friend. Find out what was going on and find out what was wrong with the soup.

CHAPTER TWELVE
RILEY

Eddie, Rita and Luc had left the house. Now it was only me and Pa left here in the chilly dining room. He said he would stay for a couple more minutes and then he had to go and sort stuff out with Eddie. The fire had burnt out a while ago, only a few embers glowed in the grate. It was late and everything felt precarious and strange.

Ma came downstairs in her dressing gown.

'Can't sleep?' Pa asked.

She shook her head. 'Come on. Help me clear the table. We can wash up tomorrow.'

The three of us began stacking dirty plates and carrying empty dishes back into the kitchen.

'So what's going to happen now?' I asked.

'Eddie and I will have to gather as many people as we can,' Pa replied. 'We'll head to Ringwood tomorrow.'

'Will you at least try to talk to Grey first?' Ma asked.

She didn't realise that James Grey wasn't a man you could talk to. He was not the listening kind.

'No,' Pa replied. 'Eddie's right. It's too late for talking. We'll have to hold him off, drive him back.'

Ma shook her head worriedly.

'Don't worry,' Pa said. 'Eddie and I can take him.' He grinned, but I didn't feel like laughing. 'Come on, you two,' Pa added. 'We've been through worse and we'll get through this.'

I stacked the glasses next to the sink.

'Cup of tea?' Ma asked.

'Mint would be good,' I replied. 'Well, at least Luc and I can help,' I said. 'We've seen Grey up close.'

'We can certainly use your knowledge,' Pa said. 'And we'll talk to Fred and Jessie some more.'

'Luc and I can go up to Salisbury with Fred and Jessie,' I said. 'We can help try to get their kids back. Hopefully we'll do better than last time.'

'What?' Pa frowned. 'No, Riley. Absolutely not. You're not going anywhere near that place again.'

'You promised Fred you'd get their kids back so—'

'And I'll keep my word. But you're not going to be the one to do it.'

'You need *us* to get in. We can pretend to be outsiders like last time.'

'I said no. And anyway, now's not the time to be running around Salisbury.'

'But that's stupid. You need me to—'

'I'm not discussing it with you, Riley. My decision's final. Anyway, you'll be recognised.'

I supposed he had a point. But there were ways around that, surely.

Ma wasn't getting involved. She didn't catch my eye and had started washing the dishes even though she'd said she was going to leave them until tomorrow.

'I'll need you here to keep an eye on things while I'm away. I've got to have someone I can trust...'

'Now you're just being patronising,' I snapped. 'I'm not a kid.'

Pa glared at me and then sighed.

'Is it because I'm a girl?' I asked.

'What? No.'

'That means yes,' I said.

'Riley... you want to know what it means? It means you're the most precious thing in the world to me and I'm not prepared to let Grey get his hands on you again.' His voice wavered as he spoke.

That shut me up for a few seconds. Pa never usually said things like that. He was a straightforward man. Not given to emotional outbursts. And since my sister, Skye, had died, he'd been more closed off than ever.

Last month, after Luc and I returned from our quest to track down Skye's killer, Pa had been beyond furious. He didn't speak to me for days. He literally blanked me. But then, one morning he told me to get in his AV and he drove us down to Cutter's Quay.

'Ma wants arts supplies,' he'd said, passing me a handful of silver bits. 'You can do the talking.'

We hadn't discussed my trip outside or why I'd done it. It was like he'd decided that he'd forgiven me and this was his way of letting me back into his life.

But that didn't change the fact that now he was back to treating me like a child. For all the trust he'd placed in me with his business, it didn't amount to anything if he kept wrapping me up in cotton wool. When it came down to it, I was still only Pa's little Riley. I couldn't believe he was side-lining me like this, especially when we'd recently developed such a close working relationship. I felt betrayed.

'Pa...'

'No,' he said, cutting me off. 'I need to go next door. I've arranged to meet Eddie. We've got a ton of planning to do.'

'Don't run away from the conversation,' I said.

'Riley, that's enough,' Ma said.

I ignored her. 'Pa, if I can trade at Cutter's, then I can—'

'We'll talk tomorrow, Riley,' Pa said, grabbing his jacket off the back of the kitchen chair. 'Get some sleep. See you later, Ellie.' He leant across to kiss Ma.

'Don't be too late,' she replied. 'You look exhausted.'

'Night,' he said, and left the house.

'Great,' I said, plonking myself down at the kitchen table. The kettle was boiling and Ma still had her hands in the sink so I dragged myself out of my chair to make us a cup of tea.

'D'you want mint?' I asked Ma.

'No thanks, darling. No tea for me. You okay?'

'Not really.'

'Must have been a shock,' she said, 'seeing that awful couple today.'

'They're not really that awful,' I replied. 'Their kids have gone missing. They did what they thought they had to do.'

'Try not to give your father a hard time over this,' she said, turning to face me and wiping her soapy hands on a tea towel.

I didn't answer. There was no point moaning to Ma about it. She wouldn't stick up for me. She only had a rough idea of what Pa did and never got involved in the business. I probably knew more about it than she did.

It was Pa and Eddie who originally set up our Perimeter after the old ways collapsed. It was Pa who'd had the foresight to build up a stockpile of goods to trade. Who made sure everyone in the Talbot Woods Perimeter was safe from the chaos on the outside. Back then, he even travelled to Ma's village in Gloucestershire to set up the Uley Perimeter to keep her family safe.

His business had grown in leaps and bounds since those early days. Pa was tough and well-connected. And I wanted to follow in his footsteps. I didn't want to be like Ma, living in ignorance of what it took to survive in our world.

So it stung that Pa was leaving me out of things now. I'd

really thought things had shifted between us. I'd thought he was finally trusting me with the important stuff.

I poured boiling water into a mug over a couple of mint leaves, wondering what Luc thought about all this. I wanted to talk to him about everything, but it was too late now that Eddie and Rita were home. And, anyway, Pa was over there too. They would all be making plans. Without me.

Right now, I was more than a little envious of Luc. He was always included in major decisions even though he was only one year older than me. I needed to stop whining about it and do something. I wasn't a total idiot; I had skills they could use. I'd just have to come up with my own ideas and maybe then they would start taking me seriously.

'Riley... *Riley!*'

'Hmm?' I replied, realising Ma was talking to me and that I was overfilling my mug, pouring boiling water onto the counter. 'Oh!' I put down the kettle and reached for a tea towel to blot the spill.

'I know someone who could get into Salisbury for you.' She'd finished the washing up and was leaning against the sink.

'What did you say?'

'Salisbury,' she repeated. 'I know who can get in there for you.'

'Who?' I asked.

'You won't like it and nor will your father.'

My interest was piqued. 'Ma, just tell me.'

'Connor,' she replied, biting her lip as she watched for my reaction. She was talking about my biological father. The man I'd only recently found out the truth about. As far as I was concerned, Connor was the reason my sister was dead.

I scowled.

'I said you wouldn't like it.'

'So why did you even mention his name?' I replied. 'I told you I never wanted to talk about that man. *Ever.*'

'Not even if he can help save our home?' she said. 'Not even if he can help reunite two kidnapped children with their parents?'

I didn't reply.

'So, do you want me to tell you how he can help?' she pressed on.

'No,' I snapped. But even as I said the word, I knew I didn't really mean it. I knew that I'd do anything to help save our home. To help save innocent children from Grey's cult. Just as I also knew it was inevitable I would see Connor again. I just didn't think it would be this soon.

And part of me was curious. Part of me wanted the chance to yell at him or at least try to make him feel guilty. And I wondered if this man, whose genes I carried, might be instrumental in changing Pa's mind about my involvement in this plan.

So even though I had said *no*, what I really meant was *yes*.

CHAPTER THIRTEEN
LISS

Over the next few days, Lissy continued disposing of the soup. She would go up to the serving hatch, receive her bowl as normal and then on her way to the table, she would slosh most of it into the large black plastic bin at the end of the hatch. Then she would tip the tiny bit she had left, into her neighbour's bowl, or just leave it in her own.

This meant she was always crazily hungry in the afternoons, having only eaten a piece of bread, but at least they were also given a main evening meal. The blonde girl hadn't said anything about not eating the other food – just the soup.

And she hadn't figured out a way to get rid of Annabelle's soup either. The younger girl seemed to enjoy it. How could she explain to her that she shouldn't have it? And even if she did think of a way of explaining why she shouldn't drink it, there hadn't been any opportunity to speak to her alone.

The initial fuzziness she'd felt during the first day had gradually disappeared and now she was almost entirely herself again. But the other girls were still half-asleep. It was weird – none of them showed any emotions or facial expressions. They merely did as they were asked. Liss thought she'd better pretend to be like them too, otherwise Leah might shout at her, but her brain was buzzing. She needed to talk to the blonde girl.

An opportunity came along quite quickly when, a few days later, Liss was sitting at her desk in the draughty classroom.

Sarah was teaching them today. It was supposed to be a history lesson, but it wasn't like the history her mum taught her, or the history she had read about in her books at home.

'This poor man lost his family,' Sarah said. 'His wife and children were taken from him. But instead of giving up and feeling sorry for himself, do you know what he did?' She paused, looking around the room. Nobody spoke.

'I'll tell you,' she continued. 'He decided that he would help others. That he would give up his life to the worship of God and the salvation of the people.'

Liss wasn't sure what Sarah was talking about, but she liked the way she spoke with excitement and energy. She spoke with a sparkle in her eyes and made you really interested in what she was saying. Not like the other boring teachers. Leah was the worst. Liss always had to force her eyes to stay open when Leah was talking.

'This good and simple man is called "James Grey",' Sarah continued. 'He never thinks about himself. All he wants is for everyone in the world to be happy and safe. Isn't that wonderful! We could all take a leaf out of his book and learn to be more selfless.'

He did sound like a good man. Liss wondered why she had never heard of him before.

'And shall I tell you something even more wonderful?' Sarah said without waiting for a response. 'If you work hard and are very well behaved, you may even get to meet him.'

Suddenly, one of the girls at the front of the class threw up all over her desk. Sarah stopped talking about James Grey and eyed the girl with a mixture of pity and irritation.

'Oh dear. I need a volunteer please,' she said, glancing around the classroom.

The blonde-haired girl stuck her hand in the air.

'Thank you,' Sarah said. 'Take Mary to the nurse please. Her room is downstairs next to the girls' toilets.'

The blonde girl stood up and the sick girl followed shakily, wiping her mouth with her sleeve.

'And ask Nurse to send someone up with a mop and bucket,' Sarah called after her.

As she walked past, the blonde girl whispered to Liss, 'Meet you in the loo in two minutes.'

Lissy tried to appear normal, but she felt as though everyone was staring at her. The smell of vomit wafted into her nostrils and made her feel like she wanted to throw up too.

She tried to count to one hundred and twenty in her head. The girl had said two minutes and she didn't want to get there too soon or too late. But when she reached seventy-five, she was convinced she'd been counting too slowly, so she took a deep breath and raised her hand.

'Melissa?' Sarah said.

'Please may I go to the bathroom?' Liss asked.

'You're not sick too, are you?'

Liss shook her head.

'Very well. Don't be too long.'

Liss scraped back her chair and walked self-consciously out of the classroom, tucking loose strands of hair behind her ears. She hurried down the wooden stairs and walked into the girls' toilets where the blonde girl was washing her hands. She threw a glance over her shoulder and her face split into a wide grin.

'Took your time,' she said. 'I'm Chloe.'

'Hi. I'm Liss.'

'We can't stay here long, someone might come in. So just listen, okay?'

Liss nodded.

'The soup's drugged.'

Chloe waited for a reaction, but Liss didn't know what 'drugged' meant. Chloe went on:

'The people here want us all to be good little girls and do what they say. The only way they can do that is by making us dopey and stupid. There are only a few of us who know about it. You have to be careful who you tell.'

'What do you mean?' Liss asked.

'How old are you?'

'Seven,' Liss replied defiantly. 'Seven and a half, actually.'

'Seven? You seem older. I'm eleven. Okay. Listen to me, Liss. The people here are evil. They put medicine in the soup to make us all sleepy. So you mustn't drink the soup or you'll end up here forever. But they can't know that you're not drinking it – okay?'

'Is that why I felt all strange before?' Liss asked.

'That's exactly right. Some of us are planning on getting out of here. I'll let you know when the time comes.'

'Have you been here long?'

'Long enough,' Chloe grimaced.

'There's another girl with me. She's only five. Can she come too?'

'Yeah, but you'll have to get her to stop drinking the soup and she mustn't blab to anyone or we're finished.'

'And my brother – FJ. He's here somewhere too, but I don't know where.'

'Sorry, we don't know where they're keeping the boys.'

'But I can't leave him here.'

'We'll get you out first and then you can always come back with help and get him out later.'

Liss decided that this would have to do. Once she got home, she could get her mum and dad to come and rescue him.

'You'd better go back up or Sarah will wonder where you are. I'll follow in a couple of minutes.'

'Okay. So when do we leave?'

'Dunno yet. But I'll send you a message soon as it's planned.'

'How can I stop Annabelle drinking her soup?'

'Don't know. You'll have to figure it out. Now, quick, go back up. And you mustn't talk to me in public – not even a smile. Remember, you have to pretend you're doped up like the rest of them.' She made a blank, staring face to show Liss what she meant.

Liss left the bathroom, her mind a whirl of questions. She felt so much better now that Chloe was helping her. But her heart hammered at the thought of trying to escape. What would the women do if they caught her? Leah especially.

As Liss came to the top of the stairs, she paused outside the classroom door. She hoped Sarah wouldn't be able to read the turmoil and excitement on her face. Inhaling deeply in an effort to calm her mind, she gave herself a shake, made her expression blank and walked slowly back into the classroom.

CHAPTER FOURTEEN

RILEY

I had been devastated when I'd found out Pa wasn't my biological father. Still was. I really wanted to block out that particular truth, but my real father, Connor, kept forcing his way into my life, whether he wanted to or not. I'd discovered Ma had been with Connor the night Skye was killed – the reason she now feels such crippling guilt and why she can never do enough for Pa or me.

Last night, Ma made things even more complicated by telling me that a few years back Connor had worked in the Cathedral Close in Salisbury. He'd been offered a position as soon as he'd told them he was an electrician. They'd treated him well and he'd stayed on for a few months, but the place had creeped him out and so eventually he'd left.

Ma reckoned they would probably welcome him back in. Skilled tradesmen were always in demand. She hadn't wanted to mention Connor's name to Pa, of course, so she'd told me instead. And now I had the unenviable job of telling Pa that Connor was the key to getting into the Close.

First, I needed a long hot shower.

I could have stood under that steaming jet all day, with my

eyes closed and my mind blank. But I was only delaying the inevitable. Finally, I turned off the water, pulled on fresh jeans and my favourite red hoodie and sloped down the stairs.

Pa stood in the hall slurping down a mug of coffee. We had an almost endless supply of canned green coffee beans which Pa hoped would be okay for at least another ten years. He was always on the lookout for a fresh coffee supplier, but none of his contacts had come good yet.

'Morning, Riles. Sleep well?'

'I s'pose.'

'Come on, don't give me a hard time. I'm going to need your help this morning. We've got a lot to do. You coming?'

'Yeah, okay.' I felt like I should probably be sulking or throwing a hissy fit, but I didn't have the energy and I needed to be on good terms with Pa so I could tell him about Connor. Then maybe he'd get distracted and let me go with them.

This time last year my life had been so simple and good. But now... now I was this other person with all these crazy emotions. And I wasn't as nice as I used to be. But I guess that's what happens. It's easy to be nice when nothing bad has happened to you.

Pa smiled and ran a hand over my hair. 'We're going next door. Come on. You can grab some breakfast over there.' He put his mug down on the console table in the hall, leaving a wet ring of coffee on the polished wood.

'Is Ma coming?' I asked.

'No, she'll only worry herself sick. It's not good for her to worry.'

'Okay.' I followed Pa out of the front door and we headed over to Luc's. 'When are you leaving?'

'Today. As soon as we're ready. Ringwood are expecting us.'

I sucked in some air.

'We need to get this done, Riley. No time to hang around.'

I wanted to protest again and tell him that I should be going too, but we had already reached the Donovans' house.

'Morning, Culpepper!' Eddie called from his driveway. He poked his head around the side of the open hood of his AV. 'Hello, Riley. You all right?' He smiled in my direction and then returned his gaze to the engine.

'What's up, Eddie?' Pa called out. 'Problems?'

'Nah. Just checking everything's good.'

'That old heap needs more than a check,' Pa replied. 'She wants putting out of her misery.'

'You don't know what you're talking about, Culpepper. Stick to your roses and leave the man stuff to me.'

Pa swore good-naturedly at Eddie. 'Sorry you had to hear that.' He grinned at me.

'Give it a rest, children,' Luc said, walking out of the front door. 'Hey, Riley. You okay?'

I nodded and flashed him a quick smile.

Everyone was pretending to be happy and normal, but I could feel the tension and see through the forced smiles.

Even with everything that was going on, I still couldn't ignore the effect Luc had on me. I looked away, sure he knew what was on my mind, and it felt even more awkward to be around him with family there. I couldn't act naturally and kept blushing which annoyed the hell out of me. Made me feel like a kid. But Luc seemed relaxed, even if he did keep a bit of distance between us while Pa was around, and I couldn't blame him for that.

'Let's go inside,' Eddie said, closing the hood. 'She's running sweet. You guys had breakfast yet?'

'Riley hasn't,' Pa replied.

Rita walked down the stairs and gave me a hug. 'Morning, sweetie,' she said, kissing my cheek. 'Morning, Johnny. Come into the kitchen, we can talk and eat. There's tea in the pot, want some?'

'Please.' I nodded, following her into the large, homely kitchen.

After a few minutes, Fred and Jessie were escorted into the house by Roger Brennan. They joined us at the table.

'So,' Pa said, stretching his hands out and cracking his knuckles. 'It seems your information was correct.'

Fred nodded once.

'We can spare a couple of guards to help you get your children back.'

'We don't know exactly where FJ and Liss are being held,' Jessie said. 'It might be hard to get them back with only two guards.'

'We need a plan,' Fred added. 'Not just a couple of guards. Grey's place is locked down tight. We need to be a bit clever about this.'

'There's no time for elaborate plans,' Pa said. 'Grey's already taken three Perimeters that we know of, and he's getting closer. You'll just have to do the best you can.'

'That wasn't the deal,' Fred said. 'You agreed to rescue our kids if we gave you the information. 'Two guards' isn't a rescue. I didn't take you for a liar.'

Pa's face turned a deep shade of red. I couldn't believe Fred had called him a liar. That wouldn't go down well. Not at all.

'Easy, Johnny,' Eddie said.

All pretence of civility had disappeared. Pa's expression was thunderous.

'The only option is to take Grey down,' Pa said through gritted teeth. 'Then we can find your children and free anyone else who's being held. That's our best chance of success. But if Grey takes this Perimeter then nobody will be rescuing anybody.'

'You could ask to speak to Grey,' Fred said. 'Try to negotiate a peace with him and in return he could give you our kids.'

I had to hand it to Fred – he didn't seem at all intimidated by Pa or Eddie.

'There's no negotiating with Grey. He's not an honourable man,' Eddie said. 'We're way past the negotiating stage. That man has crossed the line, literally.'

'We could pretend to negotiate,' Jessie said. 'Agree to his terms until we find out where Freddie Junior and Liss are. Once we have them, we can deal with Grey.'

'Do you really think we can walk into his territory and take what we want?' Pa retorted. 'He'd try to kill us before we were through the gates. Our first priority is to save the lives of everyone in our Perimeters and to stop Grey getting his hands on our oil. I know I gave you my word and I intend to keep it. But we have to be practical. Logical.'

As I listened to the conversation, chewing on a piece of toast, all I could think about was what Ma had told me. I knew I should've spoken to Pa about Connor earlier, but I hadn't had the opportunity. My mind worked double time trying to think of another plan enabling the couple to get their children back. But the only way I could see it happening, was if Luc and I did it, which Pa wouldn't condone, or if Connor helped. But I couldn't mention his name here. Not in front of everyone else.

'Maybe FJ or Liss will have some information we can use against Grey,' I said.

'I'm sure they will,' Jessie said, grasping onto my theory. 'You'll need inside information.'

I inadvertently caught Luc's eye and he gave me a brief lopsided grin. It made me catch my breath and for a second I forgot about Grey and wars and kidnapped children. All I felt was the sharp pleasure of Luc's smile.

Reality dragged me away from thoughts of Luc and, once again, he was just another voice around the table trying to get this thing contained. But his smile had given me courage.

'If you're going to rescue FJ and Liss, you'll need me and

Luc to act as bait. Like last time,' I said clearly, ensuring my voice cut through the conversation.

'Riley,' Pa's voice grew menacingly low. 'We've had this discussion already.'

'But it's the only—'

'Your father's right,' Eddie said. 'The idea is good, but it's far too dangerous and we're not risking your life.'

'It isn't your life to risk,' I said. 'It's my life and I want to do this.'

Pa got to his feet, resting his hands on the kitchen table. 'Riley, you're only here to give us information. Not to volunteer or play the hero.'

I clenched my jaw to stop myself saying something I might regret. I wouldn't be doing myself any favours continuing to argue with him in front of everyone.

'The main problem is, they'll recognise you,' Luc said to me. 'They'll for sure remember you from last time. My face is more forgettable than yours.'

There was nothing forgettable about Luc, I thought to myself, gazing at the contours of his face. I shook myself out of it. Now was not the time to be drooling over a boy. Rita raised her eyebrows and gave me a sly smile. I smiled back, awkwardly. Embarrassed to be caught staring.

'We're not using anyone as bait,' Eddie said. 'And that's final.'

'But Riley and I can do it,' Luc said. 'We would've done it before if we hadn't been tricked.' He looked pointedly at Fred and Jessie. Jessie had the grace to blush.

'I already said no.' Pa's voice boomed around the kitchen. 'We should be discussing Grey's army, not this wild goose chase of a rescue mission.'

'There is another way,' I said. The words came out before I could stop them. My heart sped up. I didn't want to hurt Pa, but I knew I should tell him. Anything that helped us to beat Grey was a good thing.

I realised everyone was staring at me.

'Umm.' I paused, gathering up my courage. 'I know someone who can help us get inside The Cathedral Close.'

'Who?' Eddie asked.

'If we have someone's help getting in, we won't be in so much danger,' I continued, avoiding the question. 'We can slip in and out without being detected.'

'Who are you talking about?' Luc asked.

'Connor,' I said in a small voice.

'Connor?' Rita said, frowning. 'Isn't that the man who...' Her voice trailed off and she turned to look at Pa. We were all staring at Pa now.

To his credit, Pa didn't even blanch. 'What's Connor got to do with it?' he asked.

'He used to work in the Close as an electrician. They know him and trust him. He could let us in and we could find FJ and Liss without any fuss.'

'Ri-ight. And how do you propose to find them? Two brain-washed kids in a million.'

'Liss'll be relatively easy to find,' Jessie said. 'She's got a large birthmark on her neck. Shaped like a half moon.'

'Well, that's a start,' Pa said, 'but it still doesn't—'

'And I'm pretty sure they're not in the main part of Salis-bury,' Jessie continued. 'That Mr Sadler gave me the impression they were living inside the Cathedral Close. Right in the heart of the place.'

'You're "pretty sure"?' Pa said. 'Pretty sure isn't enough to go on.'

'I think it's a good idea,' Rita interrupted.

Pa scowled at her. 'Well, I don't.'

'Those kids could have good information,' Rita said.

'I doubt that,' Pa replied.

But Rita wasn't put off by Pa. 'I know your feelings about

Connor,' she said. 'And I don't blame you. But we have to set all that aside. If we don't do something, James Grey is going to take over the whole country. This is more than just an opportunity to rescue two children. Luc and Riley can get inside the Close. Get information. This is important, Johnny.'

'You don't need to tell me how important this is, Rita,' Pa replied. 'But it's still too dangerous.'

'We're short on manpower as it is,' she continued. 'Riley is a capable young woman. I know she's your daughter, Johnny, but we've got no choice. We can't wrap our kids in cotton wool. Any other sixteen-year-old would be expected to do the same. If Connor's there, then they won't be alone. They'll have back up. And Luc's as capable as you or me.'

I wanted to wrap my arms around Rita and give her an enormous hug for standing up to Pa on this.

Pa sat back down like his legs wouldn't bear his weight. He turned to face me.

'Do you really want to do this? After what happened last time?'

I bit my bottom lip and nodded.

Pa sighed and I knew I had won. So why was it that I didn't feel like cheering?

CHAPTER FIFTEEN

LISS

The room contained two rows of beds. Annabelle's was next to the window and Liss slept next to her. Next in the row were the two outsiders and lastly, by the door, was Leah's bed.

That night, Liss stayed awake until she was completely sure Leah had fallen asleep. When the room felt heavy with sleepy breaths, Liss slid out of bed. She pretended to go to the bathroom so she could check to see if Leah was asleep yet. As she crept past, she saw the woman's mouth lying slack, her bottom lip quivering with the occasional snore. Everyone else appeared to be asleep too.

Now came the hard part.

Liss tiptoed back past the sleeping girls and past her own empty bed. She crouched down next to Annabelle and shook her shoulder gently.

'Annabelle,' she whispered. 'Hey, wake up.' She shook her more firmly.

The younger girl gave a moan and Liss cringed, casting a glance back over at Leah's bed. But the woman didn't move.

'Annabelle,' she hissed. 'Please wake up.' She blew on her face.

Annabelle scrunched up her nose and shook her head slightly. Liss blew again. This time, Liss was relieved to see Annabelle open her eyes.

She stared at Liss, but as usual there was no hint of recognition in her expression.

'Hey, you're awake,' Liss said. 'I need to talk to you.'

Annabelle continued to stare, but there was no glimmer of life. She simply lay there like a doll.

Liss felt scared and a little desperate.

'Annabelle, listen to me. You must not drink the soup. Do you understand?'

Annabelle nodded.

'*Yes?* Did you hear me? At mealtimes you have to tip your soup away. Don't drink it.'

Annabelle turned on her side and closed her eyes. Liss didn't know what to do. There was no trace of the sparky little girl she had met a few days ago. She had become a robot. Well, she wouldn't give up on her. She would just have to help her friend anyway, whether she understood or not.

The next day, Liss tipped the contents of her own soup bowl into the plastic bin by the serving hatch. She then deftly swapped bowls with Annabelle and tipped her friend's soup away too. This was all achieved in less than ten seconds. Liss figured that as long as Leah and the women on the top table didn't see what was going on, she should be safe. Everyone else was too dopey to notice.

Once they were at the table, Liss hoped Annabelle wouldn't kick up a fuss at her empty bowl. Thankfully she didn't question it; just ate her bread instead.

Liss stared across at Chloe's table but, to her disappointment, the blonde girl didn't look over once. Liss guessed that she was probably avoiding eye contact until the time came for them to escape.

Over the next few days, Liss continued to tip away their soup. She watched Annabelle carefully for signs that the girl was regaining her senses and sure enough, five days later, a glimmer of personality returned.

'I feel funny,' Annabelle said to Liss one evening as she was drifting off to sleep.

Liss snapped her eyes open and turned to face her friend's bed.

'Annabelle!' she cried in a careful whisper.

'I feel all funny and dreamy and not nice,' Annabelle said too loudly.

'Shh. That's okay. You'll feel more normal in the morning.'

'Promise?'

'Cross my heart.'

'Okay,' Annabelle replied. 'You're Liss, aren't you?'

'That's right. I'm your friend. Everyone thinks we're sisters.'

'Why are we still here?'

'Don't worry. You just have to be quiet and good for a while longer, and then we can go home.'

'Why can't we go now?'

'Because we can't. And you can't tell anyone else that you want to go or they'll get cross.'

The younger girl looked serious, thinking for a moment.

'Okay.'

'And the soup will make you sick so you mustn't drink it.'

'I like the soup.'

'I know. But it's not good. So only eat the bread, all right?'

Annabelle sighed. 'I don't like it here.'

'Me neither.'

.   .   .

When Liss walked into the classroom the following morning, something had already been written on the blackboard in large letters. A woman stood by the board waiting for the girls to sit. She wasn't one of their usual teachers.

'I am Naomi,' the woman said. 'I am here to tell you about "the Listeners".' She pointed to the two words on the blackboard.

Naomi was quite old, older than Liss's mum anyway. She wore her grey hair in a bob and had quite a few wrinkles on her face. But she seemed less stern than most of their teachers. Her voice was softer.

'We have all done things in our lives that we are ashamed of. All of us. Including me. But from this day forward you only do good as decreed by Our Father. You will not be tempted to do wrong.'

She began to walk between the rows of desks, looking each girl in the eye. Liss wanted to flinch from her gaze, but she had to remember to stay unfocused and vague.

'But what of our past transgressions?' Naomi asked. 'What about the bad thoughts we've had and the wrongs we have committed already? How can we know God when we are so flawed? Can we be forgiven for our sins?'

Liss didn't really understand what Naomi was talking about. It all sounded a bit scary and she wondered if they were going to have to do a test on it.

'The answer is yes,' Naomi said with a beaming smile. 'Yes, we can be forgiven. Yes, we can start again with a clean slate. Yes, we can know God. For today, the Listeners are here and each of you will have the privilege of speaking your sins to them.

'Girls, you will take it in turns to go next door and tell the Listeners of every wrongdoing you have ever committed. You must leave nothing out. This is your chance to be pure again.

You will only have this opportunity once in your lifetime, so make the most of it.

'After today, you will be one step closer to joining our family. So go and unburden yourself. Free your souls.' Naomi's eyes shone with joy and Liss didn't know whether to be terrified or excited. She still didn't really understand what she was supposed to do, or who the Listeners were.

'When I call out your name, you are to leave this classroom and enter the room immediately to your right. You will see only an empty room with a chair. Sit on this chair and speak aloud every sin you are guilty of, no matter how big or small. You will not be judged. You will not be punished. You will only be absolved of these sins.

'Did you ever steal? Did you ever covet someone else's belongings? Did you lie or cheat or wish harm on another? Did you inflict harm on another? Did you kill?'

As Naomi ran through the different wrongs, Liss felt immediately guilty. She didn't think she had ever done any of the things mentioned, so why should she feel this way? Her cheeks burned with guilt for things she hadn't done and she was sure she would be punished despite what Naomi said.

'I will give you some time to sit here and think about your wrongdoings. And then in a while I will begin calling names and you will go and confess your sins to the Listeners.'

Naomi strode back to the front of the classroom and stood by the blackboard, her eyes roaming across the girls' faces. They sat in silence, presumably thinking about all the things they'd done wrong. Liss worried that Annabelle wouldn't know what to do, or worse still that she'd tell them she hadn't been eating the soup. That the Listeners, whoever they were, would know she wasn't drugged like the others.

After a while, Naomi called out a name: 'Tessa'.

It was one of the girls from Liss's dormitory. The tall girl who hadn't cleaned her hands properly that first day they were brought here in the truck. Tessa pushed her chair back, stood and left the room. She was gone for a while and Liss wondered if she would be coming back. Eventually, she heard footsteps and Tessa returned to her desk.

Liss was relieved. At least she had returned, so whatever happened out there couldn't be all that bad. More girls' names were called. They left the room and then they returned. Some were gone a very long while, others were only a few minutes.

'Annabelle,' Naomi called out.

The young girl hesitated, so Naomi spoke to her. 'Annabelle, go into the room next door and tell them all the bad things you have ever done.'

Liss prayed she wouldn't kick up a fuss. That she would go next door and say a few things to keep them happy.

Annabelle stood and left the room. Liss was more worried about her friend than about herself. What was she saying in there? What would the Listeners make of her? Would they realise she wasn't drugged? Would they take her away? She was gone ages and it took all Liss's willpower not to run out of the door and see where she was.

Sweat formed at her breastbone and her palms felt clammy. She prayed to God to bring her friend back to her. But it wasn't James Grey's God she was praying to. No. She imagined Grey's God as a stern giant with thunder in his voice, whereas her God was a kindly old man with a beard and twinkly eyes.

And then she heard the sweet sound of footsteps approaching. She would know that hesitant tread anywhere. It was Annabelle returning. At last, Liss could relax a little.

Hours seemed to pass, but she couldn't be sure. Her eyes grew heavy and she would have loved to rest her head on the desk and sleep. She widened her eyes to try to keep them open, shook her head and flexed her fingers. But she was soon jolted awake when Naomi called her name.

'Melissa.'

CHAPTER SIXTEEN

LISS

Liss placed her hands on the desk and pushed herself upright, aware of Naomi's eyes on her. She turned and walked out of the room. What would she find next door? Who were the Listeners? There was only one door to the right and it was closed. Liss turned the handle and pushed open the door.

It was dark in here with only a single spotlight pointed at a small wooden chair. Heavy black curtains had been pulled across the window, blocking out the sun. The room was similar in size to their classroom, the difference being that it was empty, apart from the chair and an odd-looking electronic device with a strange glass eye.

Liss's footsteps sounded too loud as she crossed the wooden floor. She sat on the chair facing the device. The thing seemed to stare back at her. It was almost exactly at her head height, raised off the ground on three spindly black legs.

She had a vague memory of what this thing was. Something to do with photographs perhaps. But then her mind flew into a panic. She shouldn't be worried about the machine, she should be speaking about the things she had done wrong in her life.

Only she really couldn't think of any. Her mind had gone blank. And she mustn't show fear either. They must not guess she hadn't been drinking the soup.

'Speak. We are listening.' The voice seemed to come from everywhere. It made Liss's scalp prickle and she wanted to flee the room. But instead she gripped the chair with both hands, forcing herself to remain seated.

There was nobody in the room, so where was the voice coming from? And it was so loud. Louder than a normal voice. It was a man's voice and it hissed and crackled like a snake or maybe a dragon. She noticed a red light had appeared on the machine. Maybe it was the machine talking. But she didn't think so.

'I ... I left the yard when I shouldn't have,' she said. 'Our parents said we were never to leave the yard. To never to go outside onto the road. But we did it anyway. I'm sorry,' she added.

'We are listening,' the voice said again.

Did they want more? Liss trawled her brain for more sins, but she couldn't think of anything. Should she make something up?

'There's nothing else,' Liss said. She thought about the soup she tipped away every day and was sure that would count as a wrongdoing. But there was no way she would tell the Listeners about that.

'You may go,' the voice said.

Was that it then? Great. She left the room and returned to the classroom, pleased to be back in the daylight again. That hadn't been bad at all.

The next day, Liss had a shock.

Chloe wasn't at breakfast. She also wasn't at lessons or at lunch or dinner.

Perhaps she was ill. Or maybe it was something to do with the Listeners. Maybe she had said something that had made them suspicious. But Chloe seemed really smart. She would never have given herself away.

Surely, she wouldn't have escaped without her and Annabelle. Would she? Liss would have to wait and see, and hope that the next day Chloe would return. But she didn't. And she wasn't back the following day either. Or the one after that.

Chloe had gone.

Liss felt terrified all over again. She would be stuck here forever. And the women would eventually realise that she and Annabelle weren't drinking the soup and they would force them to take it until they became zombie robots like the other girls.

The days blurred into one another. Breakfast and lessons and tipping away soup and lessons and soup and bed. On and on for days and days with no change. Annabelle had become listless again and this time it wasn't down to the soup. It was the boredom and monotony and hopelessness of everything. Would it be like this forever?

One morning, after breakfast, Sarah stood at the top table and cleared her throat. Liss was beginning to realise that Sarah was someone important. More important than mean old Leah. More important than any of the other women. And she was nicer than them too. The girls immediately turned their gazes up towards her and she smiled, a radiant beaming smile that made Liss feel instantly less sad and worried.

'You have all been here for over a month now and I am happy to tell you that you have passed.' Sarah paused and cast her eyes over every girl in the room.

Liss made sure to make her face blank and unfocused like everyone else's. Sarah continued to speak.

'You will all be welcomed into His arms today. Be very proud, children, for not everyone is afforded this opportunity.'

Despite the warmth of her smile, Liss shivered at Sarah's words. She had no idea what they meant, but she did not like the sound of them. Not one bit.

CHAPTER SEVENTEEN

RILEY

Pa was due to leave for Ringwood any minute. The AVs and trucks were weighed down with guards, volunteers and weapons. They would stop en route to pick up more supplies and recruits from other Compounds.

I'd been helping to load up and now they were finally ready to go. I stopped for a moment to swig some water. Shielding my eyes from the autumn sun, I scanned the vehicles until I saw Pa. This was him at his best – giving orders, checking and double-checking supplies.

'Hey.'

I turned to see Luc coming towards me.

'Hey,' I replied.

He gave a soft smile.

Our picnic at Coy Pond – was it only the day before? It felt like forever ago that I was laughing and mucking about with him. Talking about trivial things and thinking of love. Now the only thoughts I had were of war and kidnap and rescue and danger.

'Is there anything else I can do to help?' I asked.

'Nope. Don't think so. They're pretty much ready to go.'

A couple of engines started up. Low throaty rumbles.

'You okay?' Luc asked.

'I honestly don't know.'

'Me neither,' he said.

'Is everything really as bad as it looks?'

'Well, Grey hasn't taken over our Perimeter, so things aren't majorly bad.'

'Just minorly bad.'

'Maybe somewhere in the middle.' He gave me a lopsided smile.

'Do you think he will? Take over Talbot Woods, I mean.'

'I hope not. We'll do everything we can to stop him.' Luc took my hand, folded my fingers over and stroked my knuckles, sending sparks along my skin. 'Are you nervous?' he asked. 'About meeting your real father again?'

'I don't really think of him as my father,' I replied.

'No. Of course not. Sorry. I meant... Connor.' He let go of my hand.

'I haven't really given it much thought,' I lied.

In truth, I thought about him all the time. I didn't know how I was going to act around that man. The last time I saw him, I'd yelled and said some really horrible things. He probably hated me. But, whatever our feelings, we'd have to get over them because we'd be seeing one other sometime later that day.

It had been decided – while Pa, Eddie and the guards travelled in convoy to Ringwood by road, Luc and I would go by copter to the outskirts of Salisbury where we would rendezvous with Connor.

Fred and Jessie were also coming. Not to break inside the walls with us, but they wanted to be nearby when we brought out their kids. Only I supposed they weren't kids anymore. I kept thinking of them as these young children, like in the photos on Fred and Jessie's Welsh dresser. But they were the same ages as me and Luc. I couldn't imagine what their lives must have been like all these years.

Doubt was beginning to creep in. Before now, I had only been concerned with getting Pa to agree to my plan. But now it had become real, I started to imagine how hard this was actually going to be. How in the hell were we going to locate two people in a city of thousands? We didn't even know what they looked like and they could have changed their names. But I couldn't voice my doubts. I had to be positive and hope that luck would favour us.

Luc gave me a nudge. I looked up to see Ma tottering down the road towards us like someone out of a movie. She was dressed up for the occasion. Her hair and make-up were immaculate and she wore crazily high heels. She waved at us, her face cheery and bright. Since Skye died, Ma had two settings – fantastically happy or terrified and miserable. It seemed she'd chosen happy mode to wave Pa off. I was relieved. I couldn't have coped with a weeping mother today.

Pa spotted her and headed over to me and Luc. 'Ellie,' he said. 'You look so beautiful.' He kissed her on the lips.

'Just gonna see if Dad wants any help,' Luc said, walking away.

'Hang on a sec, Luc,' Pa called after him. 'Charlie's going to drop you and Riley outside Salisbury in the copter. You need to be ready to leave in three hours. Connor will meet you at the drop-off point.'

'Are Fred and Jessie still coming?' I asked.

'Yes. But Charlie will keep them in the copter. If you do find their kids, you'll need to get information out of them. We have to find out what Grey's plans are. See if they know anything.'

'And please be careful,' Ma added, enveloping me in her arms and kissing my cheeks.

'Yes,' Pa said. 'Lucas, I'm counting on you to look after my daughter.'

'Of course,' Luc replied. 'But she's pretty tough, Johnny. She got me out of a couple of really bad situations last month.'

'Yeah, Johnny.' I grinned at Pa. 'She's pretty tough.'

'Well, I should think so,' Pa replied. 'She's a Culpepper, isn't she. We don't breed no weaklings.'

We smiled, but inside I started to quake. It was all happening so quickly. Would we get through this? Would I ever see Pa again?

'They're waiting for me,' Pa said. 'I'd better...'

I fell into Pa's arms, and he, Ma and I squeezed each other tight while I tried my hardest not to cry. I tried to block out all thoughts of what could go wrong. If I gave into my worries, I would turn into a blubbing mess. Pa broke away first.

'Right,' he said. 'I'll see you soon.' He strode over to his AV and swung himself into the driver's seat.

Luc had walked off a little way and was talking to his parents. He was saying goodbye too.

The AVs moved off slowly. Pa hadn't activated the blackout mode yet, so we saw him as he rolled past, his mouth turned up in a smile, his sunglasses hiding his true expression. It was too much for Ma and she let out a sob. Turned her back while her shoulders heaved. The smile left Pa's face, but he kept going. Eddie and Rita drove past next. I raised my hand, but they were deep in conversation and didn't notice.

And then there was a blur of huge wheels, trucks and faces sliding in and out of focus. The deep roar of engines and the intermittent squeal of brakes. There were quite a few of us lining the road. All there to wave off our friends and family. To wish them luck. To hope they would come home safe. Soon.

CHAPTER EIGHTEEN

LISS

She had seen its tall spire from a distance, but they had never been right up close before. And now they were to go inside. And they were actually going to see James Grey.

They had learnt about Salisbury Cathedral in their lessons, but all Liss could remember was that it was the most important place in the country and it was nearly eight hundred years old. And now all two hundred girls walked two by two in a line towards this ancient building. Away from the familiar courtyard, through an iron gate and along a wide gravel path. Their teachers walked alongside them, silently and slowly, shingle crunching underfoot. A few large drops of rain fell and somewhere above them, a mistle thrush sang.

It felt strange to be out of their usual confined area. All Liss had seen over the past few weeks had been the dormitory, the dining hall, courtyard and classroom. Now they suddenly came out into the open. Trees swayed in the distance, and their path cut through great swathes of glistening emerald green lawn. Impressive buildings lined the walkways and beyond them in the middle distance towered the imposing cathedral. Liss suddenly realised how much she'd missed open spaces.

The rain came harder now and it felt good on her face. A couple of the women hunched their shoulders and scowled at the weather, but Liss welcomed the cold rain; it reminded her of working at home on the farm. She liked being outdoors.

The girls trudged on in silence. Liss tried not to stare as a robed figure passed them. The person was covered from head to toe in a cloak with a deep hood so their face was concealed. Several more identically dressed figures walked by.

And now they came to a wide road with proper pavement on either side. It was all smooth and clean and well kept. The road went on for a long way, but they passed nobody else. Liss suddenly caught her breath as she glanced up and saw the face of a young boy at a window. They locked eyes for a brief moment before Liss had to look away. Maybe FJ was somewhere near here.

Walking through a wide stone archway, they came upon a narrower road where ancient buildings and tall trees lined the pavements. Her parents had said that when they were growing up, most people lived in brick houses on long streets with roads and pavements. Liss wondered if this was the sort of thing they meant. She didn't think she would like living like that. She preferred the fields at home and their old stone farmhouse with its sunny yard. Even if she did get lonely sometimes.

The girls left the narrow roads behind and came back out onto a path flanked by rectangles of close-cropped grass. They soon came to a halt on a wide stone square, right in front of the cathedral entrance. Liss gazed up at the building. It was like something out of a fantastical dream.

It didn't look real with all its arches and columns and pointy bits of stone. It reminded Liss of lots of fish bones stacked up on top of each other. She had to remember not to gawp. The other girls weren't showing the slightest bit of interest. They stood listless and disinterested like a herd of sleepy cattle.

They were all soaked through to the skin now. Annabelle

shivered next to her, but Liss wasn't able to rub her shoulders or smooth her dripping hair away from her face as she would have liked to. They had to stare straight ahead and carry on pretending to be spaced out. One of the wooden doors was ajar and the girls were led into the cathedral, out of the rain.

The inside space was as amazing as the outside. Cavernous ceilings amplified their footsteps on the polished floor and hundreds of candles flickered in the gloom, casting long shadows all around. There were arches and columns and windows with coloured glass pictures. They walked past row upon row of empty red velvet chairs, until they were almost at the end of the aisle. Sarah stood in the centre and directed them to the chairs near the front.

Once seated, Liss heard more footsteps from behind. She wanted to risk a glance. All the other girls had their eyes firmly facing forward and she knew that if anyone saw her turn her head, they would know she wasn't drugged. She noticed some small leather books on the ledge in front of them. Liss picked one up and let it fall near the aisle. She bent to retrieve it and at the same time, turned her head to look behind.

And what she saw made her pulse begin to race. Behind the now-seated girls came a long line of boys.

FJ.

He might be here.

He must be here.

The boys began to take their seats. But Liss had to sit up and face forward again. She couldn't draw any attention to her and Annabelle. They sat for an age. She heard more and more people enter the cathedral. No one spoke, but she could sense the vast space filling up. She could hear more footsteps and dry coughs and the swish of damp clothing.

Suddenly there was a scraping and clatter of chair legs as everyone rose to their feet. Now an eerie silence hung in the steamy air. Not a sound could be heard. Liss felt the tension like it was a living thing. Annabelle stared up at her, wide-eyed, and she gave her what she hoped was a reassuring look. Thank goodness the younger girl had learned how to be quiet and blend in.

A robed man appeared at the front of the cathedral. He was tall and thin with a long nose and hooded eyes. He looked very important and very scary. His face was in shadow, but he seemed to be staring right at her. Right into her eyes. Into her mind. He must know about her. He must know that she wasn't drinking the soup. Liss thought she might faint. But then a big light came on illuminating his face and she saw that he wasn't staring at her after all.

He stood before a wooden post which looked a bit like a tall table. Fixed to the table was a small roundish metal object. He leant forward and spoke into it. Liss almost cried out in terror. The man's voice was so loud. It was like thunder. Annabelle squealed, but luckily, his voice drowned out her cry. His words filled the whole cathedral right up to the rafters.

The shock of the noise meant she missed the beginning of his speech, but now, as she listened to his words, she began to shake.

'...I am your father now. And I will care for you and love you as if you were my own children. You shall want for nothing. I will feed and clothe and keep you until you are taken from this earth. I was put here for that very purpose and you are blessed to have arrived in this heavenly place. And now you will be named and you will become part of our great kingdom, never to be parted from me.'

This was James Grey, the man Sarah had told them about in their history lessons. But he didn't look or sound like the great man Sarah had described. That man had sounded wonderful and kind. Sort of like Father Christmas. But this man in front of them wasn't like that. He was scary and horrible and she didn't like him at all. His eyes were mean, his face thin and pointy and his skin all shiny and smooth. His dark robe was trimmed with red, like crows' feathers dripping with blood. He looked like a bad man, even though he was trying to seem like he was good and kind. His smile wasn't even a proper one.

Liss trembled, she couldn't help it. Her teeth chattered and she felt as though she might faint with terror. This man was saying they must stay with him forever. He was saying that he was supposed to be their father now.

He wasn't her dad. He wasn't anything like her dad. Liss realised that Annabelle was gripping her hand, but she had to pry it off before one of the women saw.

She darted glances around the church. All the girls were staring at James Grey like he was the most beautiful thing they had ever seen. They seemed happy, enraptured.

Liss wanted so much to run right out of this creepy church. To grab Annabelle and sprint as fast as they could and as far away as they could. But there were girls in front of her and girls and boys behind her and there were grownups standing every-where. There was nowhere to go.

She wished she was a tiny insect who could slip away unno-ticed. Or a sparrow who could flit up to the rafters and hide. But instead she was a useless girl – too big to hide, too slow to run, too stupid to escape.

She sensed he was saying something more important now. His voice had gone a little quieter. A little scarier.

'It pains me to tell you that before I can welcome you into my church, there are some matters to attend to. Some unfortu-nate events which need to be dealt with. You will see that I am not afraid to do what must be done. Lesser men would shy away from such things, but I am not a lesser man.

'I speak to you today of betrayal and evil. Of bad people in this world who would like to destroy heaven. Who would ruin our quest for perfection. I must make an example of these selfish people who try to disrupt our peace. For if I spared them, they would leave here and bring others to destroy our beautiful life and that cannot be allowed to happen. I am here to protect you and in order to protect, I must also pass judgement.'

Liss didn't want to hear his words, but they bored into her brain like a thousand drills. She knew he was leading up to something bad. Something she would have to witness and she didn't want to. She wanted to crawl under her chair and cover her ears with her hands.

'It hurts me to pass judgement on these lives, but before we can move on and make ourselves clean and good for God, we must purge ourselves of the evil within these sacred walls.'

Suddenly Liss sensed movement close by. She flicked her eyes over to her left and saw Sarah walking down the aisle, tears running down her face. Behind her came half a dozen women and girls, shackled together in chains. Their ankles and wrists in iron cuffs, their eyes wide and terrified. But some looked more angry than scared. Their hair had been shaved off and they were filthy, covered in cuts and bruises

'See how my beautiful disciple Sarah weeps for their souls,' Grey's voice boomed. 'I weep too for the tragic waste of life. They could have had everything I have to offer, for you must know I would give each one of you the shirt off my back. But they have foolishly squandered their good fortune.' He pointed a long accusing finger at the prisoners who were guided up onto the platform. Sarah and two other elders helped them before retreating into the shadows.

And then a chill ran through Liss's body. A coldness which froze her limbs and made her head swim.

She recognised one of the girls.

At first she couldn't place her as her hair had been shorn and her face was bruised and swollen. But she did know her. And with recognition came the realisation that she and Annabelle had just had a very narrow escape.

CHAPTER NINETEEN

LISS

Liss heard a knocking sound. She looked down and realised her right leg was trembling, vibrating against the chair leg. She pressed her palms down on her knee to try to keep it still.

The prisoners on the platform had their eyes cast downward except for one – a young woman who cast filthy glances at James Grey. She looked as though she wanted to strangle him, her hands flexing open and closed.

But Liss's attention was pulled towards the end of the line-up, where a terrified girl stood. She knew that girl. It was Chloe. Her pretty face bruised and hollow, her ash blonde hair all gone; shorn away to nothing.

So she hadn't escaped as Liss had previously thought. No. She had been here in the Cathedral Close all the time. A prisoner.

One of the shackled girls let out a sob which echoed around the cavernous cathedral.

Grey left his stand and walked over to where the prisoners stood. He carried the loud speaking device in his hand, trailing a black wire behind him.

'Look at these, the faces of traitors,' he said, his voice

booming as he gazed out across his congregation. 'Remember these faces. They are faces of sadness and fear and confusion and anger. These are the emotions which mark out a traitor. If you feel these emotions, you may tremble, for your fate will seek you out.'

Liss's other leg began to shake and she pressed her forearms down against her thighs. She was sure Grey must know about her intention to escape. She was convinced he was about to have her hauled up to join Chloe and the others.

Annabelle had shoved her thumb in her mouth and her eyes had glazed over. Liss felt bad as she knocked the young girl's thumb away, worried that it would draw attention to her.

'These foolish females would seek to destroy our way of life,' Grey continued. 'Given the chance they would leave our walls only to return to wage a war against us all.'

'That's a lie!' one of the women shouted. 'We only want to—'

'Silence, traitor, or I will cut out your tongue.' Grey slapped her face with the back of his hand.

Liss felt as though he had slapped her own face. She put her hand to her cheek, but quickly let it drop back into her lap.

The woman opened her mouth and then closed it again.

'I have prayed for an answer,' Grey said, lowering his voice and bowing his head. 'And I have wept at the answer I received.' He lifted his head as a single tear rolled down his cheek.

'Say goodbye to these traitors for this is the last day of their earthly lives. We must sacrifice a few for the good of the many. Their only sentence can be a merciful death. We will pray for their souls.'

At this, the congregation dropped to their knees. Liss followed suit and pulled Annabelle down with her. As Grey recited his prayer, Liss had to clamp her jaws together to prevent her teeth from chattering. Grey had said this was the last day of the prisoners' lives. That their sentence was death. Did that mean he was going to...

'Amen,' Grey said.

'Amen,' they all repeated and rose to their feet.

When Liss looked up at the platform, the prisoners had been joined by four cloaked figures with swords at their belts. One of the figures pushed at a shackled girl, trying to get her to walk, but none of the prisoners would move. Eventually, all six were dragged by their chains from the Cathedral, screaming and sobbing, stumbling and falling. Liss had to turn away. She couldn't bear to see the disbelief and terror in Chloe's eyes.

The congregation appeared calm and apparently unaffected by the display they had witnessed.

Liss wondered if FJ sat somewhere behind her. If only she could run and find him. They could make a plan to get out of this nightmare place together.

Grey moved back to his spot behind the stand, his eyes glittering.

'We must put this unpleasantness behind us. We must move forward.' He paused. 'And the best way to do this is to welcome our blessed initiates into our family.

'Today, five hundred young souls are to join my church and I am so happy and filled with the light of the Lord.' He smiled. 'You will come forward one at a time and I will name you.'

Liss realised she would have to go right up close to this man. She didn't think she would be able to do it. All the girls were now on their feet. The first row was being led up by one of their teachers. How could she face Grey? Surely he would guess that she too was a 'traitor'? And what about Annabelle? What if she couldn't keep her face blank? Liss inhaled deeply.

'Annabelle,' she muttered under her breath. 'Annabelle.'

The younger girl turned to her, her eyes still glazed, her thumb back in her mouth. Liss pulled her hand away again.

'You mustn't speak or cry or look at anyone,' Liss hissed. 'Do you understand?'

Annabelle nodded. There was nothing more Liss could do but hope the younger girl would understand the importance of what she'd said.

Up on the platform, Grey was telling each girl which name they would take, then he placed something around each of their necks. The lines of girls were moving fairly quickly now. In turn, they were named and then each left the building via a side exit.

Liss wondered if the boys were also to be named today. If they were, Liss realised she wouldn't get to see it, for she would already have left the building. If FJ was here, she would never know. But perhaps he would see her. Perhaps, once he knew she was here, he would come and find her. Unless he too was drugged. But FJ was smart – smarter than her. He would know about the soup. She was sure of it.

Liss's row was ushered forward along the aisle and up a set of wooden steps. Onto the platform, where only moments ago the prisoners had stood in chains. Were those poor girls even still alive? Or had they been killed already? Liss gave a shudder and tried to clear her mind.

And now, suddenly, she was next in line.

CHAPTER TWENTY
RILEY

'It's you and me back on the road, Riley,' Luc said, punching me lightly on the arm. 'Except this time I'm with a blonde instead of a brunette.'

I grinned. He was referring to my rushed dye job. My brown curls had vanished, to be replaced with a pale blonde ponytail. Scissor Sue had done a great job and I had hardly recognised myself in the mirror. In the unlikely event that James Grey saw me, I was hoping he wouldn't recognise me either.

While I was going blonde, Luc had gotten over-friendly with the clippers and now had army-short hair. I ran my hand over his head. 'Feels like a mole,' I said. 'All velvety.'

The copter was here. A Eurocopter Panther, the only one Pa had access to that would seat all of us. Charlie Duke was piloting and his huge frame filled out one side of the cockpit. Luc could also pilot if he needed to and I decided that copter lessons were next on my 'to do' list.

Charlie gave us a wave. Fred and Jessie were already inside. Luc helped me in and I smiled half-heartedly at the couple. If we were going to be in each other's company for a while, we might as well be civil. They smiled back, unsure and a little confused.

'It's me, Riley,' I said.

'Riley?' Jessie said, frowning. 'Oh, yes. It *is* you. Very nice hairstyle. Different.'

'It's so no one recognises me in Salisbury.'

'Sensible idea,' Fred said.

There was hope in their eyes. Barely contained excitement in the looks they passed between each other.

I considered what we were about to attempt – to reunite these people with their children. It was a huge responsibility. Despite what Fred and Jessie had done to us, it was still the right thing to do and, in a weird way, it was something I *needed* to do. We'd had no luck finding Skye's killer, but maybe if we could save these two kids, it would redress the balance a little. I needed to do this for Fred, for Jessie, for me and for Skye.

We strapped ourselves into the seats behind them and stowed our bags underneath. I slid my sunglasses off the top of my head down onto my nose, picked up the headset and slipped it on.

'Luc,' Fred said in greeting.

'Hi,' Luc replied. Then the blades started up and after a few moments we lifted off from the helipad outside the guards' building.

There was no one to wave us off and I was glad. I'd told Ma to stay at home. I didn't think I could take another dramatic goodbye. I was still reeling from the last one.

Everyone else was busy fortifying our Perimeter in case the unthinkable should happen and Grey reached Bournemouth.

I peered out of the window and saw the guards' building receding, the H of the helipad, a couple of vehicles, some guards walking across the yard. And as we climbed higher I caught my breath at the shrinking roads of our Perimeter, the trees and large square houses. Down at Coy Pond, the silver stream peeked out from beneath lush green foliage which merged into the dark woods at the southern boundary.

I'd never seen my home from this angle before. It looked like a toy town. I could see the full extent of the fence surrounding it; wire and metal glinting in the sunshine.

The demarcation line was incredible: inside the Perimeter, all lay neat and orderly. Straight tree-lined avenues, jewel-green lawns, elegant houses with turquoise swimming pools. And throughout, there was a sense of beauty and safety.

But outside the fence a wasteland sprawled out into infinity. Scrubby brown earth and low bushes. No roads. A pack of scavenger dogs trotting along. Clusters of dilapidated buildings. It was impossible to tell if anyone lived in them or if they were abandoned.

Our Perimeter was truly cut off. A floating paradise island in a sea of desolation. Seeing it like that, it was a wonder we'd survived untouched for as long as we had.

As the copter tilted and banked north, I dragged my eyes away from home and stared ahead at the tall imposing outline of the Charminster Compound in the distance, with its towering brick walls and metal ramps. Beyond that, lay the road which led northward. Pa and the others would be on that road. Perhaps we would pass over them. Perhaps he might look up and know it was us.

But as we left Bournemouth and continued on our journey, there was no sign of him down there. Maybe they were still inside Charminster trying to drum up volunteers. I hoped everyone would realise how serious the situation had become. I hoped they would want to join the fight against Grey. We wouldn't be able to win this on our own. We needed numbers. Massive numbers.

I glanced back. Jessie appeared nervous. She gripped her husband's arm and he took her hand. Then I turned to look across at Luc who was deep in thought. After a while he noticed my gaze and smiled.

The journey took much less time than I thought it would. As Charlie brought the copter down, I didn't feel nearly prepared enough to meet up with Connor again. What on earth would I say to him? At least we'd have more pressing issues to deal with than Ma and Connor's messy history. I decided I would ignore the emotional stuff and concentrate on doing the job we were here to do.

We finally set down in a field on the edge of a wood. Charlie killed the engine and after a while all was quiet. We were a couple of miles south west of Salisbury, praying that none of Grey's men had seen us land. Charlie had flown in over the least populated areas, but the noise of the copter would have carried so we were all a little on edge.

'Stay put for a while, till we know it's all clear,' Charlie said in his thick Dorset accent. 'Keep the doors closed.'

And so we sat and waited. There was no sign of Connor yet, but that didn't mean he wouldn't come.

'Here,' Charlie said. 'He turned around and handed us a cloth bundle over the top of his seat. Inside were some green pears. 'The missus picked 'em fresh this morning from the garden. Last ones of the season.'

'Thanks,' Luc said.

We took one each and I offered them to Fred and Jessie. We sat quiet for a few minutes, munching our pears. They were perfect – sweet and tart.

'Any chance of using nature's facilities?' Fred said after a while.

'I suppose,' Luc replied. 'One at a time though. And watch your backs. We don't know who might be outside.'

'Or *what*,' Charlie added.

'What do you mean 'what'?' I asked.

'I believe he's talking about the wildlife,' Fred said.

'There used to be a safari park near here,' Luc said. 'But the animals aren't behind fences anymore.'

'What? Like a zoo? How come I'm the only one who doesn't know this stuff?' I asked.

'I guess you never needed to know,' Luc replied.

I thought back to the time I had stopped outside Fred and Jessie's farm a few weeks ago – it had been dark and I'd heard a creature howling. Maybe there had been wolves nearby. Perhaps it was a good job I hadn't known about the wildlife back then. I'd been freaked out enough as it was, without adding wild creatures into the mix.

'So what animals are we talking about?' I asked Luc. 'Lions?'

'And tigers and bears...'

'Oh my.'

Luc grinned.

'There are a few big cats left out there,' Fred said. 'But most of 'em got shot. We sometimes see monkeys in the trees near our farm.'

'For a couple of years there were zebras and bison,' Jessie said. 'But you don't see them these days. I think they were probably hunted for food.'

'The wolves are the main problem,' Charlie said. 'They bred fast and there's a lot of them round these parts now.'

'So?' Fred said. 'Can I go and find a tree?'

Charlie opened his door and climbed out of the copter. I held my breath, almost expecting a pack of wolves to descend on him. But he came around and opened Fred's door without a wild animal in sight.

'Rest of you lot, stay put and keep the door closed.' Charlie said. He took Fred a little way off.

Once they were back inside, I decided to brave the wildlife and go and find a tree of my own.

'My turn,' I said.

'I'll come with you,' Luc said.

'No, you won't.'

'Okay, but stay in sight,' Luc said.

'I don't think so!'

'Take this then.' He offered me a revolver.

'Got my own,' I said, tapping my side. I scanned the vicinity for some privacy. We were adjacent to a wood, but a thick high hedge meant I wouldn't be able to get to it easily. I spied a small copse of trees a few hundred yards away.

'Those trees are too far away,' Luc said following my line of sight. 'Stay closer.'

I was mortified. This was way too embarrassing. But the trees were a long way away and I didn't think I'd be able to pee and shoot straight at the same time, should the need arise.

Dusk was creeping across the meadow and if there were any hungry wolves or big cats in the area, I imagined they would be on the prowl right about now. That settled it. I would do what Luc suggested and pee close by.

I got out of the copter and scooched around the back. At least we were right in the corner of the field and so I had the hedge behind me and the copter's tail in front. But before I had the chance to worry further, there was a rustle and snap from behind.

In the split-second I turned around, a dozen thoughts flashed through my mind: wild animals... raiders... attackers... no, it'll be nothing, just my imagination... Grey's men... wait, it must be Connor...

But when I finally did turn around, I found myself staring at a face. And it was a face I recognised.

Not Connor.

It was somebody I didn't think I'd ever see again.

CHAPTER TWENTY-ONE

LISS

'I name you Dinah.' Grey lifted a thin chain from a large wicker basket and placed it around the girl's neck. She moved off slowly and then suddenly Liss was standing in front of him.

She didn't dare make eye contact for fear he might read her mind. She kept her eyes facing down and prayed he couldn't hear her hammering heart.

'I name you Deborah.' Grey's hands brushed her hair as he lowered the chain over her head and she suppressed a shiver of revulsion, managing not to look up.

Soon it was over and she found herself walking through an arch into a dimly lit passageway which ran down the side of the cathedral. Liss, or Deborah as she was now supposed to be called, touched the chain around her neck. She lifted out her ponytail which was trapped under it. Then she examined the small metal cross which hung from the delicate links.

Liss touched the simple pendant. It was light and small, but to her, it felt as though it weighed a ton. As though her body was being held prisoner by it. As if she herself was now in shackles. She let go of the cross and it fell back against her pinafore.

Annabelle should be along soon, as long as she had remembered to be quiet and not draw any attention to herself. Liss heard a soft tread behind her and couldn't help turning. She breathed a sigh of thankfulness. It was her friend. She was safe. They were both safe. For now.

Liss learned that her new name 'Deborah' was the Hebrew name for Melissa, the Greek word for 'bee'. She had to remember to answer to her new name and also had to remember to call Annabelle 'Anna'. They were told that these were more Godly names, more fitting for servants of Grey's Church of the Epiphany.

After the naming ceremony, things returned to what now passed for normal. The two girls continued with their lessons and continued to avoid drinking the soup. There were no opportunities for escape and no one else approached them like Chloe had done. Liss and Annabelle were on their own.

Liss had hoped that after the naming ceremony, she might have heard something from FJ, but she hadn't had any indication that he was even here. Perhaps that man outside their farm – Mr Carter – perhaps he had killed FJ, or taken him somewhere else, or let him go...

Weeks dragged on. Winter came around and then spring and still nothing changed. Liss even had moments where she considered drinking the soup. At least she wouldn't have this constant fear of discovery rolling around in her stomach. But she couldn't bring herself to do it. What if she drank the soup and then FJ turned up to break them out? She would be a zombie, unable to think for herself. Unable to escape.

Annabelle behaved as though she was spaced out most of the time anyway. She wasn't anything like the lively feisty girl she had been a year ago. But the other girls in their dormitory were gradually becoming a little less docile. More aware. Liss had an idea that the women had stopped putting so much stuff in the soup. Maybe they had decreased the doses over time.

After all, none of the women seemed as drugged up as the children.

One year became two years became three years became four and soon Liss could hardly remember what life had been like before the Close. She had an image in her head of two kindly parents and a farmhouse bathed in sunshine. But beyond that the details were fuzzy, a half memory.

They only saw James Grey three or four times a year for religious ceremonies and that was three or four times too much as far as Liss was concerned. More girls joined them and their living area expanded. They were allocated more space and Liss was often called upon to help with the building work and decoration. She enjoyed this part of her life more than any other. The lessons were boring, the church services bewildering and a little scary, but the manual labour soothed her mind and allowed her to forget the fear for a few blissful hours.

Liss wished she were brave enough to approach some of the new girls, as Chloe had done with her. Brave enough to whisper to them not to drink the soup. But after witnessing Grey's harsh judgement in the cathedral, she knew she didn't have the courage to risk her life like Chloe had. Perhaps if Chloe had known where her words would have led her, she wouldn't have been so brave either. Even if Liss *had* plucked up the courage, there hadn't been any opportunity for escape. Not one. They were locked in, constantly watched, and the fear she felt at being discovered was debilitating.

When Liss was fourteen years of age, she realised that she had lived at the Close for the same number of years that she had lived at home. Seven years on the farm with her parents, seven years under the rule of James Grey. Was this going to be her whole life now? Would she be here forever?

One day at lunch, out of the corner of her eye, Liss saw

Sarah and another of the women whispering frantically and glancing over at her. Liss's stomach dropped to the floor. Was this it? Was this the day she had been dreading? The day they discovered she hadn't been drinking the soup? They must have found out. What should she do? Could she run? But her legs were jelly.

Sarah was heading over to their table. She was definitely staring right at her. Liss hastily looked away, adopting a semi-glazed expression.

'Come with me please, Deborah,' Sarah said, her voice too neutral for Liss to determine whether or not she was in trouble.

Liss's breathing grew shallow and her head swam, but she forced herself to stand. She felt Anna's eyes on her and was able to quickly squeeze the younger girl's hand in reassurance. Anna was twelve now. Old enough to understand that what they were doing was forbidden. Yet they both still continued to tip their soup away. A small act of defiance. A way to keep a little piece of their old selves alive. It was a miracle they'd got away with it for so long.

Following Sarah out of the dining hall, she left by a different exit. It was the way Liss had come in, seven years earlier. They walked out into the lobby, past the wash basins and coat hooks and left the building. The sun was bright and she screwed up her eyes against its glare. They were in the small courtyard. It was empty and still, apart from some trees swaying beyond the wall.

'Follow me,' Sarah said. 'Quickly.' She strode over to a metal gate set into the wall, drew out a key and clicked open the lock. The gate opened and Liss followed her through.

As Sarah locked the gate behind them, Liss cast a surreptitious glance around before quickly lowering her eyes again, for this courtyard was filled with robed guards and workmen. The only man Liss had seen for years was James Grey. Even the boys had never attended cathedral services at the same time as the girls since that naming ceremony. So it was shocking and a little scary to be in the presence of so many males after so long. It made Liss more convinced that she was about to meet her death. For what other explanation could there be for this trip out of the women's quarters?

It was rumoured that all girls would be married when they reached the age of eighteen. But Liss didn't know if this was truth or gossip. However, it was true that the majority of girls did leave the dormitories at eighteen.

Sarah crossed the courtyard and entered a building. This time, Liss kept her eyes fixed either on the flagstone floor or on Sarah's back, too terrified to take in these strange new surroundings. Their footsteps echoed in her ears as they continued on through the entrance hall and along wooden corridors. Soon they emerged into the open air once more.

Liss hazarded another glance around. A middle-aged man in a suit stood outside the building. It looked as though he had been waiting for them as he visibly relaxed when he saw Sarah.

'Wait here,' Sarah said to her. She approached the man and they spoke for a few moments. The man looked as though he was enjoying the conversation, but Sarah sounded annoyed. Liss strained her ears, but only caught odd snatches of conversation:

'...for a few minutes,' the man said.

'...bad idea,' Sarah snapped.

'...not your decision. Come here, girl.'

Liss realised the man was now speaking to her. She forced one foot in front of the other. If they were going to kill her she hoped they would do it quickly. She didn't think she could bear to be paraded in front of everyone in the cathedral, humiliated and terrorised by Grey.

'Wait here. I'll have her back in ten minutes,' the man said to Sarah.

Liss's heart lifted a little. Maybe she wasn't to be killed after all.

'Deborah, is it?' the man asked.

She nodded.

'Follow me and you're to do exactly as I tell you. Do it right and you will have a free day to yourself tomorrow. Do it wrong and you will suffer the consequences.'

Liss gulped and nodded, remembering to keep her face blank as always. The man pulled a piece of cloth from his jacket pocket. He shook it out.

'Stand still,' he said. 'I'm going to put this over your head for a minute.'

Liss realised it was a hood. She balled her fists and willed herself not to scream as he slipped the material over her head. She could see a faint sunshiny glow through the dark material which smelt of the Close – that musty, dark scent of old class-rooms and corridors.

'There's a good girl,' he said, talking to her like she was one of her dad's horses. 'We're going to walk a few paces and then I'll take off the hood. When I remove it, you are to stare straight ahead without turning around. Do you understand?'

Liss nodded.

'Whatever you hear, you are not to turn your head or strain your eyes to look. There will be a door in front of you. Look at the door and at nothing else.'

She felt his hand on her elbow.

'Walk slow and steady until I tell you to stop.'

She did as he asked, the fear threatening to topple her. A faint shout came from the distance and then a woman's scream. Liss tried to concentrate on her breathing and on trying to remember the man's instructions. She was to stare at the door. Nothing but the door.

He told her to stop and then removed the hood. The light made her momentarily blind and then the wooden door bloomed into focus. She stared at it as though her life depended upon it. Which it probably did. Her eyes bored into the metal bands and studs of the door which merged with the dark knotted wood. Her gaze then slid down to the iron handle and the key-shaped hole. Then to the lintel and the doorframe and the grey bricks surrounding it.

She knew the man had told Sarah she would be returned in ten minutes, but perhaps that had been a ruse. Meaningless words to keep her calm. Perhaps he had no intention of returning her. Any minute now he could slit her throat or shoot her in the head.

Was this where they would kill her? Was this where it all ended? She closed her eyes. And then she heard her name being called. Her real name.

'Lissy! Oh my God, Lissy! Is it you?'

Liss opened her eyes, but she didn't dare turn her head. She recognised that voice. It was her mum.

CHAPTER TWENTY-TWO
LISS

The desire to turn her head was so overwhelming that she couldn't breathe. What would they do to her if she did? Would they kill her? But her mum and possibly her dad were nearby. Close enough to shout to her. After all these years.

Then again, what if it wasn't her mum? What if it was only someone who sounded like her and this was all a trick to see if she would disobey her keepers and turn around.

Liss continued to stare straight ahead at the wooden door. It faded in and out of focus as old memories crowded her brain. Things she hadn't thought about in years. The soapy smell of her mother's cheek as she kissed her goodnight. Baking cakes together in the kitchen. Holding Mum's hand so tightly as they visited the market at the Compound. What she wouldn't give to turn and see her mother's face right now. To collapse into her arms and be swept up in kisses. To leave this place.

But how could she be sure it wasn't a trick?

She would do it. She would look...

But in that split-second between decision and action, the cloth hood came down over her head once more and everything went dark. Liss wanted to scream and rip the hood from her head. But she didn't. She stood and let the man lead her away. A tear fell and she used the hood to blot it away.

As she stumbled, blind, alongside the man who held her arm, guiding her away from the thing she had dreamed of all these years. She began to convince herself that of course it hadn't been her parents. If they'd known she was here, they would have got her out years ago. And why would the man have made her stand there while her mum called out to her?

It had to have been a test. And she had passed. She didn't let herself think about the alternative – that her mother had come to see her and she, Liss, had been too afraid to turn around.

After that incident, Liss hadn't let herself think too much about anything. She threw herself into her chores and lessons and even drank a little of the soup from time to time. Whenever she did this, Anna became agitated, so she stopped again. If it weren't for Annabelle, Liss was sure she would have had drunk two full bowls of the stuff every day. But it had little effect on her anyway. Liss was convinced that it was just normal soup now. The other girls she had arrived here with were no longer spaced out, even though they were still fairly docile.

Again, life in the Close became slow and predictable. Things occasionally happened which started speculation and a little whispered gossip. Accidents occurred or sometimes someone went crazy and lost their mind. Once a group of armed raiders broke in and tried to steal from their stores. They got caught, but Liss never did find out what happened to them.

Over the years, many young girls disappeared from their quarters to be replaced with new girls. Liss didn't know where they went and she was never offered an explanation. She certainly couldn't ask. The rumours were that they were given new jobs in other areas of the city. Liss wondered if she or Anna would ever be moved. Part of her hoped so and part of her hoped not. They hadn't been outside the Cathedral Close since she had arrived here. She wondered if the main city was much different.

At age fifteen, her lessons ceased and Liss was put in charge of a group of much younger girls. She taught them to sew, to grow vegetables and to cook. She much preferred doing this to enduring the interminable lessons and time now passed more pleasantly. The best thing was that she had been put in charge of her dormitory. The awful Leah had been sent elsewhere.

A few months after her sixteenth birthday, Liss was in the dining hall with her girls. As group leader, she was no longer given the same soup as the others, but she still only ever took a couple of tiny sips. Anna still sat at the same table and still slept in the bed next to her, although they were no longer in lessons together. Anna had to continue on for another year until she reached the age of fifteen. Everyone still assumed they were sisters and Liss hoped this meant they would never be separated.

As Liss sat at the table chewing on a piece of bread, a sudden shriek from the top table made her start. She snapped her head up. It was Sarah. And a robed man stood facing her! A man. Here. In the women's quarters. Sarah was staring at him, ashen-faced, as though she had seen a ghost. And then she ran from the room, holding her skirts to stop herself tripping.

The hall was always quiet, but now a shocked hush fell over the room. Another of the elder women rose from the top table and walked out, followed by the man.

Liss's heart began to pound. What was going on? She caught the eye of several other group leaders, but they turned away, not showing any worry or distress in their expressions.

After lunch, Liss mulled over the strange events. She and her girls were in their workroom, busy hemming robes. Something shocking had obviously occurred. What could it have been? Would anybody tell her? Probably not. But the desire to find out overcame any sense of self-preservation. She needed to know.

'Wait here, girls,' she said. 'I'll return shortly.'

The girls obediently continued sewing, unquestioning.

Liss left the room. She now wore the long skirt and grey blouse which marked her as a group leader. She had been secretly thrilled to wear these new clothes as she was sick of her worn-out pinafore. Her skirts swished along the wooden floor as she made her way to the infirmary. Nurse was the most approachable person in the Close. Hopefully she would know what was going on.

Liss stood outside Nurse's office door and knocked twice.

No reply.

She waited and then knocked again. Harder.

Maybe this was a bad idea. She turned to leave.

'Can I help you, Deborah?'

Liss turned to see one of the elders coming out of another room. It was Naomi. Liss had never spoken directly to her before. She was quite old with a stern expression. She vaguely remembered her as the teacher who had told them to confess to the Listeners. But that had been years ago when she'd first arrived here.

'Oh. No. Sorry. I came to see Nurse.'

'Nurse is busy.'

Liss bowed her head and turned to go.

'Wait, child.'

Liss stopped and looked up.

'Are you ill?'

'A headache, that's all,' Liss lied.

'I may have something for you. Come.'

Liss hesitated and then followed Naomi into her room – an office. Beneath a frosted window was a light-coloured wooden desk. Shelves lined the left hand wall, but there were no books on them, just stacks of numbered box files.

Naomi walked behind her desk and pulled open a draw. She rummaged around for a few seconds before pulling out a small white pot.

'Magic pills,' she said with a smile.

Liss assumed she was joking and tried to smile back.

'I take it you haven't heard the news,' Naomi said.

'News? No.'

Naomi gestured to the faded wooden chairs. Liss sat in the closest. Naomi sat in her chair and sighed. She poured a cup of water from the tin jug on her desk and pushed it across to Liss. Was this stern woman about to tell her what was going on?

'Hold out your hand,' Naomi said.

Liss did as she was asked. Naomi pried open the lid of the pot and tipped a tiny white stone onto Lissy's palm.

'What... what is it?'

'No need to look so terrified. It's a headache pill. You're lucky. This is my last pot of tablets. After these, it's back to the vinegar wraps and Feverfew.' She wrinkled her nose.

'Oh no,' Liss said. 'I couldn't...' She didn't even have a headache. It was simply an excuse she had used.

'Psht,' Naomi said. 'Wash it down with water.'

Liss thought she had better do it. Gingerly she placed the small stone tablet thing on her tongue. She tasted sugar and then an awful bitterness. Quickly she took a swig of water and swallowed. Naomi did the same.

'I've been watching you, Deborah. You're a good girl. Bright and hard working. I think it was God's will that I bumped into you today.'

Liss noticed a ticking sound. She hadn't heard that noise in a long time. Not since she was a young child, back home. She gazed around the room until she located the source of the noise. On one of the shelves sat a small brass clock. Liss suddenly pictured the sitting room at home with the grandfather clock in the corner. She and FJ used to take turns winding it up and setting the pendulum swinging. She hadn't thought about that clock for years.

Naomi was still talking: 'Something terrible happened today. Something that has shaken our whole community.'

Liss wondered if Naomi would tell her more.

'There has been the most terrible attack. I can't quite believe it's happened. But it may mean a big change. We must prepare ourselves for the worst.'

'What attack?' Liss asked, Naomi's words only beginning to sink in.

'You would have found out soon enough anyway. It pains me to tell you, but Our Father has been grievously hurt. That's why Nurse isn't here. All medical staff have been called to his side.'

'Will he be all right?' Liss asked. She had the unchristian thought that she hoped he wouldn't be all right. That this would be the end of him and she could finally go home. But then she suddenly realised she wasn't totally unhappy here anymore. That she actually enjoyed her work. This realisation shocked her more than the news about James Grey.

'We must all pray for his fast recovery. Matthew is at his side doing everything he can.'

Matthew was James Grey's son. Not his true son, but his chosen head disciple who had taken on many of his roles. It was said that he was as beautiful as an angel and that the light of God shone from his eyes.

'What happened to Our Father?' Liss asked.

Naomi hesitated before answering. 'Intruders attacked him this morning. They tried to kill him at breakfast. They were children by all accounts.'

Liss gasped. 'How?' she asked, before she could stop herself. 'Sorry.' She shook her head and stared into her lap. It did not do to ask too many questions. It was not looked upon favourably.

'Don't you have a class to attend to?' Naomi asked.

'Yes. My children are—'

'Well, then you must go. Headache or no headache, we must not shirk our duties.'

'Of course. I'm sorry.'

'You're a good girl. We will pray for Our Father and I will see you later.'

Liss stood and left the room, her mind spinning with all she had heard.

CHAPTER TWENTY-THREE
RILEY

My shock turned to pleasure, but I realised my mouth was still hanging open like an idiot. I quickly turned my gawp into a smile.

'Denzil, I don't believe it! How did you get here? How come... I don't get it.'

'Hey, mate,' Luc said, coming around the side of the copter.

'You weren't supposed to be looking!' I said to Luc.

'What's going on?' Charlie Duke called, stepping outside. 'That's not Connor.'

'It's okay, Mr Duke,' I said. 'We know him.'

Charlie puffed around the side of the copter, his gun in his hand. He had it pointed down at the ground, but it was ready to fire. 'You sure?' he said. 'This isn't part of the plan. I don't like surprises.'

'Don't worry, sir,' Luc replied. 'He's a friend.'

After grinning like crazy people for a few seconds, Luc and I gave Denzil a huge bear hug. His handsome face looked exactly the same, minus the split lip he'd had the last time we saw him. The time he'd put himself in danger to save our lives.

Luc laughed. 'I don't believe it. This can't be a coincidence. What are you doing here in the middle of nowhere?'

'Back in the copter,' Charlie ordered. 'It's almost dark. I don't like us all standing around out here. Too exposed.'

'I still need to... you know... pee,' I said awkwardly.

'We'll leave you to it,' Luc said.

I did what I had to do without being attacked by wild creatures and then climbed back into the copter.

Denzil was still kitted out in his military gear and I wondered what he'd been up to and how he'd managed to get free of the army.

'So good to see you,' Luc said.

'I almost didn't recognise you, Riley,' Denzil said, touching a lock of my hair. 'Blonde? It looks good, but I preferred your natural colour.'

'It's a disguise.' I smiled.

'Aah,' he replied, and then tilted his head towards the seats behind us, raising his eyebrows.

'Oh,' I said. 'That's Fred and Jessie.'

He leant over his seat. 'Hi, I'm Denzil.' They shook hands. 'Yours are the kids we're gonna rescue, right?'

'How do you know about that?' Luc asked. 'We're supposed to rendezvous with someone else.'

'Yeah, I know,' Denzil replied. 'Connor, right?'

'How do you—'

'Basically, I wound up at the Uley Perimeter.'

'Uley?' Luc and I said together.

'Yeah. Four of my unit had to go up to Hullavington to pick up some supplies. I made sure my name was on that list. Figured I'd try to get up there and see if any of my family was still in the area. But then I saw Uley was close by and I remembered it's one of Eddie Donovan's Perimeters.'

'It is,' Luc said.

'My grandparents live there too,' I said.

'I know. I've been staying with them. Me and your grandad, we get on great.'

On hearing this, I smiled. Last month, I told Grandma and Grandpa all about Denzil and what he did for us a few months ago. I'm sure they must've treated him like a king.

'Anyway,' Denzil continued. 'I met Connor up there. He told me about what went on last month. That's some serious story.'

'So how did you get away from your unit?' Luc asked.

'That part was easy. They're a dozy bunch. It was having a place to go that was the hard bit. But I'm hoping your offer of becoming a guard is still good.'

'Course it is,' Luc said. 'Of course. We need all the help we can get, with everything that's going on.'

'It's crazy,' Denzil said. 'Grey's not right in the head.'

'Where's Connor?' Charlie asked bluntly.

'Oh, sorry, sir,' Luc said. 'This is Denzil Porter. Denzil, Charlie Duke. Mr Duke will probably be your boss.'

'Will I now?' Charlie raised a bushy eyebrow. 'Good to meet you, lad.' He extended a beefy hand over the back of his seat. 'Now tell us why you're here and Connor isn't.'

They shook hands and I felt real joy that this lovely man had finally found his way back to us after putting himself in jeopardy and saving our lives.

'We decided it would be better this way,' Denzil replied. 'There wasn't time to let anyone know, cos we were already on the road with no comms. We thought it made more sense for Connor to go into Salisbury first. Suss the place out. That way he gets a head start. He can ask a few questions, see if he can locate the kids before we get there.'

'Good plan,' Charlie said.

'Connor sent me to meet up with you. Let you know the score. Now I'm here, I can lend a hand.'

'Yes, you can,' Charlie said. 'We could certainly use an extra man. Any more like you?'

'Not where I'm from,' Denzil said. 'They're all a bunch of tossers.' And then he broke into that loud infectious belly laugh of his and we couldn't help joining in.

'Right,' Charlie said, breaking up the party. 'I suggest we eat and then Luc and Riley need to get going.'

'I'd like to volunteer to go with 'em,' Denzil said. 'If that's all right, sir. Make sure they get to the walls safe and sound.'

Charlie didn't speak for a moment. It was dark now. Properly dark, and I could hardly make out anyone's face. We couldn't turn on the interior light for obvious reasons.

'That would put my mind at ease,' Charlie finally said. 'I didn't like the thought of these two going to that place without backup. My orders are to stay here with our two guests.'

'Riley and I don't need backup, sir,' Luc said. But there was no fight in his voice.

'I know you don't, Lucas. I just said I'd feel more at ease knowing you had someone else.'

'Yeah, me too,' Luc admitted. 'Denzil's a good man to have around.'

Reaching under the seat, I fumbled about for my rucksack and heaved it onto my lap. I undid the top zip, grabbed my torch and shone it into the bag.

'Bread and cheese all right for everyone?' I asked.

There were murmurs of agreement so I broke off chunks of the crusty bread and handed it out along with thick slices of hard cheese. Then I brushed the crumbs off my lap, switched off the torch and popped a piece of bread into my mouth.

'How long will it take to get there?' I asked with my mouth full.

'Just under an hour on foot,' Denzil replied. 'Connor showed me which entrance to watch. We've got to wait for his signal. If he doesn't manage it, we'll have to think of something else.'

'No,' Charlie said.

'What do you mean?' I asked.

'No thinking of anything else. Your Pa was very clear. Connor lets you in, or you turn around and come straight back. You do it stealthy or not at all.'

'Johnny Culpepper gave me his word he would get my kids out of there,' Fred called from the back.

'I don't care who told you what,' Charlie replied. 'I have my orders and that's what we're doing. No one said nothing about any other plans. There'll be no improvising, d'you hear me?'

'Them's our children in there!' Fred cried.

'Yes. And Luc and Riley will try to get them out. Let's not worry about anything else for now. We stick to the plan and that's that.'

Luc took my hand and I felt instantly confused. Was this just a friendly gesture, meant to reassure me? His fingers were warm. Mine were freezing. Whatever his reasons, his touch gave me confidence in what we were about to do. And I realised that, despite my nerves, I wasn't in this alone.

As we had headed further into this journey, rescuing FJ and Lissy became more and more important to me. It made me feel closer to my sister somehow. As though rescuing them was a way of bringing a small part of her back again. I wondered if we would succeed this time. Last time we'd tried it had been a disaster.

'You will do your best though, won't you?' Jessie asked, her voice small and pleading.

'Of course,' I replied.

'It's just... they're my babies.' Her voice was breaking.

'If it all goes well, we'll be back by morning and you can go home with your children,' Luc added.

'Sounds like a wonderful dream,' Jess said.

'Might take a bit longer than that,' Denzil said. 'Just so you know.'

'I'll give you seventy-two hours and then I want you back, kids or no kids,' Charlie said. 'That's plenty long enough. If you can't bring them out in that time frame, we'll regroup. You hear me?'

Luc, Denzil and I gave Charlie our word.

'You ready?' Denzil asked. 'Don't want to miss our opportunity.'

'Yeah,' I said, but the word came out too quietly for anyone to hear. 'Yep,' I said, too loudly this time.

'And don't forget,' Denzil added, 'this is all Grey's territory. He catches us and we'll have a lot of explaining to do. So, nice and quiet.'

I nodded.

'Good luck,' Charlie said.

Fred and Jessie echoed his words.

'Let's go.' Denzil slid out of the Panther without a sound.

I climbed down after him, landing with a thud on the rustling grass. As I swung my rucksack up onto my back, Luc followed me out and closed the door behind him with a dull clunk.

The night air felt cool and damp and I was suddenly aware of my heart beating.

Denzil pointed to our right and took off at a jog into the pitch black. I hoped my fitness would be good enough to keep up and that my eyesight would adjust to the moonless night. But with Denzil ahead and Luc behind, I was sure it would be okay.

I wasn't even going to think about wolves, let alone the other dangers that might be waiting for us.

CHAPTER TWENTY-FOUR

LISS

In the days following James Grey's injury, there were no lessons or chores. Every waking hour consisted of prayers. From dawn to dusk, Grey's disciples stayed on their knees fervently begging the Lord to spare their Father.

But Lissy could not bring herself to pray for a man she suspected of being evil. Instead, as she knelt, her muscles cramping, she used the time to let her mind wander through her past. To remember who she was and what she had lost. She realised that she had almost accepted her life here. That she had become defeated. But that would not do. Something had to change. If she did nothing, she would end up dying here, either executed for treason or withering away from old age. And Liss didn't know which would be worse.

She was disappointed to discover that the mass prayers did their work and soon the cathedral bells pealed in celebration of Grey's recovery. She would probably go to hell for her unchristian thoughts, but Liss concluded that if Grey's version of Christianity was the right one, then she would go to hell anyway because in her mind she'd rebelled against just about every rule he had.

Even though James Grey survived the attack, there was a serious after-effect – their Holy Father had lost his voice. None of his followers were told how it had disappeared, merely that he could now only speak in a low whisper and sometimes not at all. Despite his new-found silence, he still wished to celebrate the miracle of his recovery, and so Grey called his disciples to rejoice with him at the cathedral.

At the allotted time, Liss joined the other group leaders as they and their children made their way through the Close to the cathedral.

The route was very familiar to her now, despite the fact that it had changed so rapidly and drastically over the years as more lost souls joined Grey's Church. Hundreds of new dwelling houses had been erected, as well as places of work and study. There were fewer trees and hardly any large green spaces that she knew of within the Close, other than the area immediately in front of the cathedral.

Liss waited her turn on the green before leading her girls into the massive building. They were one of the first groups inside and reluctantly she led them down the aisle to a row of seats near the front on the left. If she could have chosen, she would have sat as far towards the back as she could. But it wasn't her choice. They were always instructed to fill the front seats first. She ushered her girls along their row and sat at the end on the aisle seat, waiting for James Grey to make his appearance.

She would never get used to seeing him. Would never be able to master her fear and revulsion whenever he stepped up onto the platform. As she waited, her armpits prickled with sweat and her stomach gurgled.

Although she did not believe he was their 'Father', she still had the superstitious thought that he was in some way more powerful than a mere human. That he could somehow read her mind or see into her soul. Although common sense told her this was nonsense. If he could do that, she would have been hauled up onto the stage with Chloe all those years ago.

The cathedral was awash with anticipation. A fevered silence which made Liss want to scream. She could do it. She could stand up and scream her lungs out. See how loud and echoing her voice could really be. She wouldn't be the first to do so. It had happened at least twice before. But she knew she wouldn't. She would sit still and quiet and bide her time. Wait for a good opportunity to escape. The right moment would come along soon. Now that she was ready for it. It had to.

And suddenly everyone was rising to their feet. James Grey was about to walk out and greet them. Liss had another odd thought – what if everyone felt the same way she did? What if every single person in this cathedral wanted to escape, but they were just too scared to do it? The thought made her want to laugh, but she smoothed the smile from her face and studied the platform instead. Here he was.

Rather than coming out alone as he usually did, this time he was accompanied by a young man, a boy really, dressed similarly to Grey in a dark robe with a crimson trim. He must be a highly favoured disciple to be dressed in such a way. They stood side by side at the pulpit, almost identical in height, but it was the disciple who stood in front of the microphone, not Grey.

Liss realised that this boy was as beautiful as Grey was not. He had broad shoulders and good posture, flawless features, clear skin and shining eyes. It really did seem as though he were filled with the light of the Lord. Grey touched him on the shoulder and the boy began to speak:

'I am humbled to stand before you all today alongside our glorious Father.' His voice was warm and soft with a slight tremor. 'For he has charged me with an important task here in our church.' The boy's voice grew stronger as his nerves faded. 'Many of you will know me only as 'Matthew', but from this day forward, my name is forgotten. From this day I shall only be known as "the Voice of the Father".'

So this was Grey's favoured disciple, Matthew. She agreed with the rumours – he truly did have the face of an angel. His eyes roamed across the congregation and his gaze seemed to hover for a moment over Liss's face. But she must have imagined it, for why should he look at her? This boy who was to speak for James Grey.

Although his voice was beautiful, Liss did not like his words. They chilled her.

Grey leant in close to the boy and whispered something to him. As he did so Liss had a strange sense of recognition. Something about the way the boy tilted his head to listen. But it couldn't be. That would be crazy. That would be impossible. Wouldn't it?

But just as she told herself it *was* not, *could* not be true, she knew in her heart that it was. This 'Matthew', this 'Voice of the Father' who seemed so confident and had the ear of James Grey himself. This boy was her brother. It was FJ.

Liss stared hard at his face. There was no mistaking him. In fact she couldn't believe she hadn't recognised him straight away. As she stared harder, his features blurred in front of her eyes. They tilted to the side and then a rushing noise filled her ears. Liss fainted.

She was comfortable and warm, wrapped in a cocoon of soft sheets and blankets. It must be a dream. She didn't want to open her eyes, for if she did, the dream would end and she would be back in her narrow bed with its itchy blanket. She opened them anyway.

Not a dream.

The room in which she found herself was dimly lit and wasn't a place she had ever been before. Liss sat up. Where was she? The bed was huge and she lay under a heavy embroidered coverlet, plump white pillows at her back. Thick curtains covered the windows, a faint light washing in at their edges.

This room was beautiful and homely, probably the same size as her dormitory, but it contained only this one bed. By the window was a sofa, armchair and a low table. Liss didn't think she'd seen a sofa since she'd arrived at the Close. Even the word 'sofa' sounded strange in her brain. A word from another lifetime.

A clear glass of water stood on the nightstand. A glass! That was another thing she hadn't seen for years. Here, they all drank out of tin or pottery cups. She reached across and picked it up. It felt smooth and cool. Grown up. Back when she lived on the farm, she wasn't supposed to use the glasses in case she broke one, but her parents always drank from them. She took a delicate sip. It was the most delicious drink of water she had ever tasted. Like drinking cool fresh air. She drained the glass and set it back down.

Then she remembered what she had seen. Or rather *who* she had seen. *FJ*. Matthew was FJ. That couldn't be true. And then she had blacked out. Fainted. And now she was here. Wherever *here* was.

Liss gave a start as the door creaked open and someone walked in.

'Hello, miss.'

It was a girl. And she had called her 'Miss'. Nobody called anybody 'Miss' in the Close. They were only to use first names. It was one of Grey's rules. They were all supposed to be equal in the eyes of God. Well, just because they all used first names, didn't mean they all acted as equals. Liss realised the girl was nervous of her.

'Hello,' Liss replied. 'Could you tell me where I am please?'

'Yes, miss. You're in the North Canonry.'

The girl came over to the nightstand and refilled the glass with fresh water. Then she bobbed a little curtsey.

The North Canonry? Wasn't that where Grey lived? But that couldn't be right. She couldn't be in James Grey's living quarters. Could she?

'Sorry, did you say the North Canonry?' Liss asked.

'I better tell Sir you're awake,' the girl replied, ignoring Liss's question. 'He said to inform him the second you woke up.' She scuttled from the room before Liss could quiz her further.

Liss grew even more anxious. Why was she here? Was she in trouble for fainting? Was Grey going to come in here next? The thought terrified her. And what about her girls? She had left them into the cathedral. They wouldn't know where to go without her to lead them back.

And FJ... had it really been him? Or had she imagined it? Maybe she had dreamt him after she collapsed. But it felt more like a memory than a dream. It was so sharp and fresh. His face; the way it had drawn her in as always. It had to have been her brother. And he was—

'Hello.'

Liss snapped her head up and stared at the figure at the foot of her bed. He was still dressed in his robes and appeared taller and broader close up. But there was no mistaking that this was truly her brother.

'FJ,' she whispered. 'Is it really you?'

CHAPTER TWENTY-FIVE

LISS

He tutted and shook his head. 'FJ is gone. I am the Voice of the Father now. Or did you miss that part of my speech?'

Liss couldn't tell if he was joking or serious. 'But it *is* you, isn't it?'

He came around to the side of the bed. 'Yes. It is I. How are you, Deborah?'

Liss gave a giggle. 'It feels funny hearing you call me by that name.'

'Deborah is your name, isn't it?'

'Well yes, it is *now*, but—'

'Then why should it be... funny?'

Liss realised FJ wasn't joking. He was very serious. Perhaps they were being watched.

'I've been so worried about you,' she said. 'All these years not knowing if you were alive or dead. And now, here you are. My big brother. And you're... the Voice of The Father.'

'I must say, it warms my heart to be reunited with you too, sister.' There was no trace of FJ's boyish country accent. He now spoke with exactly the same intonations as Grey.

'You didn't know I was here either?' Liss asked.

He hesitated.

'FJ?'

'It was difficult.'

'So you did know I was here?'

'Like I said, it was diffi—'

'How long, FJ?'

'How long for what?'

'How long have you known I was here?'

'A while.' He sighed and walked over to the window, drawing back one of the curtains. Daylight streamed into the room making Liss squint and blink. She peeled back the covers and slid out of bed. Her clothes were warm and crumpled and she attempted to smooth them down.

'Days? Weeks?' she prompted.

He didn't reply.

'Months? God! Years?'

'Don't blaspheme, Deborah. Do you want to go to hell?'

'So why didn't you try to contact me?' she said, walking round the bed towards her brother. 'You obviously have some power now.' Liss hadn't spoken this much in years. It felt strange to hear her voice running free without fear of consequences. 'If you knew I was here, you could've sent word. Or at least a note to put my mind at rest.'

'I couldn't.'

'No. I see that. You were too busy being promoted to think about your little sister. Even though it's your fault I ended up here in the first place.'

'Enough!'

'FJ, what happened to you?'

'I'll tell you what happened to me,' he said softly. 'My life began.'

'While mine ended,' she replied.

'Careful. Those are treasonous words.'

'So? What are you going to do about it? Lock me up? Have me killed?'

'Why are you acting this way?' he asked, taking hold of her arm. 'Where is my sweet little sister? I cannot believe you have become so... so shrewish. I thought you would be—'

'You thought I would be meek and mild and placid. A drugged-up zombie like the rest of them...'

'Quiet! You are out of control. You need to—'

'What? I need to what?' A tear rolled down Liss's cheek and she wiped it away angrily.

'Sister, we have got off on the wrong foot. We should rejoice that we're finally reunited, not bicker like the children we once were.'

Liss bit her bottom lip. He was right. Of course he was right. The main thing was that FJ was alive and they had found each other. None of the other stuff mattered.

'I'm sorry,' she said. 'It was the shock.'

He relaxed his shoulders and smiled. 'Of course. Come here.' He held out his arms and she stepped into them. They hugged, something they had never done as children. Then he stepped back and looked at her. 'Do you know, you have hardly changed a bit.'

She smiled. 'Well, I hope I've changed a little. It has been nine years, you know.'

'Still the same sweet face though, sister.'

'And you're still the same old FJ, able to wrap me round your little finger as usual.'

He grinned and for a moment it was as though they were back home in the yard. But then his smile hardened. 'I must go,' he said. 'Our Father will be missing me. He needs me more than ever now. Now that I am His Voice.'

'Of course,' Liss replied.

'Rest. I'll return when I can and we'll talk more. I will find a position for you here in the house.'

'Here?'

'Of course, here. You're my sister, I need you close by.'

'If I'm to stay here, can you... could you bring Anna here too?'

'Anna?'

'She's my sister. Well, not my real sister of course. But we've been together since...' A tangle of memories scratched at her brain. A summer's day, the dark interior of a van, the stench of fear, a crying child...

'Will it make you happy?' FJ asked. 'To have her with you?'

'Yes.'

'Then of course. But I really must go now.' He kissed her cheek, straightened up and left the room, his cloak billowing out behind him.

Liss watched him go, her heart racing. She stared at the empty space he'd left, letting her eyes slide out of focus, and then she finally turned away.

FJ. She had seen FJ. He was here.

She pulled back the other curtain letting more light tumble into the room through the diamond-leaded glass. Slants of yellow sunshine sliced through the air making little kite shapes on the carpet. Liss touched the patterns with her toes. Then she climbed back onto the bed and pulled her knees up to her chest, the sun warming her face.

So FJ had been here all along. But he had become one of them. He wanted to be here. Wanted her to be here too. When all she wanted was to go home and have everything be like it was before. But it would never be like that. Too much time had passed. Too many things had happened. Her childhood had gone and her brother was lost.

CHAPTER TWENTY-SIX

We'd been moving through thick woods for a while now. Negotiating our way over tree roots and around low branches. The area was alive with night noises – rustlings and snufflings, screeches and hooting night birds. I tried not to think about it. Denzil had come this way alone to meet us and he wasn't worried, so I shouldn't be either.

The clouds thinned to let a haze of milky moonlight through and I could scarcely make out Denzil's shape ahead of me, moving quickly and silently through the trees. I was warm now, sweating slightly in an effort to keep up, concentrating on avoiding the branches and on where to place my feet.

I hadn't realised that Denzil had suddenly come to a halt, and I only just stopped myself from crashing into his backpack. He raised his right hand and cocked his head to the side. I didn't dare break the silence to ask why we'd stopped.

He turned around and raised a finger to his lips. I turned back to Luc whose eyes were wide and questioning. I slowly shrugged my shoulders. Luc moved closer and the three of us stood there. Listening.

There. I heard it. A soft steady shuffling noise up ahead, like muffled rain. The sound was distant and close at the same time. Denzil motioned for us to stay where we were and he silently disappeared ahead into the trees.

The shuffling noise was constant which made me think it couldn't be an animal. It sounded too regular.

'What is it?' I mouthed to Luc.

He shook his head. 'Whatever it is, stay close to me,' he whispered.

I nodded.

Suddenly I spied a shape moving through the trees towards us. I tensed up, stifling the urge to cry out. My hand reached for my revolver at my side, but I relaxed when I realised it was only Denzil returning.

He came up close and spoke in a low voice.

'Grey's men are on the track up ahead. Hundreds of 'em. Marching towards Salisbury.'

'*Towards* Salisbury?' Luc asked. 'But we're going that way!'

'Yeah.'

'Maybe they're coming back for supplies,' I said.

'Could be.' Denzil shrugged. 'Anyway, we'll have to wait here till they've gone. I don't want to have a confrontation. Explain what we're doing on their land in the middle of the night. This'll put our plans back a bit. Hope it don't mess things up too much.'

'Is there another route?' Luc asked.

'Probably,' Denzil said. 'But I don't know for sure and I'm not risking getting us lost or trapped somewhere. We're better off waiting; seeing if Connor can still get us in when we get there.'

The shuffling noise continued and it creeped me out even more now I knew the source of it – Grey's disciples in their long spun cloaks. Their feet tramping through the countryside, faceless figures in the night. I couldn't even think of them as people. They were more like machines created to do his bidding. Not thinking for themselves. Perhaps they were too terrified to disobey him, or maybe they really had been brainwashed and *wanted* to serve him.

Strange. If Luc and I hadn't escaped, would we have become part of Grey's scheme now? Would we have lost the power of rational thought? I'd like to have thought not.

'What if FJ and Lissy are like Grey's guards now?' I whispered.

'What do you mean?' Denzil asked.

'They've been there years,' I said. 'They must be brain-washed already.'

'Dunno,' Denzil said. 'Bit late to be worrying about that.'

'Yeah,' I said. 'Sorry.'

'No, it's a fair point.'

'It's getting quieter,' Luc said.

'We'll have to travel more slowly now,' Denzil said. 'Don't wanna catch up to that lot. Let's give it five more minutes and then we'll get going.'

I started thinking about Pa and Eddie. About how they might be getting on in the Ringwood Perimeter. Had Grey's men reached them yet? Were they fighting? Would they succeed? And I wondered if Grey was leading his men in battle or if he was safely holed up near here in Salisbury, away from any danger. I guessed that would be more his style.

The woods were quiet now, apart from the usual forest noises. The sound of Grey's men had receded and so we decided to start moving again. Darting across the track that Grey's army had used, we headed into deep forest again, travelling parallel to the track, but hidden from view under cover of the trees. It was slower going, but at least we weren't exposed.

I gave a start as a large-ish creature crossed in front of us, eying us worriedly before slipping into the undergrowth.

Then, abruptly, the woods ended and we found ourselves standing at the edge of a huge meadow, the sound of rushing water nearby. There in the distance lay Salisbury Cathedral, its tapered spire piercing the blue-black sky.

We stood in silence for a moment, taking it in. The whole building glowed eerily as though lit up from inside – a ghost building. The moon suspended in the sky above, a small insignificant dot.

'Keep to the edge of the field,' Denzil said. 'The closer we get, the more chance there is of being spotted. The walls aren't far from here.'

We did as Denzil instructed and stayed close to the hedge. There was a wooden stile at the end and Denzil vaulted over the top in a single fluid movement. I climbed after him and Luc vaulted over last. And now we'd reached the heart of Grey's empire – the walls of the Cathedral Close.

It was then that I remembered something. Something I couldn't believe I had forgotten.

The following day, Liss was transferred out of the beautiful room in the North Canonry and into a small dwelling in the grounds of the big house. FJ kept his promise and later that afternoon Annabelle was brought to her. They were shown to a room which they were to share with four other female staff.

The two girls were given two sets of clothes – shoes, socks, grey skirts and blouses, a nightdress each, towels and wash things. They each had a comfortable single bed and a night-stand containing two drawers. Liss kept asking after FJ, but every time she did so, she was met with a shrug or a quizzical look. He must be too busy to see her.

Liss sensed an opportunity. This could be the chance she'd been hoping for. A way for her and Annabelle to escape. She realised FJ would not want to come with her. Nor would he allow her to leave. She had no choice but to forget all thoughts of them leaving together to be reunited with her parents. It would be her and Annabelle together. She didn't have it figured out yet, but surely something would present itself.

As the days passed, Liss and Annabelle settled into their new routines. Liss missed caring for the children, but she didn't have much time to dwell on it. They were working as maids in Grey's house under the supervision of Mary, an older lady who lived in their dwelling. She showed them how to make the beds properly, how to sweep the fireplaces, clean the crockery, glasses and silverware and, most importantly, how to move quietly about the place.

'You must never be in the presence of Grey or his disciples without express permission,' Mary instructed. 'If a room needs to be cleaned, you wait until it has been vacated. If Our Father or His Voice, or any of his holy disciples enter a room, you lower your head and leave that room. Am I clear?'

Liss and Annabelle nodded.

'Good.'

Liss wanted to tell her that His Voice was actually her brother, but she kept her silence. Maybe Mary already knew.

Her days were full and every night Liss fell into a dead sleep as soon as she crawled into bed. There was no time to think of escape, no time for anything other than the work at hand. She barely spoke to Annabelle or the other girls. But she wasn't unhappy. The only thing that niggled was that FJ had seemed to have forgotten her. After that first conversation, the day she had fainted, she was sure they would see each other often, but she hadn't set eyes on him since.

Time passed quickly and Liss realised she had lived at the North Canonry for over a month now. Over a month with no word from FJ and no real plan of escape.

Lying in bed one night, she felt exhausted as usual, but her mind was working overtime. A cool draught from the window made her pull the covers up past her cheek and over her nose.

She heard Annabelle's regular breathing in the bed next to her. Heard soft snores from the other girls. She knew she should sleep too, or she'd be fit for nothing tomorrow, but she couldn't switch off her mind.

Liss felt frustrated and, for the first time in years, she actually felt angry. Her brother was the reason she had been abducted all those years ago. He was the reason she had been torn from her parents and lost her childhood. This whole thing was his fault.

It had all worked out nicely for FJ. He had always craved adventure and now he was second in command of a whole city, while she was an unpaid serving maid. A prisoner. It wasn't fair. But looking back on her childhood, FJ had always got what he wanted and she had always fallen in with his plans. So maybe it was her own stupid fault for being so weak-willed.

Gradually she drifted into an irritable sleep. But her sleep didn't last very long. For only moments later she awoke to feel a hand at her throat.

CHAPTER TWENTY-SEVEN

'Quick, hide,' I hissed.

'What?' Luc replied.

'Hide.'

He and Denzil followed me to a clump of bushes where we crouched down out of sight of the wall.

'Riley, what is it?' Denzil asked.

'Last time we were here, the Cathedral guards came out of the walls. They're hollow. The walls are hollow. Don't you remember, Luc?'

'Yes. Of course! Can't believe I forgot that.'

'Hollow walls?' Denzil said. 'What's that got to do with anything?'

I crept to the edge of the bush and gazed across at a section of wall, but I couldn't see what I was looking for. 'When we were here before,' I began to explain, 'there were bricks missing in parts of the wall.'

'And?' Denzil asked.

'They're peep holes. The guards are inside the walls and use the missing bricks to spy out of so they can spot anyone approaching the walls.'

'I can't see any bricks missing,' Denzil said, using his binoculars to scan the walls.

I stared hard. As far as I could see, he was right. 'This part of the wall must be different,' I said with relief. 'I think it's okay.'

'That's good information to know anyway,' Denzil said. 'We'll just have to pay extra attention as we go, that's all. Come on.'

We crept from our hiding place and ran across to the towering brick wall which stretched away in both directions. Denzil went first, then me, then Luc. We stayed close to the wall, hunched low and followed it around to the left. A barbed wire fence up ahead separated this field from the next, but Denzil pulled at the wire, and I saw it had been cut, so there was a gap for us to slip through.

'My handiwork from earlier this evening,' Denzil said, with a wink. 'Useful tip – always carry a pair of wire cutters.'

I eased my way through, careful not to get caught on the barbs.

'Not far now,' he said.

Scanning the grey bricks, I kept imagining I could see missing ones, but it was only my eyes playing tricks on me. Denzil slowed to a halt in front of a small arched wooden door set into the ivy-covered wall.

'Connor said this is where he'd let us in,' Denzil explained. 'Called it the tradesman's entrance.'

'Is it safe to wait here?' Luc said.

'No, we can't risk it,' Denzil replied. 'There's a track at the edge of the field. We'll wait over there, out of sight.'

We sat behind the track, beneath a couple of sturdy trees. I could clearly see the door in the wall, but we were less exposed here, in the darkness. It was a good place to wait. The leaves whispered and an owl hooted.

'We should try to sleep,' Luc said. 'I'll keep first watch.'

'I won't argue with that,' Denzil replied. 'Keep your eyes on that door, Luc. Wake me if you see anything.' He lay on his side using his backpack as a pillow, closed his eyes and was almost instantly asleep.

How had he managed to do that? I knew it would take me ages to feel relaxed enough to sleep out here.

'Go on, Riley,' Luc urged. 'Get some kip. I'll wake you if anything happens.'

I shuffled back against one of the trees and closed my eyes. I was aware of every little sound. Every rustle and twig snap, every breath of wind and distant fox bark. I was also conscious of Luc sitting near me, leaning against the other tree. I opened one eye. He was staring at the wall. I closed my eye again and despite my earlier claim of not being able to sleep out here, I soon drifted off.

Through the night we took turns keeping watch, but the door in the wall remained closed. I admitted to myself that I was worried about seeing Connor again. I knew I'd said I didn't care about him. That Pa would always be my father. But I realised that part of me did want to see this man, my biological father. I didn't know what I would say, but that didn't matter. I only wanted to see him. To see him without shock clouding my judgement this time. To examine his features and maybe get a sense of who he was. Perhaps see if we were in any way similar.

The sky was lightening. I stood and stretched. It had been hours and there was still no sign of Connor. No sign of anyone.

'This isn't good,' Luc said.

'What should we do?' I asked.

'All we can do is wait,' Denzil said. 'We've got two more days until Charlie Duke leaves. And if this door in the wall doesn't open, we'll have to go back to the copter.'

That's not an option, I thought to myself, thinking of Lissy and FJ kept prisoner all these years. And also, strangely, about Connor who was possibly – *probably* – in danger.

'A lot can happen in two days,' Luc said.

'Too true,' Denzil replied. 'Let's have some brekkie.'

We waited another day and another night. We spoke little. There was nothing we could do or say to make a difference, to ease the impotence we felt. All we could do was hope. But, with a knot in my stomach, I realised that something really bad must have happened to Connor.

Liss opened her eyes, her body rigid with terror. A man loomed over her. He seemed to be staring at her neck but, as her eyes opened, his stare moved to her face. She tried to open her mouth to scream, but to her horror, her mouth had been taped closed. He slid his hands beneath her back and lifted her out of bed. She thrashed her body, but he had tied her wrists and ankles. She was being taken. It was happening again! She wouldn't, *couldn't* let it happen again.

Even though he wore a cloak, her abductor did not look like a person from the Close. There was something about him that seemed more... alive. Was he a raider or a murderer come to kill her or worse? Why were her roommates still asleep? Why didn't they wake and sound the alarm?

The man had now reached the landing. He used his elbow to edge the bedroom door closed.

'Keep calm, I'm here to rescue you,' he whispered. 'I saw the birthmark on your neck. You're Lissy, aren't you?'

Did she hear him correctly? Liss stopped struggling for an instant. No one called her Lissy except her parents and, once upon a time, FJ.

'Mmmphffff.'

'Shhh,' he murmured. 'Stay calm. We'll never get out of here if you wake them. Your parents sent me. Fred and Jessie. They're desperate to see you.'

At his words, Liss felt herself go limp. The man stopped walking, sensing her confusion. He softened his expression. 'Sorry about the tape, but I couldn't take the chance that you'd scream.'

She nodded.

'We need to find your brother, Freddie Junior. I promised them I'd get you both out.'

Liss shook her head vigorously.

'Is he still alive?'

She nodded.

'Is he here? In the Close?'

Again she nodded. The man had an unusual accent. Northern. A bit like Grey's.

'I'm going to peel back the tape,' he said. 'You won't scream, will you?'

She shook her head. Who was this stranger? As he pulled at the tape, she almost yelled out with the pain.

'Sorry,' he whispered. 'That must've really hurt.'

'I'm all right,' she said.

The man carefully carried her all the way down the wooden staircase.

'Where's your brother?' he asked as they reached the bottom.

'He won't come. Grey's changed him. He's lost his mind.'

'Oh. I'm sorry.' He set her down on the hall floor and cut through her ties. 'And what about you? Do you want to leave this place?' He reached out his hand to open the front door.

Her heart raced as she understood that she was finally being rescued. After dreaming about this moment for so long, it was actually happening. Liss stretched out her limbs and stood, her nightdress untwisting from her legs.

'Lissy? Are you okay?' he asked. 'Do you want to come with me?'

'Yes,' she said. 'Yes, of course.'

'Good. Then we have to go quickly. I have some friends waiting outside.' He handed her a cloak which had hung from the bannister. He helped drape it around her shoulders before opening the front door.

She fastened the cloak with trembling hands, felt the cold night air rush in and wrap itself around her ankles. 'Won't we get caught?'

He took her hand and led her out of the house. 'I hope not. I think Grey's guards are busy with other things at the moment.' He jerked his head over towards the North Canonry and Liss gasped as she saw smoke and flames shooting up into the night sky.

'My brother! FJ is in there! Did you do that?' Much as she held little love for her brother anymore, she would not wish him harm.

'Don't worry. I piled up some dry wood against one of the empty outbuildings. The main house is safe.'

'Are you sure?'

'Yes. Now, come on. We have to run before they realise it's nothing.'

'Wait,' she hissed, her guts clenching.

'What?'

'We can't leave Annabelle.'

'Who? We have to go, Lissy.' He pulled at her hand.

'No. I can't go without her. She's like a sister to me.' Liss was panicking. She really wanted to go, but there was no way she would abandon Anna. She would rather stay to protect her than run to save her own skin.

The man let go of her hand and turned again to look at her. She stared back, defiant. He let his shoulders drop.

'Okay. Where is she?'

Relief made her feel less scared. 'She's in my room.'

He rolled his eyes.

'I'll run up and get her.' She turned back to the front door and turned the knob, but nothing happened. 'It must've locked behind us,' she said. 'Do you have a key?'

'No, I broke a window round the back. This is madness. We don't have time for this.'

Liss heard shouts from over at the main house.

'Wait here,' the man hissed 'I'll let you back in.' He left her and headed down the side path to the back of the dwelling.

Liss felt exposed and scared, standing in the small front garden. She sidestepped to conceal herself behind the hedge, pressing herself deep amongst the manicured leaves. She willed the man to hurry up. He should have opened the front door by now. Should she go around the back to see what was taking him so long?

The front door suddenly swung open. The man stood in the doorway, but Mary stood behind him, a gun trained up towards his head. His hands were raised, an expression of defeat and apology on his face.

Mary stepped around him and spoke to Liss. 'It seems the Voice of the Father was right. He told me to watch you. And that's what I have been doing. And you, his *sister*! You should be ashamed.'

Liss was seized from behind as robed guards swept into the garden. She watched as they put the man in cuffs and then her arms too were roughly dragged behind her back, cold steel snapped around her wrists.

'It wasn't her fault,' the man said calmly. 'I was kidnapping her.'

Liss was surprised at the stranger's attempt to save her.

'Don't bother lying.' Liss recognised her brother's voice. She turned as he marched into the garden and up to the man.

'What's your name?' FJ asked the stranger.

'Connor. What's yours?'

'Take them to the cellars,' FJ said, ignoring Connor's question.

'Why can't you just let me go, FJ?' Liss said. 'All I want is to go home. Surely that's not so terrible?'

'Sister, you're a fool. And fools die young in this world.'

'I hate you!' she cried. 'You've always been a spoilt, arrogant brat. God help everyone here, with *you* in charge. You and Grey are nothing but bullies.'

But one of the guards was already dragging her out of the garden, away from FJ and towards a fate she could only guess at. As she tripped and stumbled away from the house, she saw a face at the bedroom window above. It was Annabelle. Sweet Annabelle. What would become of her friend now?

CHAPTER TWENTY-EIGHT

RILEY

After another exquisite dawn, accompanied by a shrill chorus of birds, the morning sky darkened again as grey clouds gathered. It would be miserable here if it rained, but so far it had held off, other than a few teasing spots.

I continued to stare at the door in the wall, willing it to open. But it remained firmly shut. After all the build-up and tension of the past two days, this felt like such an anti-climax. Another dead-end trip.

It was already late afternoon and it really didn't look as though Connor would be coming at all. I hoped he was okay. I hoped it was simply a case that things were taking him longer than we'd thought. That he'd missed his opportunity the last two nights and was waiting until tonight to make his move.

Evening finally came and with it, my anticipation returned. I was sure that if anything was going to happen, it would happen at night. It had to. Because Luc and Denzil said that if he hadn't opened the door by tomorrow, we'd have to turn around and head back to the copter without him. That wasn't something I was prepared to do and I was formulating arguments in my head just in case.

The clouds thickened, hiding the moon, turning the wall into nothing more than a dim shape.

'Can we risk going closer?' I asked. 'We can't see the door from here.'

'I was going to say the same thing,' Luc said.

'Come on then,' Denzil said. 'Fast and low.' He crouched and ran and we followed close behind. We hadn't seen anyone the whole time we'd been here, but it was still nerve wracking, running across the field like that. I couldn't help imagining gunshots and robed men sweeping through the field after us.

But we made it to the wall without incident.

'We should wait here for the rest of the night,' I said. 'Do you think it's safe?'

'I hope so,' Luc replied. 'Doesn't seem much point in—'

But before he could finish his sentence, a rattling noise came from behind the door. The unmistakable sound of a bolt sliding across and a key turning in a heavy lock.

The three of us froze, staring from one to the other.

'Connor?' I mouthed.

The other two shrugged and I wasn't sure if we should stay or run back. We all made a grab for our weapons, Denzil planted himself to the left of the door and I stood with Luc on the right. I held my breath as the door swung open inwards.

Please let it be Connor...

But it wasn't.

It was a woman dressed in grey with an iron cross around her neck and a gun in her hand.

CHAPTER TWENTY-NINE

In the moonless dark, Liss and Connor were led away in chains by Grey's guards, their deep hoods concealing their faces. The guards' silence only added to Liss's fear and anger. She could not believe her brother would treat her in this way. That he was still forcing her to do what he wanted. He had no empathy whatsoever. He had been corrupted by power, seduced by Grey's made-up religion.

And who was this Connor person? This friend of her parents. Was he now to suffer because of her? He had come to save her and FJ both, but her idiotic brother was too caught up in his own importance to care about anyone else's life.

She realised they were heading over to the main house. She hoped she wouldn't have to see Grey. He gave her more than the creeps and she didn't think she had the mental strength to cope with facing such evil tonight. The fire Connor had started in the outbuilding had burnt out, but the air was still thick with acrid smoke and floating ash. She began to cough and shiver.

Now only two guards remained with them. They led her and Connor around to the kitchen door and prodded them inside. It was good to be out of the biting wind, but Liss's heart gave a thump of dread as she realised where they were going. The cold night would be preferable to this destination.

One of the guards unlocked the studded wooden door which led down to the basement. Liss had never been down there, but she had heard whispers that it was where Grey kept his prisoners. Where he extracted confessions. It was a place you did not ever want to end up. She caught Connor's eye, and he shook his head and mouthed the word 'sorry'. She gave him a small shrug and he looked away.

The door swung open and they were led inside. A dim light glowed, illuminating limestone steps which led to the cellars. Liss took a breath to steady her swimming head and walked downwards into the gloom.

The air smelled of decay and damp. Coughs and moans assailed her ears along with the metallic clink of chains and unidentified scuttling, rustling, shuffling sounds. Although Liss felt dizzy and strange, she did not feel the terror she would have expected. No. In her head, she was having an imaginary argument with FJ. She was shouting at him, blaming him, telling him how wrong and terrible he was for ruining her life. If he was here now, she would claw at his face and beat him with her fists. It was all him. All his fault. But it was hopeless. She was powerless against him and his guards. And now this poor Connor person was caught up in it all.

Their metal cuffs were removed and they were pushed into a dark room with a metal door. It clanged shut behind them. There was no light. She could not even see her hand in front of her face.

For the first time that night, she became aware of her bare feet. The floor was cold and damp. It felt spongy in places – wet.

'Are you okay?' Connor spoke to her through the darkness.

'What are we going to do?' she asked.

He sighed. 'I'm not sure. I'll try to think of something.'

Liss edged forward, her arms outstretched until her finger-tips touched a wall. It was rough and dry. As she slid her hands downward, the wall grew damp, slimy, wet. She shuddered and straightened up again. Hugged her arms around her body.

'The floor's wet,' Connor said. 'Don't sit down.'

'I know. I've got no shoes on.' Her legs felt heavy and tired and it was freezing down here. Even with the heavy cloak.

'No shoes? That's my fault. Sorry. Take mine if you like.'

'No. That's all right.'

'Here,' he said.

Liss heard a rustling. 'What's that?'

'I've folded up my cloak,' Connor replied. 'We can both sit on it.'

'Won't you be cold?'

'I'm okay. I'm wearing a coat underneath.'

Liss edged her way onto the bunched-up fabric. It felt good to move her feet off the slimy ground. She crouched down and leant back against the damp wall.

'So was that your brother?' Connor asked. 'Back there. Outside your house.'

'Yes. That was FJ. He wasn't always so awful.'

'I'm sure nine years in this place would change anyone... but not you.'

'I was only seven when they took me. I'm sorry you got caught too.'

'You don't need to apologise. It was me who got you locked up.'

'If I hadn't made you go back for Annabelle...'

'You couldn't leave your friend. I understand that. I'll get you out. I promise.'

How long they sat there, Liss could not tell. It could have been hours or days. No one came to see them or feed them or anything. Maybe that was the plan. Maybe they would just be left to starve or freeze.

They were huddled together now. Connor's arms wrapped around her shivering body. They half dozed, no longer mindful of the cold oozing floor.

Liss's throat was parched and dry. She was almost tempted to lick the moisture off the walls. Almost, but not quite that desperate. Not yet.

The bed was warm, cosy, safe. But she couldn't rest or sleep. Not after everything that had happened. She had a plan and she could carry it out. She could. Liss needed her now. Liss, who had always been there for her. Right from the start. Back when they were in that truck.

If she didn't have Liss, she would have nothing.

She didn't know how on earth she'd managed to get through today. It had been awful. All those lies everyone had been telling about Liss. About how she was evil and a traitor and deserved to die. And now the only person who could save Liss was *her*. There was nobody else.

Annabelle peeled back the covers and slid out of her bed. She tiptoed out of the bedroom and took two steps along the landing. Mary's bedroom door was closed. Annabelle guessed it was locked, but nevertheless she had to give it a try. The worn brass handle creaked as she twisted it, but nothing happened. The door was most definitely locked. Never mind, she would get in there anyway, somehow or other.

Heart thumping, she crept back into her bedroom and closed the door behind her. This next bit could be tricky and it would be a miracle if she didn't get caught. Annabelle held her breath as she passed the other sleeping girls, finally stopping when she reached the sash window. She peeped behind the heavy velvet drapes and was reassured to see the back garden empty and still. Good. If there had been any guards about, her plan would have been impossible.

She slipped behind the curtains so her nose was pressed up against the cold glass. Then she quickly raised the sash, praying the curtains would be thick enough to prevent too much of a draught blowing through to the bedroom and waking the other girls.

Wriggling out through the gap, Annabelle stood barefoot on the window ledge. It wasn't that far up, but her legs trembled. She couldn't fall. She had to stay strong for Liss. Telling herself not to look down, she looked instead to her right. The next window along was only a couple of feet away. It was Mary's window. And somewhere inside Mary's room lay the keys to the North Canonry and, more importantly, the keys to the cellars.

CHAPTER THIRTY

Annabelle twisted her body around so that she faced the house. Then she sidestepped across to Mary's window. Her heart pounded so loud it sounded like thunder from the sky. Mary's drapes were closed. Good. Annabelle was also conscious that the guards could come into the garden and see her at any moment. She had to be quick.

If Mary's window was locked, her plan would be doomed. Annabelle placed her hands flat on the glass and pushed upwards. Nothing happened. Despite the chill night air, beads of sweat trickled down her back. She took a breath and tried again. This time the wooden window frame moved a fraction. Annabelle smiled. She pushed the glass again and now the window slid up with satisfying smoothness.

There was no time to worry about being caught. She had to go for it. Annabelle slipped through the window and slid it closed behind her. She waited a couple of seconds, hidden behind the curtains. No sound came from within, but for all she knew, Mary could be standing in front of the window with a gun pointed at her.

Annabelle inched the curtain back. The room was dark, but

she made out the dim shape of someone lying in the bed. It must be Mary. The sleeping woman's breathing was slow and regular. Now, to find the keys. Where would they be?

On the bedside table sat a cup of water and a bible. Against the far wall stood a narrow table with a chair pushed underneath. It was strewn with paperwork, pencils and other paraphernalia. Perhaps the keys were there. Annabelle moved slowly across the floor. She trod on a loose floorboard and winced as it creaked. But Mary did not stir. Annabelle cast her eyes over the table, but there were no keys.

Clothes had been draped over the back of the chair and Annabelle ran her hands through them, checking for pockets and belt loops. But all she felt was soft material. Nothing metal or jangling. Where could they be? She tiptoed back around to Mary's bedside table. They had to be in one of the drawers.

Easing open the top drawer, the runner made an excruciatingly loud scraping noise. Annabelle held her breath, staring at Mary's closed lids. If the housekeeper opened her eyes now, she would be caught and branded a thief. Mary shifted and grunted in her sleep. And then she rolled over, away from Annabelle's terrified stare. Annabelle exhaled in relief.

She peered inside the drawer but could barely see in the dark and had to use her fingers to explore its contents. It felt like clothing. She opened the second drawer – clothing again. Where else could she search?

There was no other furniture in the room. Would Mary have hidden the keys under her pillow? She would have to find out.

Annabelle's hands felt clammy and shaky. She rubbed them against her nightdress and slipped one under Mary's pillow. Slowly, she moved the flat of her hand beneath the cool cotton pillowcase. And then she edged it further along to where Mary rested her head. She would have to slide her hand underneath it. Surely the woman would waken.

Her nerve suddenly left her, and she retracted her hand and crouched down onto the floor. This was a suicide mission. She would be caught and thrown in a cell with her friend, her sister. But she could not give up. She had come this far. She would find the keys. She would.

Gathering her courage back up, she stood once more and prepared to slide her hand under the woman's pillow again. But then something caught her eye and she almost laughed out loud.

The huge bunch of housekeeper's keys was hanging from the door. Mary had obviously locked her bedroom door and left the keys in the lock.

A scraping noise roused Liss from her morbid thoughts. Straight ahead, a square of dim light appeared.

'Hello?' Connor's voice sounded loud in the darkness. 'Who's there?'

'Hello?' Liss said. She got to her feet and took a step forward.

'Liss? Is that you?'

Liss's heart began to pound. She felt a smile curl at her lips. 'Anna!'

'Oh good, it *is* you!' Annabelle said. 'I thought I'd never find your cell. I haven't got long. I stole Mary's keys, but she only has one to the main cellar door. Not the one to your cell. Who's that in there with you?'

'Oh, Annabelle, I can't believe you're here. You're amazing.' Liss wondered how her friend had managed it.

'Can you get hold of the cell key?' Connor asked.

'Who's that?' Annabelle asked again, fear in her voice.

'It's all right. He's a friend. He was trying to rescue us.'

'Annabelle, listen carefully,' Connor said. 'I need you to go and tell my friends what's happened. They're outside the walls.

They'll be able to help get us out of here. Can you go there now? Before they leave?'

'I have to take Mary's keys back first. I hope she's still asleep.'

'No. Keep hold of the keys and go straight to my friends. Let them inside the walls. I only hope they're still waiting. That it's not too late and they haven't left already.'

***

The woman at the door in the wall was young. More of a girl really. Younger than me anyway. The gun shook in her hand. She was nervous. No, she was terrified. There were three of us and only one of her. We could take her down, I was sure of it. Her eyes darted around and finally landed on me.

'Are you Riley?' she asked.

I was taken aback. She knew my name. 'Er, yes. Are you Lissy?'

'No.' She lowered her weapon and seemed to relax a little. Stepping towards us, away from the wall, she pulled the door closed behind her. 'Your friend Colin sent me.'

'Colin?' I didn't know any Colin.

'Do you mean Connor?' Luc asked.

'Yes, sorry. Connor. I meant Connor. He tried to rescue Liss, but they got caught by the guards. They're in a cell. I couldn't get them out. They told me to come and tell you, but I better get back now or Mary will wake up and know I've gone and then I'll never be able to get back into the main house and...'

'Whoa there, angel. Slow down,' Denzil said. 'What's your name?'

'I'm Anna. Annabelle.'

'Take a breath, Annabelle, and tell us slowly from the beginning what happened and what you need us to do.'

She did as he said and took a deep breath. As she exhaled, a tear slipped down her cheek. I stepped closer and gave her shoulder a squeeze. She flinched, but then looked up at me wide-eyed and I gave her what I hoped was an encouraging smile.

'It's okay,' I said. 'We're here. We'll help, okay?'

Annabelle started talking, slower this time, but her voice was still breathless and nervy. She told us what had happened to Connor and Liss. About Freddie Junior and how he was now part of Grey's regime. And then she explained what she'd had to do that night to get here – stealing the housekeeper's keys and creeping into the cellars.

'Brave kid,' Denzil said. 'You did good.'

She ignored the praise, a terrified expression still stuck to her face.

'I can't believe Grey is actually here,' Luc said. 'I thought he'd be leading his army.'

'He's not a fighter,' I said. 'He's a coward and a bully.'

Luc turned to Annabelle. 'And you're sure Freddie Junior's been turned?'

'Yes,' she replied.

'Fred and Jess are going to be heartbroken,' I said.

'We still need to get him out,' Denzil said. 'That was part of the deal.'

'You won't manage it,' Annabelle said. 'He has guards. Anyway, I have to get back to my room now, before I'm missed.' She made a move towards the door in the wall.

'I think it's too late for that,' Luc said.

'What? What do you mean?' Annabelle looked ready to bolt.

'I just mean we're going to have to break Liss and Connor out tonight. Right now. We can't wait another day. They might move them somewhere else. Or worse. And we'll need you to help us.'

'But how?' Annabelle said. 'We have no cell key.'

'Do you know who does have the key?'

'One of the guards, I suppose.'

'Can you get us some of those hooded guards' robes?' Denzil asked.

'Yes. There are always a few in the laundry room.'

'And can you get us there without us being seen?' Luc added.

'I'll try.' She made another move to reopen the door in the wall.

'Wait,' I said.

All three looked at me expectantly.

'I've had a thought. It's risky, but I was thinking, while we're here, we should try to get Grey.'

Everyone stared at me as though I was mad.

'No, please,' Annabelle said. 'It's too dangerous. We need to get Liss out.'

'We will,' I said. 'Of course we will. But we have to stop Grey. His army is attacking our Perimeters. If we take him and FJ hostage, we can end their assault on the south. We can finish the whole thing without any more fighting.'

'He has an army?' Annabelle asked, her eyes wide.

'I'm afraid so.'

No one else spoke. I felt a drop of rain on my face. And then another.

'Well?' I stared at Luc and Denzil. 'What do you think?'

'I think it's genius,' said Luc. 'And I don't know why I didn't think of it first.'

'I think it's suicide,' Denzil said. 'I'm not disrespecting your idea, but Charlie Duke's orders were clear. He said to stick to the plan and—'

'I think the plan's already gone out the window,' I said.

'Please don't do this,' Annabelle pleaded.

'I'm sorry, Annabelle. I know it's scary, but the man has to be stopped.'

'Let me think for a sec.' Denzil started massaging his temples. 'I know what you're saying makes sense, but Charlie Duke's my new boss and if I screw this up, I'll be out on my ear.'

I put my hand on his arm. 'If we don't do this, Grey will take over the south coast and we'll all be out on our ears.'

'We'll never get an opportunity like this again,' Luc said. 'This could save everyone.'

My mind was buzzing with thoughts of how we could pull this off, but I couldn't formulate a proper plan. The rain was really coming down now and the wind shook the trees. Leaves spiralled through the air towards us like night spirits. 'Will you help us, Denzil? We need you.'

'Doesn't look like I've got much choice,' he replied. 'And there was me thinking I'd have an easier time if I was a guard instead of a soldier. Got that wrong, didn't I?' He shook his head and gave a reluctant smile.

'And, Annabelle...' I turned to her. 'We'll need your help too.'

'You are going to rescue Liss, aren't you?'

'Yes,' I replied. 'Yes of course. Don't worry; we'll get your friend out.'

She gave me a nod of acceptance.

'Right then,' Denzil said. 'I think I've got a basic plan, but we'll have to move quickly. We'll need to be out of the Close before dawn breaks.'

The rain was coming down in sheets now, so we huddled closer to hear what he had to say.

CHAPTER THIRTY-ONE

RILEY

I barely noticed our journey through the Close to the North Canonry where Connor and Liss were being held. My mind was too full of what we were about to do. Annabelle took us a circuitous route, close to the walls so we were hidden within the shadows of dark silent buildings and autumnal trees. Over the spattering rain and gusting winds, the sound of a rushing river soon became audible.

We were soaked to the skin, but I didn't care about that; the weather helped keep us concealed. Several times we had to slip out of sight as the occasional hooded figure glided into view, but we were making progress, gradually drawing closer to the cathedral. Soon Grey's impressive house towered before us like a fairy-tale castle.

We had approached the rear of the building, but it was still magnificent from this angle, even in the dark. I made out one solitary light in an upstairs window. The rest of the house was an eerie silhouette of pointed roofs and chimneys, dwarfed only by the cathedral spire behind it. The mansion and its grounds were encircled by a razor-topped red brick wall, but the house was visible through a set of spiked wrought iron gates, its dark lawns spread out before it. We stood well back, bowed and shivering behind a clump of bushes.

'How did you break out of there?' Luc whispered to Annabelle.

'One of Mary's keys opens the back gate,' she replied. 'I had to time it right so the guards didn't see me.'

'Let's hope Mary don't wake up and notice her keys are missing,' Denzil said.

I tapped Denzil on the shoulder and pointed as one of Grey's creepy guards came into view. He drifted slowly past the back gate, like a ghost, the wind pulling at his robes, making them swirl and billow.

'I think there are four of them guarding the outside of the house,' Annabelle said. 'Plus two at the front gates.'

'We'll leave those two till last and take the patrols out first,' Denzil said. 'Riley, I'll need you to distract them one by one. Okay?'

I nodded.

The guard had disappeared around the corner, but after a few seconds another one came into view.

'Annabelle, give Riley your cloak. Riley, we'll go round the side, where it's less exposed. You distract the first guard – pretend to need his help or something – and I'll clock him over the head with my revolver. Not very sophisticated, but it should work.'

'What do you want me to do?' Luc asked.

'Help me drag the bodies into the trees over there.' Denzil pointed to a nearby copse. 'Then we'll secure them. There's twine in my backpack. Once we start this thing we're gonna have to move really quick in case any of them wake up. Are you ready, guys?'

I was more than ready. I was itching to do this. As I pulled Annabelle's sodden cloak around my shoulders, I briefly wondered where my fear had gone. I raised the deep hood over my head and nodded to Denzil.

'Be careful,' Luc said.

In the small delay between patrols, we darted around the side of the house, keeping to the trees and bushes. I made out the receding shape of one of the guards drifting away to the front of the house. As soon as the next one appeared around the corner, Denzil nodded to me. The blood whooshed in my head as I stepped out of the shadows and walked towards the guard, my hands clasped together to stop them trembling,

'Please can you help me?' I called out. I didn't want to speak too loudly in case I attracted the attention of one of the other guards, but I had to make myself heard above the wind and rain.

The guard stopped and turned around to face me. His hand went immediately to his waist where I saw the glint of a sword. But his fingers curled around a pistol. Before he had a chance to draw it, Denzil had come up behind him and cracked him on the head. He crumpled to the ground and Denzil and Luc dragged him back into the trees, out of sight. I ran back with them, my heart thumping. Surely it couldn't be this easy?

Another guard came around the corner, but I wasn't ready for him. We'd only just reached the trees. I let him pass and waited for the next one.

When the next hooded figure appeared, I called out to him as before. He stopped and turned, tilting his head to the side, his hood a faceless void. He went down as easily as the first. The next two were exactly the same.

We had incapacitated all four guards. Luc and Denzil dragged the last body into the bushes while I stood watch. But then I heard a shout behind me:

'Halt! Show your face.'

I froze for a second before turning around. It was a fifth guard. I had to think fast.

'Oh, please,' I cried, approaching him. 'You have to help me. My mother has collapsed and I need a doctor.'

The figure hesitated. But his earlier cry had alerted another guard who now appeared around the corner.

'What are you doing out here at this late hour?' the guard said.

'Please, come and help me. My mother, she's over here...' I turned to lead them into the trees where the others were hidden.

'Wait.'

I stopped and the man took a firm hold of my arm.

'You wait here,' he said to the other guard. And then he walked with me into the trees, now gripping my arm so tightly it hurt. Once we were out of sight of his colleague, he received the same treatment as the others, as Denzil knocked him out.

'What are we going to do about him?' I asked, jerking my head at the waiting guard. I could see him standing there, his body hesitant, nervy. He took a step towards the trees, but I could tell he wasn't sure what to do.

'As long as there aren't any others, we'll wait,' Denzil said. 'Let him come to us.'

But the guard had other ideas and after a few more moments' indecision, he turned and ran. Denzil didn't hesitate. He took off at a sprint and tackled the man to the ground. They slid across the sodden grass. Luc ran after him, but I stayed with Annabelle, realising that if they got caught, they might need us to free them.

'I'm sorry,' Annabelle said. 'There are usually only four guards patrolling outside. They must've put more on since Liss tried to escape.'

'It's not your fault,' I replied. 'We couldn't have done any of this without you.' I chewed my nails and watched the tangle of figures on the ground, praying no one else would appear from around the corner. Rain dripped from my hood, streaming in rivulets down my face. I couldn't make out who was who. 'They'll be okay. They'll be okay,' I said, more to reassure myself than anything else.

After what seemed like an eternity, Luc and Denzil finally subdued the guard and carried him towards us. They dumped him next to the others.

'We'll have to be quick now,' Denzil said. 'Those guards on the front gates will be wondering where the patrols are. Riley, you're gonna have to do your thing.'

I nodded.

'Annabelle, Luc, wait here,' Denzil said. 'We'll be back in a couple of minutes. Luc, secure the guards with twine. Any of them wake up, you put 'em back to sleep again.'

'No problem. Be careful, Riley. You too, Denzil.'

I followed Denzil along the side wall, my whole body buzzing with nervous energy. We stopped at the end and Denzil peered around the corner. He immediately pulled his head back.

'The front guards; they're coming this way.'

'Lie face down on the ground like you're hurt,' I hissed. And before Denzil had a chance to stop me, I raced around the corner.

The front of the house was obscured by a towering brick wall in front of which lay a grassy expanse. Two guards had been heading in my direction, but they stopped mid-stride at my approach. Their hooded figures momentarily frozen beneath a swaying tree, the rain hammering down around them.

'Quick!' I called to them. 'Come quick. One of your guards is hurt. He's here on the ground. He needs help.'

My skin crawled at their faceless stares. But my words hit home and they took the bait. I led them around the corner where Denzil lay inert on the ground. The guards passed in front of me to examine the figure.

'That's no guard,' one of them said, his voice deep and monotone.

As he spoke Denzil spun around and kicked upward, catching him on the jaw. At the same time I was able to bash the other one on the back of the head with my revolver. But the blow wasn't strong enough to knock him out and the gun slipped out of my hand, tumbling into the wet grass.

The guard staggered and put his hand to his head, but he soon recovered and went straight for his sword. Before he could draw it, I pulled out my knife. I knew the theory, but I'd never actually plunged a blade into living flesh. I'd have to do it now. It helped that I couldn't see his face. I stabbed him with all the force I could muster, catching him in his side, making him stagger and fall to the ground. I held the bloody knife in my hands, staring at it. Denzil had already rendered the other guard unconscious. I hadn't seen how.

I was out of breath, but Denzil was calm, dragging the two bodies out of sight. The one I'd stabbed was clutching his side, groaning. My side throbbed in sympathy, but I told myself not to have any compassion for these people. They were kidnappers and murderers. I wiped the dripping blade on my jeans and re-sheathed it. Then I retrieved my revolver from the ground and followed Denzil back around the house to the others. We still had much to do.

'I hope no one was looking out any of the windows,' Denzil muttered.

Luc stepped out from behind the trees and wrapped his arms around my soaking body.

'You're okay,' he said.

'I think I killed one of them.'

'Don't think about that,' he said. 'Think about freeing Lissy and freeing Connor and getting that evil bastard Grey. We're going to save a lot of lives, okay?' He pulled back and looked me in the eye. 'You did what you had to.'

But shock was rising up in my throat and I felt like I was going to puke. *Got to hold it together.* I wondered if I had really killed that guard.

'We'd better go,' Denzil said. 'Good job, Riley.'

'You too,' I said, faking calmness.

Annabelle was already at the back gate. She pushed it open and we filed through, my mind still re-enacting the moment I'd stabbed the guard. It didn't feel real.

'Leave it closed, but unlocked,' Luc said. 'So we can leave in a hurry if we need to.'

'There are dogs,' Annabelle said. 'But they know me. They won't hurt you if you stay close.'

Before she'd finished talking, four huge shapes came bounding across the lawn and I tried not to show any fear. Dogs didn't generally scare me, but these were pretty vicious looking. Annabelle had said they wouldn't attack and I hoped she was right. They were large and slim, sleek and muscled with pointed ears. Not like any dog I'd ever seen before. They growled low and bared their teeth, saliva dripping and mingling with the rain, but Annabelle spoke softly to them and they soon calmed down. Then she said something harsh and they whined and trotted away.

'Whatever you do, don't come out here without me,' she said. 'I've only just gained their trust. Liss showed me how. She told me it was important.'

We followed Annabelle around the edge of the lawn, water sloshing in our boots. She led us to a back door and we slipped inside. It was a relief to be away from the constant slice of the rain, but I knew the relief wouldn't last long.

CHAPTER THIRTY-TWO
RILEY

The back door led us into a kitchen. It was unlit, but an outside light shone through the window giving everything a ghostly glow. Annabelle beckoned us through into the hall. A staircase led up to a galleried landing, but we followed Annabelle into another room.

It was pitch black in here until Denzil switched on his torch. Annabelle opened a cupboard and passed us each a towel. I peeled off my soaking hood and attempted to dry my face and hair. Next, she opened another cupboard and took out a pile of folded clothes.

'Guards' robes,' she whispered.

I undid the sodden cloak that Annabelle had lent me and let it drop to the floor. The clothes I wore underneath were just as wet, but there was nothing I could do about that now. I took the warm, dry robes and pulled them over my head. The others did the same with theirs, pulling up the deep hoods which hid their faces.

I shuddered. We had transformed into Grey's disciples and soon, once more, we would be face to face with the man himself.

I realised Denzil was speaking. His voice sounded different, muffled behind the hood.

'Before we get Connor and Lissy, we'll have to clear the house of guards.'

'Can't we get Liss out first?' Annabelle asked.

'We need a cell key to do that. Are there any guards down in the cellar?'

Annabelle shook her head.

'How many guards inside the house? In total.'

'Not many,' Annabelle said. 'Grey doesn't like them in the house. He prefers them to patrol outside. He only has his two main disciples in here, some servants and the Voice of the Father of course. He sleeps down the hall from Our Father.'

'The voice of the *what*?' Luc asked.

'Liss's brother, FJ,' Annabelle explained. 'He's the Voice of the Father now. Our Father cannot speak. He was attacked last month and lost his voice. FJ speaks for him now.'

It creeped me out hearing Annabelle refer to Grey as their father and even worse was FJ's new name – the Voice of the Father – what was all that about? And then it dawned on me.

'The fork,' Luc and I cried in unison.

'Shh,' Denzil hissed.

Last time we were in the Close, attempting to escape, Luc had shoved a fork down Grey's throat. It must have damaged his vocal chords. It was an image I still had trouble shifting while trying to sleep at night. At the time we'd thought it might have killed him, but unfortunately he was still alive to fight another day.

'Fork?' Annabelle asked.

'No time to explain now,' Luc replied.

'Let's get the two guards first,' Denzil said. 'Annabelle, we'll need you to show us where to go. Can you do that?'

'Of course.'

She was braver than I would have been at her age. I couldn't imagine what it must have been like for her, growing up in such a harsh environment. I wondered how long she'd been here and how she and Liss had managed to resist the brainwashing.

We followed Annabelle back out of the dark laundry room, re-emerging in the hallway. She pointed up the staircase. Denzil led the way as we crept up the stairs in a tight bunch. When we reached the landing, Annabelle pointed straight ahead. Beyond another small set of stairs lay a door.

'That's where Our Father sleeps,' she whispered.

'Can you lock it from the outside?' Denzil said.

Annabelle nodded and spent the next few seconds locating the correct key. She slotted it into the keyhole, but shook her head.

'There's already a key in the other side of the lock.'

'Don't worry, I'll stand guard,' Luc said. 'Stop him leaving.'

Denzil nodded.

'The Voice of the Father sleeps there,' Annabelle said, pointing behind us up another couple of stairs.

Denzil mimed a locking action. Annabelle nodded and walked up the stairs. A few seconds later, she turned back, smiled and nodded.

'And where are Grey's guards?' I whispered.

Denzil and I followed her back past Grey's room; right and right again down a narrow corridor lined with doors. Annabelle pointed to the first door and then the second. As she did so, the first door creaked open. I went for my gun and Annabelle shrieked in fright.

The man in the doorway wore a plain white robe; he was massive – tall and broad with fists like boulders.

'What are you doing?' he asked, his voice thick with sleep, confusion clouding his face. We were dressed as Grey's guards, but Annabelle's scream had tipped him off. Then he glanced down and saw my gun trained on his chest. He looked startled, but his shock soon turned to anger. His hands flailed around for a moment, then he stepped back and slammed the door in our faces. I should have used my weapon, but it was too late now.

Denzil immediately shouldered his way past us, and charged at the door, turning the handle at the same time. As the door flew open, the guard went for his gun which was hanging over the back of the chair, but Denzil kicked him in the face before he had a chance to grab it. The guard quickly recovered and dived for Denzil, grabbing him in a bear hug so they crashed onto the floor, rolling and throwing punches. After my initial shock, I gathered my wits and slammed my gun down onto the guard's head.

'Quick, Annabelle,' I shouted. 'Lock the other guard's door before he gets out.'

'Already done it,' she cried, as shouts and bangs emanated from within.

Denzil emerged from the first room, blood dripping from his nose and mouth.

'That's one sorted,' he said. 'Nice work, Riley.'

Scuffling noises now came from around the corner. Then a gun-shot.

'Luc!' I yelled. But before I could run to see what was happening, another shot rang out behind me followed by the splintering of wood. The second guard had fired his way out of the room and seized Annabelle by her hair. He held a gun in his right hand and was about to raise it when Denzil turned and shot him straight through the forehead, spraying blood over the wood-panelled walls.

The fatally wounded man let go of Annabelle, staggered and fell backwards into his room with a dull thud.

Silence descended.

Annabelle cowered on the ground, shaking. I wanted to comfort her, but there was no time. Shouts and grunts came from the direction of Grey's room and I was terrified for Luc's safety, especially after hearing that gunshot a moment ago.

Denzil turned to me. 'I'm gonna check on Luc.'

'I'm coming too,' I said, grabbing Annabelle's hand. I pulled her upright and led her out onto the landing. Luc was no longer outside Grey's door. He must have gone inside.

We now had the added problem that all the commotion had drawn the servants from their rooms downstairs. Denzil pulled his hood over his face, leant over the bannisters and shouted: 'Get back to your rooms! Intruders! Lock your doors, Father's orders!' Then Denzil disappeared into Grey's bedroom.

Meanwhile, thuds and bangs were coming from Freddie Junior's room as he attempted to break down his door. I didn't think he stood much of a chance unless he shot it open. The doors were solid. No time to worry about that now; I had to follow Denzil and see if Luc was okay. A quick glance over my shoulder showed that Annabelle had recovered herself enough to walk unaided and followed behind.

The door led into an empty office. Another door lay open at the far end and through it I heard a voice – Denzil's.

'Wait here,' I said to Annabelle. I adjusted my hood and stole through the empty room, my body tensed in anticipation of what I might see beyond the next door. Terrified in case Luc or Denzil had been hurt or worse.

As I stepped through the doorway, Denzil's back blocked my view. I inhaled and stepped around him, my gun trembling in my hands.

Grey was standing behind his bed next to the window, his bedside lamp illuminating him in a long white nightshirt, his thin hair dishevelled. But his face wore a sneer, for he held Luc in front of him, the tip of a knife pointed at his throat.

Luc's expression held no fear, only anger. Denzil and I faced them, our guns trained at Grey's head.

'Remove your hoods,' Grey whispered, pointing to us. Neither Denzil nor I made a move.

'Do it,' he hissed, his voice nothing but an empty croak. He pressed his blade into Luc's skin, drawing a bead of blood. I drew in my breath as Luc winced. Denzil and I pushed our hoods down.

Grey's eyes bored into mine. 'I know you,' he hissed. 'You and this boy.'

It wasn't good news that he'd recognised us. We were the reason for the loss of his voice. He would surely want revenge. I looked at the bloody smear on Luc's neck. Luc looked me in the eye and mouthed the word 'sorry', but I didn't think he had anything to be sorry for.

'You will pay for your attack on me and my people,' Grey said. 'You will pay in this world and the next.' His voice was so quiet and strained that I had trouble hearing his words. Speaking was costing him a great deal of effort. His Adam's apple bobbed up and down as he swallowed. His eyes fell on a glass of water which sat on his bedside table.

'Thirsty?' I asked.

'Pass it over,' he croaked.

Neither Denzil nor I moved.

'Pass it here, or this boy will have a smile from ear to ear.' He said, moving the knife up to one of Luc's ears, his breath now a rasping wheeze.

I took a step towards his bed and picked up the water.

Grey had gone very pale. I approached him warily with the glass, longing to fling the contents in his face.

Suddenly Grey broke down into a fit of coughing. And as he did so, Luc twisted neatly out of his grip and wrested the knife from his hand, turning it back on the gasping man.

I dropped the glass on the floor, but it didn't break. At that moment I wanted nothing more than to unload a bullet into Grey's head, but I knew we needed him alive to stop his invasion of the south. He was still coughing and wheezing, trying to get his breathing under control.

Denzil came over and yanked Grey's wrists together.

'You won't make it past my disciples,' Grey hissed.

'We already have,' Denzil replied, pulling a length of twine from his pocket. 'They weren't much good. In my opinion, they need to take more initiative. Oh, yeah, I forgot, you don't like them to think for themselves, do you?'

'You won't get out of here alive,' Grey rasped.

'We'll see,' Denzil replied, securing the twine tight around Grey's wrists and patting him down. He turned to Luc. 'Are you all right with him if I go and get FJ?'

'Yeah, no problem.'

Denzil left the room as Luc pushed Grey onto the bed and retrieved his revolver from the floor, training it on the wheezing man. Luc slipped Grey's knife into his robe. He pressed his fingers to his neck and studied his bloody fingertips.

'Are you all right?' I asked.

'It's just a cut,' he said. 'You okay?'

I nodded. 'I better check on Annabelle. She was pretty shaken up.'

Luc tilted his head and I turned to see the girl coming through the door. Her step faltered as her gaze landed on Grey, her mouth falling open in disbelief.

'Is that…'

'Grey?' Luc finished her sentence. 'Yeah.'

Annabelle didn't come any further and I could see that even though the man was bound and gasping for breath, he still had the power to terrify.

'I am your Father,' Grey wheezed. 'You will burn in hell for your treachery, girl.'

'Don't listen to him,' I said.

'He's not your father,' Luc added. 'He's just a sad old man.'

Luc hauled Grey to his feet and pushed him towards the door. Annabelle recoiled and so did I. His breathing was laboured and painful sounding, but he narrowed his dead blue eyes at me as he passed, probing for weakness. I glared back, but I didn't feel brave at all. I felt violated.

Denzil stood on the landing holding a young man by the shoulders. The man's hands were bound in front. I guessed it must be FJ. He wore a cotton shirt and rough linen trousers and, as he lifted his head, I saw that he was absolutely beautiful. So beautiful that it took me aback. He saw me catch my breath and smirked. I scowled. Beautiful he might be, but he was a part of this place and this place was rotten.

'Where are the cell keys?' I asked.

Neither of the prisoners replied.

Denzil pressed his gun to Grey's temple. 'Answer the question.'

'I have a set in my room,' FJ said.

'Where in your room?' Denzil asked.

'Top drawer of the dresser.'

I made a move towards FJ's room.

'You'll need the key to the drawer,' he said. 'It's around my neck.'

I approached him and pulled the neck of his shirt open revealing a thin chain with a key and a cross hanging from it. The fastening had slipped around to the front, so I had to face him as I undid the chain with fumbling fingers. I avoided eye contact, but I felt his gaze on my face, unnerving me.

Eventually I had the chain in my hands and slipped off the key.

'Could I have my cross back?' he asked.

I shrugged and dropped it into his bound hands. Then I went to get the cell keys, glad to be away from the two of them for a few moments. They were both unsettling in very different ways.

I found the keys where FJ said they would be, as well as a couple of sets of handcuffs which we used on Grey and FJ instead of the twine. Soon we were all back downstairs in the kitchen at the entrance to the cellar door.

In the cell, Liss drifted in and out of an uncomfortable sleep, all the while aware of her freezing feet and numb legs. Her neck was stiff from leaning on Connor's shoulder and her throat ached with a cruel thirst. In the midst of this discomfort, she dreamt she saw Annabelle standing before her in a halo of light. Her friend was speaking to her urgently, but she couldn't make out what she was saying. Then she felt a hand shake her arm.

'Lissy, Liss, wake up.'

Liss blinked and realised it was not a dream. Annabelle was really here and Connor was trying to get her to focus. To wake her from her trance.

'Anna?' Her voice came out weak and hoarse.

'Quick!' Annabelle squeaked. 'I've brought help, but we should leave now before anyone else comes.'

Connor stood and Liss tried to get to her feet, but her body was so numb and stiff that she couldn't move. Connor knelt down and scooped her up in his arms. She was too weak to protest.

As they left the darkness of the cell, Liss made out the shape of other figures – a girl and some men, but she couldn't focus properly. They were talking to Connor in hurried whispers, but she only caught odd words.

'Water,' she croaked. 'Please.'

Connor carried her up the stone steps and into the kitchen. Someone handed her a cup of water and she gulped it down. It was ice-cold, but she didn't care. It soothed her throat and gave her a small boost of energy, clearing her mind a little. Connor set her down gently on the flagstone floor.

'Here,' one of the men said, wrapping a thick cloak around her shivering shoulders. 'I'm Luc.' He was about FJ's age with short hair and kind eyes. 'You'll need some shoes too.'

'There are boots in the laundry room,' Annabelle said.

'Anna,' Liss said. 'I can't believe you did it. You got us out.' They hugged.

'You're so cold, Liss. You're like ice.'

'I'll be all right.'

'Wait here. I'll get you some socks and boots.'

'Sorry, we've got no time for that,' a huge black man said. 'We've gotta go.' But Annabelle ignored him and ran out of the room. He turned to Liss with an apologetic smile. 'I'm Denzil.'

'Thank you... for getting us out of there,' Liss said.

'Don't thank me yet. We've still got a way to go.'

Next to Denzil stood two shackled prisoners with pillow-cases over their heads, their clothes dripping wet. She wanted to ask someone about them, but right now everybody was moving towards the back door.

At that moment, Annabelle ran back into the kitchen. She motioned to Liss to sit on a chair and knelt on the floor in front of her. She pulled a pair of thick woollen socks over Liss's frozen feet and slipped a pair of leather boots over the top, lacing them quickly. Liss was grateful to her friend despite the fact that her feet were so cold she couldn't feel the difference.

'Hoods up, everyone,' Denzil said. He appeared to be the one in charge, but he hadn't seemed to mind Annabelle disobeying him about the boots. 'If we're stopped out there, say nothing. Leave the talking to me or Luc. Okay?'

Everyone nodded and pulled up the hoods to their robes, giving the illusion that they were Grey's guards, with the exception of the two prisoners.

'Where's my brother?' Liss asked. 'Is he okay? You didn't hurt him, did you?'

No one spoke. Denzil removed the prisoners' hoods.

Liss took a step back. Their mouths had been tied with cloth and their clothes looked like outsiders' rags, but standing before her were the figures of Grey and FJ, fury radiating from their eyes.

To witness James Grey up close, bound and gagged, was a shock. But it was even more disconcerting to see her brother like this.

'FJ,' she breathed. She knew she shouldn't feel any pity for him; not after what he had put her through. But he was still her brother and part of her still loved him. Still loved the boy he had once been.

FJ was trying to speak to her, but she couldn't make out his words through the gag.

'Could you... can you take off his gag?' she asked.

'Sorry, no time for that now,' Denzil said. 'You can talk to him later.'

Someone took Liss's hand and gave it a squeeze. It was the boy – Luc. His skin was warm and so was his smile. He only held her hand for a moment and then he let go.

Denzil slipped the hoods back over the prisoners' heads. 'I'm sorry. I know FJ's your brother, but we had no choice.'

'No. I know you didn't,' she said. 'I know.'

CHAPTER THIRTY-FOUR

RILEY

Luc and Denzil had charge of the prisoners. They prodded them forwards out of the kitchen door and into the soaking garden. Connor went next with Liss and Annabelle, and I followed behind. To any casual observer, it would look as though we were six of Grey's Guards with two prisoners.

The rain had eased a little, but the wind blew bitterly cold. I hoped our return journey would be more straightforward than the one on the way in. Annabelle moved up front to guide us back to the wall. The dogs appeared again, but they did not come close. Perhaps the presence of Grey or FJ had made them less aggressive. Annabelle sent them away with a single word.

We walked quickly and silently, the wind gusting and tugging at our robes, pulling at our hoods, threatening to expose our faces to an unseen enemy. It felt like we had been at the house for days. But, in reality, it had taken us less than an hour to incapacitate the guards, take our hostages and rescue Liss and Connor.

It felt strange to be here with Connor, working together against a common enemy. The last time I'd seen him, my emotions had been all over the place. I realised I was curious to get to know him better. But, I couldn't let thoughts of my biological father distract me. Our main hurdle right now was to get out of the Close.

It would be an amazing feeling to finally get back to the copter. To slide onto the leather seats, fly up into the air and be safe for a while. I darted a glance over my shoulder – all clear so far, the empty house now a dim black shape behind us.

The rushing sound of the river merged with the wind and pattering rain. We walked quickly through the gate and made our way back alongside the wall of the North Canonry.

As we scurried through the Close, we kept to the shadows. To the edges of the buildings where the sleepless couldn't spot us. We moved unhindered for a while and I dared to hope we might make it outside the walls without incident.

Grey and FJ still wore the pillowcases over their heads and because of this, the going was slower than we would have liked; they stumbled at every turn. Denzil and Luc prodded them onward to keep them moving. At least Grey's coughing had ceased.

Suddenly, in the dark silence, a violent clanging rose up.

Liss confirmed our fears that it was the bells ringing an alarm. Grey's people knew we were here. Someone must have seen us, or perhaps one of the unconscious guards had come to and managed to notify someone. Either way, it wasn't good. My first instinct was to run, but Denzil told us to stay calm.

'We look like guards,' he said, raising his voice to make himself heard above the ringing. 'There's no reason they should stop us.'

I hoped he was right.

Within seconds, several robed guards appeared on the streets. And then more and yet more. Did we blend in well enough? My heart knocked against my ribcage and my steps were less steady. Connor turned and ushered me ahead of him so that now I walked between him, Luc and Denzil, no longer so vulnerable at the back.

'If it gets ugly,' Denzil said, 'try not to fire your weapons. If you do, we'll have every guard in Salisbury here.'

Just then an uncloaked man stepped out in front of us and held out his hand to halt our progress. He was middle-aged and broad-shouldered and looked like a fighting man; his brow creased, his mouth stern, flanked by two robed guards. We had no choice but to stop.

He spoke a few words to Connor, but I couldn't hear what was said above the clanging of the bells. I held my breath as he took a step towards the prisoners. If he saw their faces we'd be done for.

He reached to lift FJ's hood. I felt time stand still as he stared at the boy. I couldn't tell if he'd recognised him or not. Then the man lurched at Connor and yanked back his hood. Annabelle squealed. I hoped she and Liss wouldn't bolt in fear.

Everything happened so fast. Denzil shoved the prisoners towards me. I grabbed their cuffs and held on tight. Meantime, Connor, Luc and Denzil fought the three guards. Punches flew, but thankfully no shots were fired. The uncloaked man lunged at Connor and grappled him to the ground. My heart leapt into my throat at the thought of this man hurting him. Connor head-butted the man and slid out from under him. He leapt to his feet, yanked the man's head backwards and ran his knife across his throat, making a deep crimson line. I winced, even though I knew Connor didn't have a choice. The man's face showed surprise and then anger before his head crashed back down to the ground.

Luc and Denzil had swiftly incapacitated the other guards, who were now sprawled at our feet. It had all happened so fast, I hoped we might be able to get out of here without drawing further attention.

Connor swayed next to me and I noticed with a cold horror that there was a knife sticking out of his robes. That man must have stabbed him. Maybe Connor wasn't too badly injured – he was still standing – but I soon realised that wasn't the case as he staggered, clutching at the knife in his side. I pushed the prisoners back to Denzil and put my arm around Connor while Luc supported him from the other side.

Glancing left and right, I saw several groups of guards approach, their pace quickening. Why the hell were we all still standing around, floundering like we'd already been caught? We needed to move.

'Here!' I shouted in the most commanding voice I could muster. 'I've found the intruders!' I didn't even know if Grey had female guards, but I hoped that there would be too much noise from the bells and general confusion for anyone to notice the timbre of my voice. I stepped back from the others and pointed at the fallen men on the ground. 'Seize them!' I cried.

Within seconds, a cluster of guards had gathered around the bodies. I panicked in the chaos as I could no longer tell who was a guard and who was a friend. But Luc was still at Connor's side and seemed to know which direction to head in. Together our group managed to slip away from the guards and hobble across the road. We followed Annabelle down a side-alley and did a quick head count. Then we criss-crossed our way through the Close, the bells still tolling.

Our progress was slow, but there was no time to stop and see how Connor was doing. All I knew was that he was becoming heavier to support. Less able to walk. I had no idea where we were. If we became separated from the others, I wouldn't have the first idea which way to go.

As we continued on, I threw paranoid glances over my shoulder, convinced that hordes of guards were about to appear on our tail. I could hardly believe it when we finally reached the outer wall and the small wooden door to freedom. Annabelle unlocked it and we filed through, the bells sounding much fainter out here.

We had done it. But at what cost?

Locking the door behind us, it felt as though we were shutting the pages of a scary picture book. One I didn't ever wish to open again.

Connor crumpled down onto the wet grass and I knelt and tried to ease back his robes to gauge how badly he'd been hurt. The knife still protruded from his body, pinning his robes in place. I didn't want to remove it in case I made things worse.

'We can't stay here,' Denzil said.

'What about Connor?' I asked. 'I think he's hurt really badly.' I took Connor's hand, his skin felt even colder than mine. ''How are you doing?'

He opened his eyes and tried to smile, but I could tell he was in a lot of pain. I used my knife to slit the coarse material. Liss removed her hood and knelt to help me. Beneath the robes, Connor's clothes were so heavily soaked from the rain that I couldn't tell water from blood. But I could see that the knife had pierced deep into his side. It looked really bad and, even if it wasn't fatal, there was no way he would make it back to the copter on foot.

'It's stopped raining,' he said weakly.

'Connor, how do you feel?' I asked. 'Can you stand?'

'I'm sorry,' he said.

'For what?'

'For screwing this whole thing up and getting caught. For slowing you down now. For—'

'Not your fault, mate,' Denzil said. 'We're out of there now, that's the main thing.'

I tried to think of something to say to make Connor feel better, but no words were forthcoming.

'Riley,' he said through a smile. 'You're my daughter.'

'Yes,' I said. 'Yes, I am. We'll talk about everything when we get home.'

He shook his head and grimaced with pain.

I realised Luc had his arm around my shoulder. 'Riley,' he whispered in my ear. 'I'm sorry. That wound isn't good.'

I ignored his words and grasped Connor's hand tighter. 'Can you stand? Can you get up? Or shall we carry you?'

'Listen,' he said softly. 'You have to leave me here.'

'Leave you? No. We can carry you.'

'No point. Now, listen...'

'No.' I got to my feet and turned to Denzil, refusing to consider what Connor was telling me. 'You can lift him, can't you? You and Luc, between you?'

'Yeah,' Denzil replied. 'But we have to go right now. The copter won't hang about much longer. We can't afford for it to leave without us. If we don't get to Ringwood, this whole thing will have been a waste of time.'

'So let's go,' I said, relieved that we'd soon be able to get Connor the help he needed.

'No,' Connor said.

'What do you mean "no"?' I snapped. 'You're coming and that's that.'

'Riley,' Connor's voice was a whisper now, his gaze holding mine. 'Listen to me. I haven't got long.'

'Of course you have.' I didn't want to hear what he was telling me. My emotions were sliding out of control. This couldn't be happening. This man, this stranger on the ground was my father. I had his blood in my veins. I couldn't lose him now. Not now we were finally about to get to know each other properly. 'It'll be fine. Luc and Denzil will—'

'I'm dying, Riley.'

'No,' I whispered, my throat constricting, eyes blurring. I crouched down and took his hand once more.

'I know you'd prefer it if I wasn't your dad,' he said.

'What?' I replied. 'No...'

'Shhh. Listen,' he said. 'I know and I don't blame you. But I want to say – I'm proud of you. Johnny did a great job raising you. A better job than I would've done. I'm happy I got to meet you, Riley.'

'We can still—'

'Let me finish,' he said. 'Be kind to your mum. We were young and stupid and in love and I know she loves you more than life. I'm happy I got to meet you. I feel... blessed.'

I couldn't speak. All I could do was grip his hand tightly. Maybe my tears were enough to let him know that I was sorry for not allowing him into my life sooner. That I was sorry he was dying. That I was sorry I would never get to know him. My father.

'Riley,' Luc whispered. He kissed my temple. 'I'm sorry. He's gone.'

I crouched there for a moment, listening to the wind in the trees and the distant clanging of the bells. Aware of everything and nothing. Did anything really matter at all?

'Riley,' Luc said.

I let go of Connor's hand and laid it back down carefully on his body. Then I jumped to my feet and wiped the tears from my eyes. 'We can't leave him here.'

'I'm so sorry, Riley,' Denzil said. 'He was a good man. We'll carry him into the woods. It's peaceful there.'

He passed me his gun, indicating that I was to keep an eye on the prisoners while he and Luc carried Connor's body.

Everything had felt hyper-real until this moment. Now it was as though I was standing outside of myself, looking down at the scene from above. I felt apart from everything and everyone. My mind was unravelling, but I had to hold it all together. I gripped the cold metal of the revolver and jabbed at Grey's back. Luc and Denzil carried Connor's body between them.

'Are you strong enough to walk?' I asked Liss, who was huddled next to Annabelle.

'Yes,' she replied.

'Ready?' Luc asked.

I nodded and we took off towards the trees, leaving the Close behind us.

The ground was boggy and water dripped from the trees. We'd been walking for nearly an hour now. This return journey would take a lot longer than the one on the way in.

My mind kept returning to Connor. Denzil and Luc had laid him in a hollow under an oak tree. There had been no time to bury him, but Luc had made a small cross from twigs and twine. I'd kissed his forehead, reluctant to leave him, but knowing we had no choice. How would I ever tell Ma? The image of him lying there kept coming into my head. With every step I saw his pale face, his eyes closed, his wet hair plastered to his forehead. If I didn't shake the image, I would go crazy. I forced my eyes up from the ground and stared straight ahead trying to concentrate on the here and now. I would let myself mourn Connor once the rest of us were safe.

'You okay?' I asked Liss, tapping her on the shoulder.

'I'm fine,' she replied quietly.

'You're limping.'

'I'm all right. I think it's blisters... from the boots.'

'Do you need to rest?'

'No. I don't care about my feet. I just want to get as far away from this place as possible. I've been here too long. Over half my life. I want... I want to go home.'

'Your parents are in the copter,' I said. 'They can't wait to see you.'

Liss stopped walking. 'In the copter? The one we're going to now?'

'Yes. Didn't you know?'

'Connor said Mum and Dad sent him to get me and FJ, but I didn't know they were going to be... here.'

'Are you all right?' I asked.

She nodded. 'I just... I didn't expect to see them so soon. I think I'm nervous.'

'Course you are,' I said. 'But they love you and as soon as you see them, it will be all right.'

She bowed her head and exhaled. Annabelle touched her arm.

'We'd better...' I gestured to the disappearing figures of Denzil and Luc.

'Yes, of course,' she said. 'Sorry.'

We started moving again, almost running to catch the others up. I wondered what it was like for Liss – to know she was about to be reunited with her parents after so many years. The image of Connor fell into my head again and I pushed it out. I thought how bittersweet things were for everybody. Especially for Liss, with her brother corrupted by Grey's regime. That man had tainted so many lives.

I stared ahead at the figure of James Grey. He didn't look nearly so scary with his hands in cuffs and his head covered. I could hardly believe this power-driven, terrifying man was finally our prisoner. But then he hadn't been as heavily guarded as usual. His army was away scooping up the Perimeters and Compounds of southern Britain. Well, they would just have to give them all up. And they would have to do it without bloodshed. For we had the top prize. We had Grey.

Luc had dropped back to walk by my side. 'I'm so sorry about Connor,' he said.

'I never got to know him. I never let him in. I was so horrible to him.'

'You were in shock. It was understandable.' He took my hand and we walked like that for a while.

'You were right to suggest getting Grey,' he said. 'Dad won't believe it when we show up at Ringwood with him as our prisoner.'

'I can't believe it either,' I said. 'He's definitely the creepiest guy I've ever met.'

'He's on some twisted power trip. Lissy did well to hold out all these years. Don't know how she did it. She must be tougher than she looks.'

We walked in silence for a while, our breath mingling with the cold night air.

'I was worried you were going to get hurt back there,' Luc said.

'Me too,' I replied. 'Worried about you, I mean.'

'Look, this probably isn't the time,' he said, 'but I need to tell you something.'

Here it comes, I thought. After everything we've been through, here's the moment he tells me we should just be friends. That he's changed his mind. That it's all too complicated. I steeled myself to take the blow. Upset that he could be so unfeeling right now.

'Riley, I know you don't feel the same way and that's okay. But I have to tell you something. After what happened with Connor, I know it's important to be honest. To say what's in my mind before it's too late.'

'It's okay,' I interrupted, not wanting to hear the rejection. 'You don't have to say anything. I know how you feel now and it's fine. We can just be friends.'

'Friends,' he repeated.

'Yeah. Please don't say anything else, Luc. I can't handle it right now.' I let go of his hand and marched on ahead, livid that he could be this insensitive so soon after I'd lost Connor.

'Riley...'

'Just leave it, okay.'

Our feet made squelching noises in the mud and that's

pretty much how I felt – like someone had squelched mud all over my heart.

CHAPTER THIRTY-FIVE

LISS

Liss felt sick about Connor. He had literally carried her to safety and now he was dead. Because of her. Although she had only known him for a short time, she would never forget him. And she would make sure her parents knew what he had done for her and Annabelle.

She was finally free. She and Annabelle were leaving the Cathedral Close behind them. She tried not to look ahead at the broad shape of her brother and the slim outline of Grey. This wasn't the family homecoming she had imagined over the years – one of them rescued, one of them a prisoner.

Why had FJ sucked up all Grey's lies? Deep down she knew the reason. It was because he'd *wanted* to believe them. He wanted power and respect, and James Grey's church had given him all those things. It didn't matter about the philosophy behind it all. It only mattered that it suited him. That it gave him the adventure and importance he'd always craved.

Or maybe he'd just drunk too much of the soup.

She gave a wry smile and then gasped as she tripped over a tree root, intensifying the pain of her blistered feet. When she'd been in the cellar, the cold had seeped into her bones, turning them to ice. But now her feet were on fire from the blisters. The pain was so raw she didn't know how she was able to keep moving. But move she did. Liss stumbled through the forest as if in a dream.

Annabelle grabbed her arm, stopping her from falling flat on her face. Poor Annabelle, who couldn't even remember her own parents or where they had lived before she was taken. She had only been five years old at the time and all she'd said back then was that she missed her mummy.

Now, nine years later, Annabelle didn't know who she was. She didn't even remember her surname. Liss realised how lucky she was to know where she came from, to have had memories of her family to sustain her. Well, Liss would always look after Annabelle. FJ was lost, but Annabelle was her sister now.

It had been an achingly lonely nine years, but she had never truly given up hope. She had never pictured herself growing old in the Close. And now she was only a few more painful kilometres away from being reunited with her parents.

The sky was almost light, but the sun remained elusive, hidden behind swathes of gun-metal-grey cloud. Denzil had been worried their transport would already have left, so Luc had run on ahead to ensure the copter waited.

They eventually reached the edge of the forest and entered an open field. It was unnerving to lose the shelter of the trees and Liss felt instantly exposed. But there, ahead of them, in the corner of the field sat a huge helicopter. Liss had never seen one up close before. She'd only ever seen them flying overhead, buzzing through the sky like metal dragonflies.

As they approached, her pulse began to race. All thoughts of her blistered feet and of FJ and of being locked in that awful cell were left behind. Now all she focused on was the copter and the people inside. After so many years would her parents be strangers to her? Would she recognise them? She could no longer bring their faces to mind. They had become nothing more than blurry images in her memory.

The sun suddenly found a gap in the cloud, rising above the copter, casting golden beams of light onto the field. The door opened and a figure emerged. Liss squinted and shielded her eyes with her hands. It was a woman with short hair and she was running towards them. Behind her, a man followed.

It was her mum and dad. It was really them.

Annabelle let go of Liss's hand and nudged her forward. Liss hesitated and then she too began to run, ignoring the pain in her feet and letting go of the pain in her heart.

Tears ran down her cheeks as she came close enough to see the faces that had been lost to her for so many years. How could she have thought she wouldn't have known them? Of course she knew them. They were her parents.

'Lissy!' her mum cried. 'Lissy, it's really you!'

'Mum,' she sobbed. 'Mum, Dad, you're here.'

They fell into each other's arms. Liss's mum kissed her hair and her cheeks and her eyes and her nose. Her dad was crying so hard he couldn't speak. Liss had forgotten what it felt like to be held. To feel secure and loved. She had pictured this moment every day for the past nine years, but the reality felt so much better than her imaginings.

'We never gave up on getting you back,' her mum cried. 'I can't believe you're actually here.'

Liss looked at their faces, drinking in the sight of them. Her family. It was like a wonderful dream. She couldn't help feeling that she might wake up at any moment to find herself lying in her cold narrow bed back at the Close.

'I can't believe it either,' Liss said. 'Are you and Dad all right?'

'Yes,' her mum replied. 'Having you back has made everything perfect.'

It felt strange to hug her parents now that she was grown.

As a child, they had enveloped her in their arms. Now they felt smaller and less substantial than she remembered. She was almost as tall as her dad and taller than her mum. Their faces were lined, thinner.

'Do you still live at the farm?' she asked.

'The old farm's still there, waiting for you.'

Liss pictured her old bedroom, the kitchen, the yard. She suddenly remembered that they weren't alone. 'FJ...' Liss said. 'Did Luc... did he tell you?'

'He said something,' her dad replied. 'But I'm sure he'll come round given time. He's our boy, isn't he?'

The others had caught up now and were standing a little way off, not wanting to intrude. Luc had left the copter again to join them. Liss's parents stared across at the small group and picked out FJ immediately.

'Freddie, son,' her dad called out, softly. 'What they done to you, boy?'

Denzil untied FJ's gag.

FJ wiped his mouth and spat on the ground, but he didn't speak. He glared at Liss and she looked away, worried about the distress he was sure to inflict on their parents.

'Freddie,' Jessie said, walking up to him. 'I can't believe it's you.' He had grown taller than her and she had to reach up to stroke his cheek. But he flinched and jerked his face away. 'You've grown into such a beautiful boy,' she said. 'It must have been hard for you.'

'No,' he said. 'Not hard at all. Grey is Our Father. He has looked after me; treated me like his son.'

'Well, that's good,' she said. 'I'm glad he treated you well. That you weren't unhappy all these years.'

'I was never unhappy. Until now,' he said. 'Being forced to come here. To see you.' His words were designed to hurt.

Jessie took a sharp intake of breath and looked down. Then

she turned to look at Fred who tried to give her an encouraging look.

FJ's eyes glittered with rage and hate. Liss couldn't bear it. Couldn't bear that he was being so nasty and unfeeling. Breaking her parents' hearts all over again.

'I am the Voice of the Father,' FJ cried. 'We are creating a better society. One where there is no war or hunger or barbaric behaviour. Just peace and the chance to know God. You should have joined us, but instead you're trying to thwart us. I will pray for you, but I think it's too late. The devil has you in his arms and you are all destined for hell.'

'Shut up, FJ,' Liss cried. 'That's Mum you're talking to, not one of your brainwashed servants.'

'I should have killed you when I had the chance, sister,' he sneered. 'You've betrayed God and don't deserve to live in His world.'

'Oh!' Liss's mum took a step backwards, shocked by the vitriol spewing from FJ's mouth.

'Now, son, that's no way to speak to your sister or your mother.' Liss's dad squeezed her shoulder and strode towards his son.

'You don't understand anything,' FJ said. 'So let me put it into plain English for you – *you* are not my mother and *you* are not my father. You are both dead to me.'

'Right,' said Denzil. 'That's enough of that.' He pulled the gag over FJ's mouth and slipped the hood back over his head.

Liss went over to her parents and hugged them again as they stood there, bewildered and upset. 'I'm so sorry about FJ,' she said. 'I tried to talk to him before, but he's a different person now. I know it must be hard to hear him talk like that.'

Her parents didn't speak. They were shocked.

'Let's get back in the copter,' Luc said, breaking the awkward silence. 'It's not safe out here. The guards could be tracking us.'

Liss went over to Annabelle who had tucked herself behind Riley. She held out her hand and pulled the younger girl over to meet her parents. As they made their way back to the copter, she introduced them.

'This is Annabelle. We were taken at the same time. She's my friend and she helped me escape tonight. Along with... Connor.'

Liss's mum stopped walking and smiled at Annabelle. Her voice was shaky when she spoke: 'I'm very grateful to you, Annabelle. And I'm glad you and Liss were friends in there. Glad you had each other for company. For support.'

Annabelle nodded.

'She can come home with us, Mum, can't she?' Liss said.

'Of course.' But it was clear that Liss's parents were too shaken up by FJ's behaviour to pay Annabelle too much attention. Liss could have kicked her brother for his arrogance and self-obsession. He always ruined everything.

As they approached the copter, the blades started up, creating a forceful wind. Liss stayed close beside her parents and held Annabelle's hand. A man sat in the front of the machine – she assumed he must be the pilot.

Liss's dad was about to climb into the copter when he stopped and turned around, looking for something. His eyes soon found their target and he strode up to Grey.

'Is this him?' her dad cried. 'Is this the bastard that took our kids and ruined all our lives?' He ripped the hood from Grey's head and stared him in the eyes. 'You're a thief and a murderer and I should stick a knife between your ribs for what you've done.'

Liss watched her dad as he trembled with anger. But Grey's eyes were mocking and cold. Fred returned his stare, drew back his fist and punched him in the face. Then again in the stomach. Grey doubled over and Fred looked ready to dish out some more, but Denzil stepped in and pulled him away.

'Okay, that's enough,' Denzil said. 'We need him alive, or I'd give you the knife myself.'

Fred turned back to the copter. He didn't look at FJ as he walked past him. The broken expression on her father's face made Liss want to weep for all they had lost. Her dad climbed straight into the copter and held out his hand to help Liss up. Annabelle and her mum followed. They all squeezed into the back and waited while the others boarded. Denzil and Luc shoved the prisoners inside and finally the doors were closed.

Again, Liss wished she could have given her parents the pure happiness of a perfect reunion with both her and FJ. But it wasn't to be.

In the front, a heated conversation was in full flow, but Liss couldn't make out what was being said above the engine noise, and she didn't much care to hear it either. She and Annabelle were now sandwiched safely in between her parents. After years of fear and uncertainty, they were finally leaving Salisbury and the Close behind them.

CHAPTER THIRTY-SIX
RILEY

We crammed into the copter, buckled up and slipped on our headphones, Charlie Duke was relieved to see us, but he was also worried about our two hostages. They weren't part of the plan and Pa and Eddie had been very specific about sticking to the plan.

'It was too good an opportunity to pass up,' Luc explained.

'You were lucky to get out alive,' Duke said. 'I don't mind telling you, I was more than a bit worried waiting here.'

'We didn't all make it,' I said.

Denzil filled Duke in on what had happened to Connor. He spoke quickly and quietly and I tried in vain to tune out his words.

'We couldn't have done it without Denzil,' Luc added.

Duke threw Denzil an appraising glance. 'Right, let's get out of here and drop these people back at their farm. There's too many of us in this copter for my liking.'

I was up front with Duke, while Denzil and Luc sat behind with the two hostages. It made me uneasy to think of them in this confined space with us, but they were unarmed and outnumbered so I tried to relax. Grey must be weak after our long journey and the beating he'd just received from Fred.

We finally rose up into the morning sky, the copter blades whirring in time with my thoughts. Connor was dead. Pa was in Ringwood facing Grey's army. And Luc and I were over before we'd really begun. I'd given him a get-out clause and he'd taken it. He just wanted to be friends.

Ugh.

Since the moment Luc had made his feelings clear, nothing felt worth fighting for anymore. It all seemed so pointless. I tried not to think of the softness of his kiss and how good his hands had felt on my back. The strong smooth feel of his fingers entwined in mine. I glanced behind me and he returned my gaze, but he didn't smile. I was still mad at him, anyway, for being so insensitive in the forest. I needed to let him go. To let these feelings go. I had to try, or they would eat me up from the inside out.

My head felt like a muddy river with its flood defences about to collapse. I couldn't let myself think about Luc and I couldn't let myself think about Connor. If I did, I would break down again and I couldn't afford to be a mess right now. I had to choke back all my emotions and stay focused.

It seemed we'd only just taken off into the air before we were descending again. Below, I made out the mellow brick farmhouse, the yard and the cow field where we were about to land – Fred and Jessie's place.

Everyone climbed out of the copter except Duke and the prisoners. The air smelt fresh, the scent of damp grass in the breeze. Jessie had an arm around each of the girls and kept kissing the top of Liss's head. Liss's eyes were as wide as the sky, drinking in the landscape of her home. I felt happy for her. But there was still one major problem we needed to discuss.

'I'll get the lad out, shall I?' Fred said, turning back to the copter.

'Can I talk to you about that,' Luc said.

'What's to talk about?'

'We need a favour.'

Fred's mouth hardened into a thin line.

'It's FJ...' Luc began. 'We need him.'

'No.'

'What's going on?' Jessie detached herself from the girls and came over.

'They want FJ,' Fred said. 'But it's not gonna happen. The deal was—'

'The deal still stands, Fred. We only need him for a short time.'

'Look,' Fred said taking a pace towards Luc. 'Whatever he might have done, it's not his fault. He was taken when he was a boy. They've twisted things in his head. We can get our old FJ back. *I'll* get him back... even if I have to tie him to a chair till he remembers who he really is.'

'And you can do all that, Fred. A deal's a deal. But if we take him with us now, we can save a lot of lives. It'll just be for a day or two. We need him to barter for our people's freedom.'

'No!' Jessie cried.

'We won't let anything happen to him,' I said. 'We only need to show his face to Grey's guards. Threaten them.'

'Threaten them with the death of our son, you mean,' Fred growled. 'You've got Grey, haven't you? He's the real villain here; not our Freddie. Why d'you need 'em both?'

'To be honest, Grey doesn't look too good,' Luc said. 'He might not last the day.'

'Good,' Fred said.

'Please, Fred,' I said, resting my hand on his arm. 'You've waited nine years already. Another day or two won't be so hard. And at least you can have a couple of days with Liss without... without any stress. Please do this one thing for us. To help save our people. You owe us that.'

Fred's shoulders suddenly sagged. 'We do owe you, but—.'

'No, Fred!' Jessie clutched at his arm.

'Let them take him,' Liss said to her parents.

They turned to stare at her.

'I don't want him here,' she continued. 'I need... peace,' she added, pleading with them.

Jessie's eyes filled with tears. She shook her head slowly, but it was more in disbelief than in protest.

'Thank you,' Luc said, taking advantage of Lissy's intervention. 'We'll bring him back to you as soon as we can.' He held out his hand and Fred reluctantly shook it. Jess looked devastated.

'You're not thinking of staying here, are you?' Denzil said to the couple.

They stared back at him, dazed. 'Yeah, course we are,' Fred said. 'This is our home.'

'Denzil's right,' I said. 'You can't stay here. Grey's men know where you live.'

'Thanks for your concern, but we can keep 'em out,' Fred replied tightly.

'This is the first place they'll come,' Denzil said. 'And you won't be able to stop them. If they can take out fully guarded Perimeters, they can take out your farm.'

'What about the local Compound?' I asked. 'You told us there was a place for you there. You could go and ask. It's safer to be around people. You said yourself that you were only staying here until your children came home.'

'Maybe...' Jess said.

'Thanks, but we're not your problem anymore,' Fred said.

'Just say you'll think about it,' I said. 'Please. After all that effort to get them back to you, don't risk getting them getting kidnapped again.'

'Noted,' Fred replied grudgingly.

'If everything goes well,' Denzil said, 'you'll be able to come home eventually.'

"Take good care of Freddie, won't you,' Jessie begged. 'No matter what he seems like now, he's still our son and we love him. He's a good boy.'

'Two days,' Fred said. 'We want him back in two days. We'll either be here or at the Compound.'

Liss walked into the yard in her socks. She had already discarded her uncomfortable boots in the copter. She stood and took a breath, inhaling wet grass, manure and cut logs. She heard the cows and the rooster and smiled as a couple of collies joyfully circled her parents and sniffed at her and Anna's legs. The farmhouse looked the same. Maybe a little smaller and little shabbier.

The others had gone. Taken FJ with them. It had been so hard for her parents, she could see that. But there was nothing else to be done. Liss had dreaded his return. She was relieved Luc, Denzil and Riley had taken him back with them, certain her parents wouldn't have been able to manage him. Freddie was a danger to all of them.

She and Annabelle had been hugged farewell by her new friends. Such kind, warm people with so much life. They were different to the people in the Close. They were... vibrant as though a light shone within them. The people of Salisbury were the opposite – like something inside them had died. Shadows and wraiths.

'So, Lissy darlin', is it like you remembered?' her mum asked, taking her hand and giving it a squeeze.

She nodded.

'We kept your room for you. It's just like you left it. You can share with Annabelle if you like, or we can sort something else out.'

Liss smiled and leant into her mum's shoulder. 'Thanks, Mum. I don't mind either way.'

Annabelle was crouching on the ground, petting the dogs. Scratching behind their ears and talking to them in soft soothing tones. Liss couldn't wait to show her around.

No bells rang out for morning service here. No hooded figures glided past, provoking fear in their wake. No stern-faced women told her off for standing still and doing nothing. No threats hung in the air. The atmosphere was sweet and untainted.

She would teach Annabelle how to farm the land and tend to the animals. She would be a good daughter and care for her mum and dad. She would have the life she had always yearned for, but never thought would come to pass. She would erase the past nine years from her mind. After all, those years had just been spent waiting for this moment. Waiting to come home.

CHAPTER THIRTY-SEVEN
RILEY

The original town of Ringwood had been decimated by rioters and looters years ago. While all that was going on, the River Avon decided to burst its banks, flooding the area and finishing off any hopes its inhabitants might have had to rebuild. So Ringwood became a no-go area for most. Some people still lived there, but it was dangerous, unprotected, a marshland concealing raiders and pirates.

The Ringwood Perimeter had been created at about the same time as the collapse of the main town. It had been founded on the site of a traditional private school to the north of its namesake. Much smaller than the old town, but heavily fortified and extremely wealthy.

Pa, Eddie and Rita should have arrived at the Perimeter days ago, but we had no idea whether they'd been successful in holding back Grey's army. We'd had to land out of sight as we couldn't risk being shot down, which had meant another trek through the countryside.

Charlie Duke stayed with the copter, an automatic machine gun on his lap. So once again it was me, Luc and Denzil on the move. But this time we had hostages. After some debate, Luc had removed their hoods.

Grey was weak, struggling to match our strides, and Denzil had to prod him along. FJ stayed at Grey's side although I'm sure he could have moved quicker if he'd wanted to. The afternoon was dull and still, quiet apart from the sound of our feet tramping up the grassy hill and the low whine of the wind. Except that was odd, because I couldn't feel even the faintest breeze on my skin. A thin grove of poplars lined the top of the hill. They wouldn't provide us much cover, but they would have to do.

As we neared the summit, Denzil crouched and scooted up to the top, sinking to his belly and pulling out his binoculars. Luc waited with the prisoners as I crept up to join Denzil, flattening myself on the ground beside him.

Spread out before us at the base of the slope lay the Ringwood Perimeter, with scrub in the foreground and dark forest in the distance. The fence was almost an exact replica of our own – a high metal electrified mesh with evergreen trees inside, screening most of the interior from prying eyes. But that wasn't what drew my attention. The thing that made me take a breath was the sight of hundreds, no, thousands, of Grey's soldiers surrounding the settlement. They must have been twenty or thirty deep.

And I realised that the low moan of the non-existent wind was actually coming from down there. The soldiers were chanting. An eerie sound which filled up the valley and sent shivers across my shoulders. Denzil turned to me and raised his eyebrows.

'Nutjobs,' he whispered.

I gave a small smile despite the chill that crept up my spine. He passed me the binoculars and I wheeled the focus until the fence became sharp through the lens.

'They haven't breached the fence yet,' I said. 'Hope Pa and the others made it inside okay.'

'They could have arrived, seen that lot and turned right around,' Denzil replied. 'I wouldn't blame 'em if they had.'

I shifted the binoculars and focused on the soldiers now. Why were they standing there chanting? What would that achieve? It was like they were waiting for something to happen. I passed the bins back to Denzil.

'I'll send Luc up,' I said and hurried back down the hill.

Luc took my place next to Denzil. It felt odd to be standing here on my own with FJ and Grey. They were sitting with their backs to each other, still cuffed, with their faces covered once more. I kept my gun trained on Grey's head, not wanting to take any chances.

A couple of minutes later, Luc and Denzil were back by my side. We moved a little way from the prisoners and spoke in whispers.

'There's no point waiting, is there?' I asked. 'We should just go down and do it.'

'Agreed,' Denzil replied. 'We'll need to stay real close to each other. No one moves off even a couple of foot.'

Luc nodded. He'd been unusually quiet. Hadn't said a word to me since our short conversation in the forest outside Salisbury.

We headed back to our hostages.

'Up you get,' Denzil said, hauling first Grey to his feet and then FJ.

Grey was the important one here, so we decided that Denzil would be the one to hold him at gunpoint. I was to train my weapon on FJ, and Luc was to go first, waving his T-shirt as a white flag so the soldiers wouldn't shoot us on sight. Lastly, we removed the prisoners' hoods. FJ fixed me with a stare.

'Walk,' I said.

We crested the hill and began our descent. There was

nothing to stop Grey's soldiers opening fire and slaughtering us all, but I was too numb to feel fear. If they had spotted us they didn't show it. They were focusing all their attention on the fence and on their chanting.

'Over there,' Luc said. 'Look left.'

I looked and saw a detachment of six soldiers break off from the rest and turn towards us. Now my heart pumped a little quicker. Not totally numb then. One of them held out a hand to halt our progress. We did as we were bid, stopped and waited for them to come to us.

They took their time, moving as one. Their cloaks merged together making them appear as though they were a single huge creature crawling across the hill. Once they got within six feet of us, they stopped. One of them stepped forward, his face concealed by his hood, a heavy iron cross hanging from his neck.

The faceless guards were still for a second before they realised who our hostages were. As one, they reached for their weapons – machine guns hidden beneath their robes.

'Put those away,' Luc said. 'Or we'll shoot them both.'

They were both still gagged, but I could see FJ itching to speak. I pressed my revolver into the side of his head.

'You're gonna need to withdraw your soldiers,' Denzil said. 'All of them.'

Their leader turned his head to Grey and although I couldn't see his face, I guessed he was seeking his approval.

'Don't look at him,' I said. 'He's not giving the orders. You all need to leave now and you need to tell your other freak-show soldiers to abandon the other Perimeters and Compounds too. Do it now, today, or we'll stick James Grey's head on a spike.' I spat out the words.

'I cannot act until I hear from Our Father,' the soldier said. His voice low and monotone.

'Do you want us to shoot him now?' I said. 'Because we will.'

'I cannot act until I hear from Our Father,' he repeated.

Denzil, Luc and I gave each other a quick glance and a nod. Luc stepped towards Grey and began to undo the knot in the gag, but it was tied too tight. He drew out his knife and sliced through it, letting the material fall to the ground.

Grey sucked in a lungful of air. He opened his mouth to speak, but no words came out. He was unable even to whisper.

'Oh yeah, right,' Denzil said. 'We need the other one to talk.'

Luc came over and sliced off FJ's gag next.

'Our Father must not be harmed,' FJ said to the guards, his voice soft and raspy. 'Do as these people say. Do you understand?'

The soldier bowed and they all turned away, returning to their comrades.

'When they've gone, you'll set us free,' FJ said.

None of us answered.

'You need to release all the Perimeters,' I called after the soldiers. 'All of them. Without harming anyone.'

Grey's face was pale and he swayed on his feet. He looked as though he might topple over.

Denzil grabbed at him with his free hand. 'Whoa there. Can't have you dying on us yet. That wouldn't be helpful.'

Luc took out his canteen of water and pressed it up to the man's lips. Grey gulped it down, half of it dribbling down his chin.

We stood and watched as the six soldiers made their way back down the hill. As they did so, the chanting suddenly stopped. I hadn't realised how oppressive the noise had been and it was a relief to have the natural silence of the day back.

As one, Grey's army turned and filed away from the Perimeter like a black river flowing back to its source. As they left, they gathered up dark shapes from the ground.

'Bodies,' I said, pointing. 'There must have been a battle. I hope our people are okay in there.'

'We'll find out in a minute,' Luc replied. 'I'm looking forward to getting rid of these two.'

'You can't kill us,' FJ said. 'You gave your word that we would be released if we gave up the Perimeters.'

'No,' Luc said. 'We gave our word that we wouldn't lop your heads off.'

'So, what then?' FJ said, outrage in his voice. 'You intend to keep us prisoner?'

'Pretty much,' I said.

'If we let you go,' Luc said. 'You'd start this whole thing all over again. And I'm not about to let that happen.'

'I'm sure there's a nice cosy cell waiting for you,' Denzil said. 'Maybe they'll let you and James bunk in together.'

FJ's expression was impressively blank, but his jawbone flexed with fury.

'Come on,' Denzil said. 'Let's go down and see if they're okay in there.'

Grey's soldiers were now nothing more than a thin trail disappearing into the horizon. They had left quickly. If they were that well organised, I shuddered to imagine what damage they could inflict in a battle situation.

We moved down the hillside towards the settlement. The gates were shut with no one manning them. There wasn't a guard in sight. The light was slowly dimming and a thin breeze began to stroke my face. The Perimeter was alarmingly quiet. Where was everyone?

Then, as we drew closer, through the gates, I saw further signs of battle. Charred trees and scorched ground inside the fence. Perimeter guards on the ground. Several of them.

'They've been using grenades,' Denzil said.'

'Where's everyone else?' I asked.

Luc cupped his hands together and shouted 'Hey!' His

voice reverberated through the valley. 'Hey! Eddie! Johnny! It's Luc Donovan!'

One of the bodies on the ground inside the fence moved. I tapped Luc's shoulder and pointed as the figure – a guard – struggled to his knees. He turned his head.

'Luc?' he croaked. Luc Donovan?'

'Seb!' Luc cried. 'You okay?'

'Not sure. Something hit my shoulder. Have they gone?'

'Yeah. Can you open the gates?'

'What's that?' Denzil said, shoving Grey across to Luc. He darted a little way off and crouched down over the only one of Grey's fallen soldiers who'd been left behind. Denzil pulled at something under the body.

'What are you doing?' I asked.

He rolled the soldier over and then backed right away.

'Move!' he yelled.

CHAPTER THIRTY-EIGHT

RILEY

I stood outside the Perimeter gates in the semi-darkness, wondering what Denzil had discovered.

'Get back up the hill,' he ordered. 'It's a bomb.'

'You're kidding,' Luc said.

'Nope. I don't think it's armed. I gotta check. There might be more.'

'Denzil, you can't!' I cried.

'Don't argue. Just go,' he said. 'I'll neutralise them.'

'Riley,' Luc said. 'I'll help you get these two up the hill, then I'll come back to help Denzil.'

I called out to Seb, the guard on the ground. 'There's a bomb out here! Get back! Can you move?'

'I'll try.'

'Where's everyone else?' Luc called to him.

'Inside, taking cover. Arming themselves.'

'Is Eddie here?' I called as we backed away. 'And Johnny? Johnny Culpepper?'

But Seb didn't reply. He was crawling away to safety.

We staggered back up the hill, pushing Grey and FJ between us. The darkness was settling fast. Once we were behind the trees, Luc pushed the prisoners together, made them sit back-to-back and cuffed them to one another.

'Gag them again and put their hoods back on,' Luc said, taking the pillowcase hoods from his pocket and shoving them into my hand. 'And stay alert. We don't know how far away Grey's soldiers are. You're nicely hidden here anyway. I'll come back once we know the bombs are safe.'

'Luc...' I began.

He took a step towards me and grasped both my hands. I thought he would say something, but he let go and turned away.

'Be careful,' I whispered as he disappeared back down the hillside.

My heart was hammering. Any second now I expected to hear an explosion. I prayed Grey's soldiers weren't anywhere nearby. That they were still on their way back to Salisbury. Not hanging around here secretly watching our every move. What if they were watching me right now?

'Scared?' FJ asked.

I glanced over. He had a smirk on his face. I tucked my gun into my waistband and began to rummage through my bag searching for something to gag him with.

'You should be,' he continued.

'Quiet,' I said.

Grey had slumped forward, unmoving. I wondered if he was still alive.

'Those bombs will blow your friends apart,' FJ said, a smile in his voice.

'If that happens, I'll kill you,' I said, wondering how someone with such a beautiful face could have so much malice in his heart.

I pulled a length of twine from my bag, but I needed something thicker. A strip of material or something. Anything to quiet his needling voice.

'And Luc?' he said. 'He's a special friend, isn't he. His body parts will be decorating Ringwood tonight.'

'I said, shut up. Unless you'd like me to blow your kneecaps off.'

'I'll enjoy taking you back to the Close with me, Riley.' His voice was soft and teasing.

Maybe if I used my knife to cut a strip from his pillowcase hood? That could work. I just needed to stop him talking. His voice was making me crazy.

'I'll enjoy making an example of you,' he continued. 'Have you ever stood in front of ten thousand people, Riley? I have. It gives you quite a thrill.'

If he didn't shut up, I would have to shoot him. I took out my knife and made a slit in the pillowcase. Then I tore the material right the way around. It ripped easily and soon I held a long strip of cotton in my hands.

FJ's eyes bored into me as I approached him. I tried not to catch his eye. I was annoyed that I'd allowed him to get under my skin, to unnerve me. At least it had stopped me worrying about Luc and Denzil for a couple of seconds.

I crouched beside him and looped the gag over his head. As I did so, my heart gave a jolt as his hands flew round to meet mine, grabbing my wrists.

'What! What are you doing? How...' He was free! I tried too late to reach for my revolver, but he was now squeezing my wrists so tight I thought they might snap.

He jumped to his feet, dragging me up with him and twisting me around so he now had both my wrists in one hand. He deftly reached beneath my coat and retrieved my gun. How? How had he got free?

I raised my foot and stamped down hard with my heel onto the top of his boot, but he kicked out with his other leg, knocking my feet from under me. I fell to the ground and he straddled me, ripping the gag from my hand and pulling it down hard over my mouth, holding my gun in his right hand. I tried to bring my knee up, but he had me pinned too tightly.

I saw that Grey, too, had staggered to his feet. It was almost dark now, but Grey's pale features loomed above me. He pointed a long finger at my face and mouthed something I couldn't hear.

FJ's fingers fumbled, trying to tie the gag. Eventually, he quit trying and balled up the material, stuffing the whole thing into my mouth, making me choke. It was pushed so far into my mouth, I could barely breathe. He straightened and pointed the revolver at my head as I lay on the ground.

'And now we will call back our disciples and finish what we started,' FJ said. 'Father...' He spoke to Grey without taking his eyes off me. 'Are you well, Father?'

Grey put his hand on FJ's shoulder.

FJ had the cuffs in his hand. 'Get up,' he ordered.

I glared at him.

'Up, or I will shoot you now.'

I stood.

'Hands out,' he said.

I held them out in front of me, taking deep breaths through my nose, furious with myself for getting into this situation. But also bewildered as to how it had happened.

'Want to know how I got free?' he asked.

I did want to know, but I wouldn't give him the satisfaction of looking interested. Instead, I stared down at my hands.

'The cross saved me,' he said, hooking the cuffs around my wrists.

What was he talking about?

'You remember, back at the house?' he said. 'I wore my cross around my neck along with the key to my drawer...'

I did remember. And I slowly began to understand what he was telling me.

'I asked you for my cross back,' he said, clicking the cuffs shut around my already bruised wrists. 'And you obliged. What you didn't know is that my cross is also a key.'

He held the small metal object out to demonstrate, but it was so dark I could barely see. All I heard was the click as he undid my cuffs and another click as he closed them again.

'Clever, eh?'

Very, I thought. And I cursed myself for being an idiot. I'd thought he had wanted his cross back for sentimental or religious reasons. How had I let this happen? We'd been so close to ending this invasion and now I'd ruined everything. I couldn't let Grey and FJ call their soldiers back. If they did, we were all dead. I had to at least try to salvage the situation.

I didn't give myself any more time to think. Jerking my handcuffed wrists upwards, I knocked the revolver from FJ's hands. He squeezed the trigger in the process and for a moment I wondered if I'd been shot. If I would feel a sudden explosion of pain before collapsing. But all I felt was the sharp crack in my ears from the gunfire. A deafening, echoing, shock of noise.

FJ and I locked eyes for a half a second. And then everything spooled forward in a tangle of arms and fingers as we scrambled to catch the weapon. The revolver somersaulted out of reach and tumbled into the dark undergrowth. I couldn't risk staying here to try to find it. FJ was far stronger than me. My best bet was to run.

CHAPTER THIRTY-NINE
RILEY

I pelted down the hillside, pulling the balled-up gag out of my mouth and yelling to Luc and Denzil for help. My chained wrists messed with my balance, making me stumble and skid. Finally, I rolled downwards on my side, accelerating towards the Perimeter fence where I slid to a stop. I lay on my side, my breath ragged and my body bruised from the violent descent.

'Luc!' I yelled again. 'Help!' I prayed Denzil or Luc would hear or see me. Instead, a shot skimmed my ear. Another shot and then the thud of footfalls following behind. I crawled a little way and then struggled to my feet, heading left where there was more cover from the trees and bushes. I shouted again for Luc and Denzil, but either they were too far away to hear, or something had happened to prevent them coming. Either way, I couldn't risk shouting anymore or I'd give away my position. I had to lose FJ.

I moved fast, hugging the Perimeter fence. If the bombs were live, then at least FJ would be blown up too. I remembered seeing woodland behind the settlement. If I could reach it, I could lose him. Another shot filled up the darkness, making me wince. After a while, his footsteps were no longer audible and I wondered if he was still following. Without slowing, I tried to think what to do. Finding the others would be the best thing, but I didn't know if FJ was still somewhere behind me. I couldn't turn back. I had to keep going. If I circled the fence, surely I would catch up with Luc or Denzil eventually.

I heard the thud of footsteps behind me once more and increased my pace, my lungs straining at the effort. I ran for my life. Another crack of gunfire. My feet smashed down onto the ground as I willed myself onward, gasping for breath, tears of cold streaming from my eyes.

I came to a dense clump of foliage which I had to force my way through. Disturbing a bird from its slumber, it flapped away into the night sky, screeching in protest. Sharp twigs clawed and ripped at my face and clothing, but somehow I managed to stay upright and I pushed on, uncaring.

And then I heard a noise so loud it shook my bones and rattled my teeth. My whole body vibrated.

The bomb.

Oh my God. What did that mean? Luc? Denzil? I wanted to turn back. To see what had happened, to make sure they were okay. To make sure they weren't... But if I turned back, I would be captured and that wouldn't help anyone. My ears rang and for a few seconds the air felt quieter than it had ever felt before. As though the very night was in shock.

And then, once more, the thud of footsteps behind me. The crack of breaking branches and the swish of leaves. I couldn't stand here all night. I had to keep moving.

Looming ahead, the dark shape of the forest beckoned. If only my hands weren't cuffed, I would be able to move quicker, but there was nothing I could do about it. If I could make the treeline it would be easier to lose him. And then I could double back to search for Luc and Denzil.

After a time, I couldn't tell if FJ was still in pursuit. There were no further gunshots and I heard no footsteps, but perhaps that was down to the violent pounding of my pulse and the rasping breaths which filled my ears. My chest felt tight as though it would burst. I had to stop, just for a second to catch my breath. Daring to slow, I strained my ears, but all I heard was the clattering wind in the trees and the thumping rhythm of my heartbeat.

And then I heard them.

A moment of terror came upon me when I realised what it was – chanting. They were back. They were coming for me. Grey's disciples. Was FJ with them? Had he somehow called them back from their retreat? Or was I imagining it? My feet gripped the earth in fear and my thoughts jumbled. What should I do?

Run.

I wasn't far from the forest now. Maybe I could lose them in there.

As I ran, I had the strangest feeling of déjà vu, as though I had been here before in this exact same situation: Heading towards a dark wood where capture was inevitable. But I couldn't let myself think like that.

I finally reached the forest edge. Slipped into its velvety darkness. The chanting grew more muffled. It became all at once louder and quieter, the eerie sound winding its way through the trees, rustling the leaves and wrapping itself around me. I had the sense that time was running out.

As I travelled deeper into the wood, the way grew increasingly more dense and tangled, slowing my progress. It was beginning to look as though I could go no further, when suddenly I stumbled onto a narrow track and heard the strangled gurgling of running water. I flew along the path, throwing glances over my shoulder, but the darkness made me blind.

The ground was now becoming boggy with sucking mud, and the rush of the stream was getting louder. Within seconds, I found myself in a grassy clearing, exposed on all sides. A small herd of wild ponies had been startled awake by my sudden arrival. They snorted, whinnied and trotted away into the forest. Retreating.

Take me with you, I silently pleaded. But they disappeared and the clearing lay empty, except for me, my breath coming in tight gasps, sweat drying on my forehead. A cloud moved to reveal a quarter-moon. The stream bubbled and the branches creaked and moaned.

What should I do? I didn't know which way to run. I couldn't go back and I didn't want to run right through the open space. I decided to veer away from the stream and back under the canopy of trees, but the chanting had grown louder. It had penetrated my body and filled up my mind, drowning out my thoughts.

They were coming...

They were here.

I had let myself be herded like a helpless lamb. Somehow, I'd known this was going to happen. A premonition perhaps. Either way, the fight had disappeared from my body. I let my shoulders slump as the dark hooded figures bled out of the trees encircling me. They seemed to glide forward, taking their time, closing in. I was rooted to the spot, surrounded. Rather than witness their approach, I turned my gaze up towards the racing clouds as they smothered the briefly hopeful moon and every-thing went black.

'I'm impressed.'

I lowered my gaze and came eye to eye with Freddie Junior.

'So now it's just you I have to deal with,' he said. 'Looks like your friends got blown up.'

My body trembled with shock and rage and exhaustion I couldn't let myself believe that what he said was true. In the darkness, I made out the dark shapes of a hundred or more of Grey's guards circling the clearing. They had fallen silent. No more freaky chanting.

'Perhaps I should kill you here,' FJ said. 'You've caused me a lot of trouble tonight. It would be the best thing all round.'

'Where's your precious Grey?' I asked. 'Did you leave him on the hillside to die? Are you taking over now, is that it? Going after the top job.'

'Our Father is perfectly safe. He is with his disciples. They are caring for him. But that's not your concern.'

I shivered, the sweat from my exertions suddenly turning cold and chilling my body. I had so many thoughts flying around my head: Luc, Denzil, Pa, Eddie, Rita… were any of them left alive? If not, I would be better off dead. But what about Ma? She didn't know about Connor yet. I couldn't let FJ kill me – Ma would never recover.

'You need me,' I said.

FJ raised an eyebrow.

'As a hostage. I'd be a useful bargaining chip.'

'Maybe. But your little band of Perimeter guards are all dead. Who else would want you?'

I bit my bottom lip, trying not to let his words get to me. I knew he was trying to goad me. He couldn't know for certain what had happened to the others. There hadn't been time for him to find out. Surely he was bluffing.

'You're pathetic,' I said, overtaken by a surge of anger. 'Really pathetic. You're supposed to be a Christian, but all you do is hate and bully and kill. You're the opposite of a Christian. It's just an excuse to terrorise innocent people and make yourself feel big.'

As I spat out the words, FJ strode over to me and grabbed my face, squeezing my cheeks so hard I thought my bones would shatter. 'Shut up, you stupid bitch.'

'Truth hurts,' I managed to hiss.

'Let her go, FJ.' A voice cut through the clearing. Luc's voice. My heart leapt and I felt like laughing and crying at the same time.

FJ spun me around and pulled me close to his body. He stuck a gun under my chin, jamming the cold metal against my skin.

'Let her go or we'll kill the old man.' Luc and Denzil appeared out of the darkness, propping up the half-conscious Grey between them. Grey's guards parted to let them through.

'Seems you were right about the hostage situation,' FJ hissed in my ear. 'But make no mistake, I am going to kill you. Even if it's not today. I'll take great pleasure in hunting you down, humiliating you and executing you publicly and painfully.' He radiated anger. The level of his hate shocked me.

'You can try,' I said.

'Let. Her. Go,' Luc said, his words icy cold.

I had never seen Luc look so furious. His eyes glittered with rage as he approached us.

'You first,' FJ said.

'Here's what's going to happen, *Freddie*,' Luc said, stopping only a few feet away. 'You're going to let Riley go and then you and your weirdo guards are going to leave Ringwood. Once you're back in Salisbury, I'll drop Grey outside your gates.'

'How do I know you won't kill him?'

'You don't know. But you've got no choice because that's what's going to happen.'

'Father?' FJ said. 'Father, can you hear me?'

But Grey was totally out of it. His head lolling.

'He's ill,' FJ said. 'He needs help.'

'You're telling me,' I muttered.

'Don't make me shoot you,' FJ whispered in my ear, tightening his grip.

'He'll be fine,' Denzil said.

We stood like that in silence for a while. I could tell FJ was weighing up his options. Wondering if he could trust Luc. Suddenly, he released his grip and shoved me away from him with such a force, I tripped and almost fell.

'Take her,' he cried.

Denzil took hold of Grey as Luc held out his arms to me. I staggered into them, trying to keep it together, breathing in Luc's familiar scent of spicy warmth and soap.

'Everyone's safe,' he whispered. 'Your Pa and my parents. They're okay. I haven't seen them yet, but one of the guards told me.'

The weight of everything bad evaporated and I was overcome with a lightness of being I hadn't felt in a long, long time.

'Let's get out of here,' Denzil said.

Luc smoothed the hair away from my face, kissed my forehead and clicked open my cuffs. It felt good to have my hands free again.

Denzil hoisted Grey over his shoulder and we began to back away from FJ and his guards. But just as we were about to leave the clearing and slip away into the forest, FJ called after me and spoke six words I never thought I'd hear:

'I know who killed your sister.'

CHAPTER FORTY

RILEY

The entrance to the Ringwood Perimeter was much like our own, with a basic brick guards' hut and a smooth tarmac road. I didn't pay it too much attention for up ahead I saw Pa striding towards me, his face crumpled and tired.

'Pa!'

He lifted me off my feet and squeezed me close. 'Riley, thank God. Thank God you're okay.'

I hadn't realised how much I'd been missing Pa. Worrying about him. It felt so good to know he was safe. My whole body sagged with relief, my emotions threatening to overwhelm me. It would have been a luxury to cry, but I took a breath and managed to keep my tears contained. As we hugged, Luc filled him, Eddie and Rita in on all that had happened.

'Grey?' Pa said, letting me go. 'You've got Grey?'

'How the hell did you manage that?' Eddie asked, incredulous.

'It was Riley's idea,' Luc said.

Denzil came over with Grey still slung across his shoulder.

'Pa,' I said, 'this is Denzil.'

'Denzil? The man who saved you when you went AWOL?'

'Yeah,' I replied sheepishly.

Pa stuck out his hand and Denzil shook it.

'I owe you,' Pa said.

'Got someone here for you,' Denzil said, turning so they could get a look at Grey's face.

'He doesn't look too good,' Rita said, stepping forward and lifting up one of Grey's eyelids. He was completely out of it, his chest and throat making a hideous rattling sound.

'Definitely needs medical attention,' Denzil replied. 'Sooner rather than later.'

'Can you put him in that truck?' Pa said, pointing to one of the vehicles. 'Carefully.'

'Sure,' Denzil replied.

'We'll get the medic to take a look at him in a sec.'

'I can't believe you guys got Grey,' Eddie said, shaking his head in admiration. 'And you saved our asses. We thought we might be toast for a while back there.'

'What about the bomb?' I asked. 'I heard an explosion...'

'Denzil couldn't diffuse it,' Luc replied. 'He took it out of range.'

'What? He carried it?' I couldn't imagine doing something so terrifying.

Luc nodded.

'Does he want a job?' Eddie asked.

'Funny you should say that,' Luc replied.

'Where's Connor?' Pa asked.

No one spoke for a second, but Luc gave me a look that was charged with empathy.

'He didn't make it,' I said quietly.

'I'm sorry, Riley.' Pa took my hand and kissed the top of my head.

'Is everyone else okay?' I asked, changing the subject. I couldn't let myself think of Connor yet. 'Was anyone in the Perimeter hurt?'

'Three guards dead, six injured.'

I glanced over to the man who had spoken.

'Lloyd Trassic.' The man held his hand out and took a step towards me. 'Thank you for everything,' he said. 'You saved our Perimeter, Miss Culpepper, Luc.'

'And Denzil,' I replied as our friend returned.

'Grey's cuffed and I took the liberty of locking the truck,' Denzil said, tossing the keys to Pa who caught them and nodded his thanks. Denzil shook Trassic's hand.

'Thank you doesn't begin to cover it,' Trassic said. 'Without you, we'd have been overrun in minutes. Please stay the rest of the night. Or longer if you'd like.'

'Thanks, but we'd better get back,' Pa said. 'This thing still isn't over. Lloyd, you'd better start reinforcing your defences. None of us were properly prepared for a full-on assault like the one Grey planned.'

'But it's over now,' Trassic replied. 'Surely... I overheard them say you captured Grey. We could execute the man and finish it all.'

'Not as simple as that,' Luc said. 'I wish it was, but there's a second-in-command. Someone who'd make you wish Grey was back in charge.'

The engine thrummed steadily. Luc and I sat quiet in the back of the truck while Pa drove us home. Denzil was travelling with Eddie and Rita, Grey was in the medic truck and Pa had sent a couple of guards to let Charlie Duke know it was safe for him to fly the copter home. I knew we were lucky to have come through this alive. Back there outside the Ringwood Perimeter, I'd thought Luc had been killed. It was only hitting me now that I could have lost him. I couldn't imagine a world without him in it. Grateful as I was to have Luc here beside me, there was something else playing on my mind. Something so huge that it dominated all my thoughts.

Luc tapped my shoulder. 'You don't believe it, do you? What FJ said... about Skye.'

I barely heard his words, suddenly feeling like my whole body wanted to shut down; I was physically exhausted, but my mind wouldn't let me rest.

'Riley...'

'I don't know.' I lowered my face and stared into my lap.

'He just said it to wind you up. You know that, right?'

'What if it wasn't to wind me up? What if he really does know who killed her?'

'How? How could he possibly know?'

'But he must because—'

'No, Riley. Don't you see? This is what he wants. He wants you to be torn up by this. He wants you to wonder and drive yourself crazy.'

'I know that, but—'

'He was just saying it because he had nothing left to bargain with.' Luc took hold of my shoulders and turned me to face him, lifted my chin and made me look at him. 'It was just some off-the-cuff desperation,' he said. 'He wants you to go looking for him so he can set a trap for you; get his revenge. FJ is sick. He's a poor twisted boy whose mind's been warped by Grey. You need to put it and him out of your mind.'

'Just listen a minute,' I said, needing to stop the torrent of words pouring from his mouth. 'Listen.'

He stopped talking and stared at me, his eyes boring into mine with a look I couldn't fathom.

I took a breath as I tried to marshal my thoughts. 'He must know something,' I said, 'because he'd never met me before tonight and so how would he know about Skye being killed? How could he possibly have known that information? I never even told him I had a sister.'

'Fred and Jessie,' Luc said. 'They would have told Grey's people about Skye, back when they were busy betraying us.'

'Why would they have done that? Getting their kids back was their priority, not talking about me and Skye.'

'Okay,' Luc replied. 'Why don't we ask them? Fred and Jessie will give us an honest answer.'

'Not when we inform them we had to let their son go,' I replied. 'They won't want to tell us anything after we give them that piece of news.'

'We didn't have a choice,' Luc said. 'They'll realise that. Eventually.'

'Maybe.'

I turned away from Luc and gazed through the window into the darkness, traces of my reflection staring back at me as my mind began to clear. I wasn't so stupid that I didn't realise FJ was the type of person who'd take great pleasure in making things up to mess with my mind. But... the way he'd said it... a deeper part of me believed he really did know the identity of Skye's killer. And I'd already decided I was going to take the bait and follow it through. Until I got the answers I'd been searching for.

Either way, FJ and I had unfinished business. I owed it to my sister to bring her killer to justice. No matter what anyone said to try to dissuade me, no matter how terrified I was at the thought of seeing FJ again, I promised myself that I would finish what I'd started. Whatever the price.

A LETTER FROM SHALINI

Dear reader,

Thank you for reading *The Clearing*. If you enjoyed it, you can find more action, romance and dystopian adventure in *The Perimeter*, book 3 in the Outside series.

If you'd like to keep up to date with my latest releases, just sign up here and I'll let you know when I have a new novel coming out.

www.secondskybooks.com/shalini-boland

I love getting feedback on my books, so if you have a few moments, I'd be really grateful if you'd be kind enough to post a review online or tell your friends about it. A good review absolutely makes my day.

When I'm not writing, reading, walking on the beach or spending time with my family, you can reach me via my Facebook page, through Twitter, Goodreads or my website.

Shalini Boland x

KEEP IN TOUCH WITH SHALINI

www.shaliniboland.co.uk

facebook.com/ShaliniBolandAuthor
twitter.com/ShaliniBoland
goodreads.com/shaliniboland

ACKNOWLEDGEMENTS

Huge thanks to my wonderful publisher, Natasha Harding, for taking this series and making it shine. I'll be forever grateful.

Endless thanks to the dedicated team at Second Sky: Jenny Geras, Ruth Tross, Jack Renninson, Noelle Holten, Sarah Hardy, Kim Nash, Melanie Price, Mark Alder, Alex Crow, Natalie Butlin, Jess Readett, Mandy Kullar, Emily Boyce, Saidah Graham, Lizzie Brien, Occy Carr and everyone else who helped relaunch this book.

Thanks also to Madeline Newquist for your fantastic proof-reading skills. Thank you to designer Eileen Carey for another incredible cover.

Big thanks to Tantor Audio and Henrietta Meire for creating fabulous audiobooks for the series.

Thank you to all my lovely readers who take the time to read, review or recommend my novels. It means so, so much. I'm so grateful. Thanks also to all the fabulous book bloggers and reviewers out there who spread the word. You guys are the absolute best.

Lastly, thanks to my family who are my inspiration, comfort and joy!